THE
FEARFUL GATES

Also by Ross Lawhead

The Ancient Earth Trilogy
The Realms Thereunder
A Hero's Throne

THE ANCIENT EARTH TRILOGY

BOOK THREE:

THE FEARFUL GATES

ROSS LAWHEAD

THOMAS NELSON
Since 1798

NASHVILLE   DALLAS   MEXICO CITY   RIO DE JANEIRO

© 2014 by Ross Lawhead

Published in Nashville, Tennessee, by Thomas Nelson. Thomas Nelson is a registered trademark of HarperCollins Christian Publishing, Inc.

Thomas Nelson titles may be purchased in bulk for educational, business, fund-raising, or sales promotional use. For information, please e-mail SpecialMarkets@ThomasNelson.com.

Publisher's Note: This novel is a work of fiction. Names, characters, places, and incidents are either products of the author's imagination or used fictitiously. All characters are fictional, and any similarity to people living or dead is purely coincidental.

Library of Congress Cataloging-in-Publication Data

Lawhead, Ross.
  The fearful gates / Ross Lawhead.
    pages cm. -- (An ancient earth trilogy ; Book 3)
  ISBN 978-1-59554-911-2 (pbk.)
1. Imaginary places--Fiction. 2. Good and evil--Fiction. 3. Knights and knighthood--Fiction. 4. England--Fiction. I. Title.
  PS3562.A864F34 2014
  813'.54--dc23

                   2013047138

Printed in the United States of America

14 15 16 17 18 19 RRD 6 5 4 3 2 1

FOR DAD,
WHO TOLD ME MY FIRST STORIES, AND WHO
STILL WRITES MY FAVOURITE ONES

PROLOGUE

They lay in wait, all of them absolutely still, the barest breath of air passing between their gaping lips. They were unruly, undisciplined, but terrified of the thought—the very graphic thought—of what would be done to them if they did not remain completely hidden and undiscovered. Long, dreary hours passed; hours of lying in the dirt and mud. Their only comfort and consolation was the promise of what was to pass in a very short time, and their place in the world once it did.

"It has been two thousand, eight hundred minutes without even a shimmer," a nasal voice whined tetchily.

"I don't need you to tell me the time. I may not even need you at all. Our team has a one hundred percent efficiency rate without you."

A snort. "With an abnormally high fatality rate," came the response. "Necessitating myself. Don't you fret, I shall prove myself capable. Were there anything to prove myself against." A ragged sigh. "How many more hours shall we stay? I do not desire to be long from the main force. I've a position there that needs constant reinforcement."

"I've no doubt of that. Your moaning would make all suspect that you lacked the action to match it."

A growl of disdain. "Do not doubt—"

"Silence."

"If you—"

"I said *silence*," the other ordered in a low hiss. "Listen. Feel that?"

The ground started to tremble, a sort of rolling, vibrating pulse. The rest of the team raised their heads, alert, as their captain lifted his hand in a silent signal. His subordinates tensed but remained prone on the ground as adrenaline shot through their systems. Eyes tilted upward, they remained tense, poised, gazing intently on the dim shadow that hung like a black, vertical cloud. It was a tear in the sky that sometimes issued a foul, sulphurous stink, depending on how the wind was blowing on the other side of whatever world it connected to.

"When it arrives," the captain said to the new recruit beside him, "stay close to me and take in as much as you can of what is going on around you. Next time you will be on the end of one of the lines."

The scar darkened, giving a fluttering flicker as something passed along it, and then a thin, angular shape the length of a bus burst out of it, streaking down toward the forest hillside. They all leapt up, in motion before it even hit the ground, coming at it from all sides.

The beast gave a confused cry, tore into the hillside headfirst, and floundered. Its long neck and sharp, beaky head thrashed violently from side to side as it fought to orient itself, desperately trying to find which direction was up. It wasn't used to the hard substance it was encountering—solid ground was something totally unknown to it, so unlike the stratified pockets of dense air and smog that rose from boiling oceans of metal on the world it had so abruptly left.

Long upper limbs, webbed like enormous bat wings, flapped, flipping it over several times as the powerful tail that made over half its length corkscrewed behind it. Finally its talons found pur-chase on the ground and gripped it with vicious, reptilian tenacity, long and sharp claws burrowing into the soft turf.

Which was exactly the opportunity the yfelgópes were waiting for. They attacked, throwing lines with sharp, arm-sized hooks across it. Spinning to meet them, the grounded creature's action tightened the ropes that constrained it, pulling it closer to the trees they were anchored to as it became entangled. It screeched in anger and frustration.

"A dragon! A real dragon!" the new recruit exclaimed, stand-ing close to his captain, who sneered back a response.

"That's no dragon—that's a wyvern. This is like a guppy to a whale, compared to a dragon. Dragons, now—you'd know when you saw a dragon. Not that you're likely to. The true ones are too well hidden, I've heard. Older than the mountains, and just as cold and indifferent. Smarter than Satan, they are. They're said to con-trol the spirit of nations and a breath from their snout will snuff you clean out of existence. No, pray that this wyvern here is the closest you ever get to a true dragon. Small bugger he is too," the captain said as he spat, an unconscious habit he had when lying. "Still. It'll be harder to throw it back in so may as well keep— Its head!" he called out suddenly. "Get a line on its head!"

Another rope was thrown across its shoulders, from one yfel-góp to another, and they slowly and with great difficulty walked it forward, forcing the neck to the ground until the line was at the base of its skull and the creature's mouth was snapping at the dirt and grass, the rough tongue darting out both sides of its mouth. Other yfelgópes went to kneel on the thick rope to minimise the effects of the thrashing.

"Bring the bit! Bring the muzzle and harness!" the yfelgóp cap-tain commanded as he watched the tail slow, now making loping, irregular arcs in the air. Feeling the helplessness of its situation, the animal began to conserve its strength. But the captain knew that given the opportunity it would break for release with even more power than it had yet displayed. Before that happened he would have to teach it pain, pure and excruciating; pain that he had control over, pain that would rule the beast.

The harness was fitted—a gruesome metal and leather contraption that contained interior studs that pressed on certain pressure locations of the animal's head. A steel bit was jammed into its mouth, which would force it always slightly open, filling it with a sharp, metallic tang that it would continually try to flush from its mouth. The thing would never stop drooling as long as the bit was in place.

Bewildered by the unpleasant sensation, it stilled for a moment and the captain took the opportunity to dash past its tail, dance along the tough membrane of its wings, and straddle its tough, sandpapery neck to seize the harness. This action was designed to impress those under his command as much as instill a concept of superiority into the beast.

He dug in with his heels, forcing forked prongs into the dense but loose neck skin. There was a wide bar at the back of the harness, just above where the rope was pinning the neck to the ground. The captain gave it a one-sixths twist and the creature howled in agony but could do little more than flex its corded muscles. It thrashed against the hooks, ropes, and yfelgópes, all of which only held more fast.

The captain gave the wheel another turn, pushing the bolt even farther into the base of its skull. A gut-watering bellow sounded from the beast, and then it started panting, its movements now no more than automatic twitches, its breath coming out in wheezes.

"You did it—you broke it," the novice yfelgóp trapper said in awe. "You tamed a dragon."

"It's not a dragon, idiot. And it's not tamed, it's stunned.

Never make that mistake again." He twisted his spurred feet in the wyvern's neck and gave the bar another turn, eliciting a renewed screech of pain and thrashing.

These actions were repeated several times—the torture, the thrashing, allowing the wyvern to calm again, then digging in the spurs and inflicting more pain with the tightened harness.

"You have to associate the two in its murderous little brain," the captain explained. "The spurs," he said, thrusting them once more inward, "and the bar," he said and gave it another turn again. This time the wyvern only whimpered—a hoarse, ear-splitting whimper, but a whimper nonetheless.

"Let go," the captain commanded.

The yfelgópes looked at each other in doubt. "Let go completely? But—"

"I said do it!" their captain barked.

Almost as one they shrugged, each of them coming to the same conclusion. Their commander was obviously trying to impress the new recruit for some reason. And if he died, that would be no bad thing. Yfelgópes were uniformly ambitious and corporately welcomed the thinning of those at the top. They let go of the ropes without a further thought.

The wyvern immediately charged into the air, coiling its tail underneath it and then springing forward in a sharp twisting motion, spinning its whole body like a propeller. In less time than the space of a heartbeat it was in the sky, darting sharply through the sparse, white clouds. The yfelgópes looked after it with interest to see if their commander had been thrown off to fall and break his neck, or if the violence of movement had simply snapped his spine and he would be flapping like a rag doll on the creature's back. But a screech of pain and a sudden stiffness that made the wyvern drop thirty or forty feet confirmed that he was still alive, at least enough to be able to twist the harness bar.

For long moments the alien animal swooped and darted through the air, releasing intermittent howls of pain as the captain fought for control on its neck. Between its cries they could hear the yfelgóp captain whooping with excitement.

"What were you wrangling before you came here?" one of the yfelgópes asked the recruit, eyes still following the battle of wills in the sky.

"Immediately before this I was a giant trapper. Before that it was trolls."

"Huhn. Difficult to capture, are they?"

"Eh, your standard troll is dead simple—just need some human flesh for bait. We put it on a stick and waved it under their nose. Easy enough to lure them down into the under realm and into a pen. Got so's we could manage it without the despised thing even tasting a morsel. We started to keep competition with how many we could lure with the same rotting limb."

The company ducked reflexively as the wyvern and its whooping rider swooped low over their heads and then vanished above the tree cover. They turned and tried to catch sight of them again.

"Giants much different from trolls, then? Not much, I'd wager."

"You'd lose that wager. Giants are an entirely different matter. Giants are reasoning creatures, technically at least, and that means you have to trick them away—persuade them, coax and cajole them. No, compared to trolls your giant demands a very high degree of . . ."

The wyvern suddenly reappeared just then, gliding low over their heads, throwing them into shadow. It then tucked its wings up in a neat fashion and gently lit on the ground before them. The captain was on its back, beaming a repulsive expression of self-satisfaction.

". . . finesse."

"Don't stand around there gawping," the captain barked at them. "I need one of you to get this one back to the aviary. Any volunteers? You, I saw that hand! Get o'er 'ere."

The switch was made with swift delicacy and soon the wyvern and its new rider were a distant speck in the sky. "The rest of you, let's get this gear stowed. We have just around three thousand more minutes to stand this post and then our orders are to return and prepare for the invasion."

CHAPTER ONE

A Song of Leaving

I

Beneath the archway of the Langtorr's outer defensive wall Freya crouched over Daniel's unconscious body. He was as loose as a ragdoll, lying on the cold stone beneath the arch that led into the Langtorr courtyard. She watched his chest as it very slowly, almost imperceptibly, rose and fell. His lips were dry and cracked and his forehead glistened with sweat.

"We know not how long he has been imprisoned," one of the knights was saying. "But you can see that he is in a bad way."

"You idiot," Freya said quietly to Daniel. "I told you not to go off by yourself. What have they done to you now?" Freya looked up at Vivienne and Alex, standing around her with several other knights and a cluster of curious children. "He left us . . . what? Three or four days ago, at least." She laid a hand against Daniel's cheek. His skin was cooler than hers, but he was still warm.

Vivienne consulted her watch. "It's been more like ten days ago now."

"Ten days? That long?" The vivid trances she had been in had taken more time than she realised.

"That's about when we parted," Alex, standing above them, said. "Did he go straight out and get himself caught?"

"It seems so," Vivienne said. "He was going to try to kill Kelm. He thought he could catch him off guard."

"I'd say that didn't pan out so well," Alex said. "I'm surprised he's still alive. But what happened to him? It looks like he's been hit by a truck."

"Let's not just stand around and talk about him," Freya said, hot, angry tears welling underneath her eyes. She awkwardly tried to rise and lift Daniel at the same time. She struggled with his weight and the two knights leant in to help, taking him out of her hands.

"Get him inside the Langtorr," Freya ordered. "Make him comfortable, keep him warm. Find someplace dry and out of the way. Ealdstan's study is probably best. It's up there. See that window, where the light is? Take him there."

"I'll get him settled," Vivienne said. "And try to get some water and food in him." She led away the two knights who carried Daniel's limp body between them.

Freya turned to Alex, who was still looking on. "The most important thing now is to find places for these kids to stay until we can get them all back home. I can see to rounding up the rest of them. Can you arrange your knights into some sort of guard?"

"Already done. We're seeing what we have in the way of natural defences, and I've posted sentries and scouts to seek out any hostiles that may be extant."

"Excellent. That's really great, Alex." She bit her lip and took a second to consider. "But they're going to need breaks, aren't they? Could you schedule them into watches?"

"Ah . . . that's a good idea. I'll get on it."

"Thanks, Alex, that'd be great. I'm glad you're here."

"What about all these kids? Shouldn't we—"

"I'm going to look into that right now."

Alex nodded. He looked as if he wanted to say something else but turned away. He went a few steps and looked back at her. "You've changed a lot in just ten days," he said, reaching to his head where the dragonhelm silver crown of the Hero of Niðergeard rested. His fingers pushed it along the top of his head, fidgeting with it. "Are you sure you don't want this? You seem to know best what you're doing."

Freya shook her head. "I haven't earned it. You're the liberator. But I am certain that we can work together, you and I. So long as you can tell a good idea when you hear it."

Alex gave her another smile and went to round up his commanders.

The only people left in the Langtorr's courtyard were Freya and the eight children, who were trying to stay out of the way of the bustling knights.

"Okay, let's find the rest of you," she said to them, stepping into the city. "How many did you say you were? Hundreds? Really?"

They looked at each other. "Maybe a thousand!" the smallest of them, a boy, said.

"Okay, let's find them, quickly. Which way?"

They retraced their steps, the children arguing over which way they had come. They went, by Freya's bearings, vaguely east.

"So . . . tell me where you're all from, and how old you are. How about you, where are you from?"

"Me? I'm from Thurso, in Caithness," the heavyset girl said. "In Scotland. I'm thirteen."

"And it's Gretchen, right?"

"Right." She nodded.

"We're from the Isle of Man. He's fourteen, I'm twelve."

"Fergus and . . . ?"

"Kieran. We're brothers."

"I can see the resemblance. You?"

"Cardiff. In Wales. Thirteen."

"I know where Cardiff is. What was your name again?"

"Gemma. Gemma Woodcote."

"I'm David Murray, fifteen. Southampton."

"Amanda. I'm from Scotland as well, from Glasgow. I'm twelve."

"Michael Page. Bournemouth. Fifteen."

"I'm Jodhi Gale. I'm from Bristol. I'll be fourteen next week."

Freya went over their names as she scanned their faces. "Do any of you know each other? Apart from the brothers?"

They all shook their heads.

"Really? And you said you heard a voice? All of you?"

They all agreed they had heard a voice.

"What did it say?"

"It said, 'You are the next army, I summon you.'"

"No, it said 'You *of* the next army—I summon *thee*.'"

"Same thing."

"What did it sound like?" Freya asked. "Was it a man's voice?"

They were less sure of this.

"It wasn't really a voice," Fergus said. "You couldn't hear it with your ears, it was mostly in your head. But it was loud."

"And when you heard it, what happened?" Freya asked, kicking through a pile of dust that was once Niðergeard's outer wall. Dread was starting to cover her—dark and icy dread. This was the first time since she was little that she had properly entered the city and Niðergeard was in even worse shape up close than what it looked like from the top of the Langtorr. It would be incredibly hard to defend completely for any meaningful length of time—what could they do to help them? Walls were demolished, buildings collapsed. Did they have time to arrange the rubble into barricades of some sort? She doubted it. And the ground was solid stone, so trenches were out of the question. Niðergeard's long years of weathering any sort of siege were well and truly behind it. Whoever wanted to take the city could just walk right into it—just as she had. These children had to be got out of here. "Sorry, could you repeat that?"

"I said, we followed it—the voice."

"Did you mean to? I mean, did you have a choice?"

"Yeah, of course. Everyone in my dormitory heard it."

"You go to a boarding school?"

"Yes. We all woke up at the same time. We were arguing about whether to follow it or not. Only a few of us did in the end."

A few from every school. Every school where? In Britain? Farther? It really would be thousands in that case.

"What happened then?" Freya could hear a hubbub of children's voices in the darkness—it sounded like the start of a school assembly.

"It was like we already knew where to go," Jodhi said. "It wasn't like anything was guiding us, we just followed the way that we already knew—like going home. I walked through a hill to get here. It was really weird, but it felt natural. It felt like I was—"

The noise was loud enough now that Freya couldn't even hear Jodhi talking next to her. It was the chatter of a large group of confused children and was therefore nearly deafening. They didn't seem to be scared or upset yet, which under the circumstances was impressive.

There were also knights shouting to each other above the din. They weren't urgent voices, but commanding, trying to herd them all together. As Freya swung her flashlight's beam ahead of her, she started to get an idea of what nearly a thousand children looked like.

A knight in odd European armour approached her. "Mistress," he said. "There are untold scores of children gathering here from the tunnels. I did not think there could be so many in all the world. And there are more of them arriving by the moment. We are trying to keep them quiet—we do not know what other enemies may be abiding within the deep dark."

"What is your name?"

"Matěj."

"Thank you, Matěj, you are doing the right thing. Keep trying to round them together. I will address them all."

"Did you know what he was saying?" asked Fergus, who was standing next to her.

"Yes," she said. "There was an arch, when I was your age, I walked underneath it . . . Stay here."

Freya had spotted a large rock and started to climb up it. Gretchen, Fergus, Kieran, Jodhi, and the rest followed her and waited at its base. She looked out over the sea of bobbing heads, only dimly visible in the darkness, and gave a piercing whistle. Everybody fell silent. She turned her flashlight onto herself and raised her voice.

"Hello, everybody, my name is Freya! I know you all have a lot of questions! You want to know why you're here! So do I! You want to know how you're going to get back—me too. But right now, we need to get you all to safety. If you follow me, and follow the knights, and follow each other, I will take you to Niðergeard where there is food, shelter, warmth, and, I hope, a way to get you all back. This is a dangerous place, but if you all act calmly and sensibly, you should be safe. I made it out of here once when I was your age, and I'm going to do everything I can to make sure that you get back home as well. So everyone stay together and follow my light!" She raised her arm and shone her flashlight out over their heads, then clambered down from the rock and started to lead everyone back to Niðergeard.

"Miss Freya," one of the boys—Michael—said. "I definitely want to get home, but what about defeating the pixies?"

"The what?"

"The—you know, the pixies and things. A friend of mine and I ran into them a couple weeks ago—they were playing tricks on us, and they actually tricked him into killing himself. I escaped, but I'd like to get rid of them if I can. If anyone can help me."

"I fought a witch," one of the girls said. "She tried to steal my brother."

"There was this troll thing . . . in the woods."

"—Sort of floating light that would confuse people."

"There's a whole island of shape-changing seals. I barely escaped with my life. I'm pretty sure they were going to eat me."

Freya's pace slowed. "Really? You all fought these things?"

"We got rid of a couple giants. Boy, were they stupid! My brother and I are giant-killers! *Rahh!*"

"*Shh*, Fergus, calm down."

"But then what's it—what's it like up there? Is everyone freaking out or anything? Is the army hunting these things down?"

"No, you know adults—they only see what they want."

"They have an excuse for *everything*."

"Plus, everyone's so depressed now. They're so miserable they just wake up, go to work in their cars, come home, watch TV, and then go to bed. They never know what's going on around them—not really."

"Even when they watch the news—it's money this, money that. Terrorists everywhere. Politicians doing wrong things. They just ignore us."

"Well, it'll be harder to ignore now that they've found that you're all missing," Freya said. "And when we get you back, they'll know all about this place. Then we'll get some people down here to sort this out." *If I can just keep everything together until then,*

Freya thought, *then I'll get everyone through this. After that it will be someone else's problem. God willing, they'll completely obliterate everything down here.*

"But we don't want to go home," Gemma said.

"What?"

"We want to stay," said Gretchen. "That's why we answered the summons. We *know* why we're here, just like we knew where we were going—we're the next army. We're going to fight."

II

He was paralysed, terrified. He didn't know how long ago it was that Ealdstan had used him as a gateway back to his own world. Every moment passed in almost unbearable pain. It felt like he was being stretched—every cell and fibre of his body was being stretched out, pulled like bread dough, always expanding but never quite breaking, becoming thinner and thinner. Every nerve ending was on fire and every second was torture.

He would have very quickly lost his mind, he was sure, except that he had a focal point of fear to keep him centred. Over the vast plain he was being dispersed across, the Silver Rider was moving toward him, as tall as the mountain behind it, a titanic entity. When that figure had appeared to him in his visions in the Night, it had brought visions of death. But all of that had been . . . hallucinations, or so he had come to believe. And now he was seeing it again, in the daylight, or so he thought. But even if it was still a hallucination, Daniel didn't like what the Silver Rider represented.

The shining knight approached him, step by step. He tried to measure the distance between them, and the length of the steps the apparition was taking. Was it just one second between those steps or hours? He couldn't say, but he dreaded every one.

The conversations Daniel had had with the Silver Rider were

circular, surreal things that haunted his memory. He tried to banish them from his thoughts whenever he rematerialised in Elfland, but snatches of them crept back.

Wish for pain, the Silver Rider told him repeatedly. *Pain will save you. Pain is your future.*

He had been right about that last part. Daniel was certainly feeling the pain now. As for it saving him, he wasn't so certain.

The Silver Rider took another step forward and another wave of fear hit Daniel. With a staggering effort of will, he turned his head away—he couldn't bear to look at it. Death might be coming for him but at least he didn't have to watch it arrive.

He looked to the forest that he'd travelled through on his first trip here and saw a glint of sunlight rising from the treetops. To his astonishment, another apparition was approaching him. This was the Gold Rider—the one that had offered him dreams of victory. He had accepted those visions and tried to take strength from them. He wanted to reach out to it, to drag it closer, but he couldn't move. He sent all of his desire out to it, as though he could bring it closer by pure virtue of wishing.

He wanted victory to reach him before death did.

III

Sir David Malcolm awoke, for a change, in his own bed. He crept into consciousness timidly. Reality was something huge and intimidating that he felt would punish him very shortly.

As a young man, he had not avoided thinking about the future. But now it was something he blinded himself to. Even living from moment to moment was a strain. What had happened to him last night? He called it that to himself, "last night," although it was just as likely to have been in the daytime that he came home. Or was he brought home? He couldn't remember either way—that is, he could remember just as many times that he returned home as when he was sent home, but he couldn't tell which was the most recent remembrance.

After an hour and a half he rolled himself across the enormous bed that dominated his now very sparse Edinburgh apartment—it was like his wife had even removed the soul of the place when she left—and used his mobile phone to call his car service. He calculated a time for pickup and then set about his normal routine for putting himself together.

At 11:35 a.m., a cream-coloured BMW 760Li saloon car pulled into the small driveway outside his building. Sir David watched as the driver exited, buzzed at his door, and then returned to the car before he made his way downstairs. Without saying a word he climbed in and slammed the door shut. There was a package on the seat next to him that he pulled onto his lap. Leaning forward, he gave two thumps on the tinted-glass partition that separated him from the driver and then he settled back into the seat and tried not to twitch. As the car pulled away, he fiddled with the air-conditioning controls, causing icy-cold air to blast out of the seven vents around him.

The rides between his office and house were getting more and more intolerable. Not only did it seem to take forever, but it was always so miserably hot outside. It didn't matter that he couldn't feel it, he could see it—see the heat waves bouncing off the pavement, see the homeless men and single mothers sweating in the sunlight . . . the sweaty discomfort got inside him.

He turned his attention to the bundle of papers on his lap. In the age of computers, why was there still so much paperwork? He rarely read the stuff anymore. He found it hard to concentrate on words. He had long ago suspected that there was no need to actually comprehend what he was given each day, and he had been proven right. The company knew what was best for itself. If it wanted for staff it hired them. If it had too many it just as simply got rid of some. The system ran itself, and it ran itself very well. On very rare occasions did the machinery jam and all it usually took was a few more signatures, or at the most a meeting with the board, and the problem would be fixed. The Alba Banking Society, PLC, was a geyser for money, and he was sitting right on top of it.

But even as CEO, there were rules and limits to his abilities, at least if he wanted to stay CEO in the long-term. But it was getting harder and harder to keep the long-term in mind now. There were too many unknown factors of the present day in order to even consider the next day.

The car crawled its way through the Edinburgh streets, from his apartment in the Grange, down Lauriston Street, and across the bridges—starting and stopping, starting and stopping, a sound-proofed, tinted-glass, air-conditioned bubble of solitude within the hot, bright, busy, choking city. It arrived at the ABS building and turned into the underground car park. A series of bollards lowered as microchips in the front of the car were read by the building's computers, which also unlocked the private elevator and sent a command for it to descend to the parking level.

The distance from the car door to the private elevator could be crossed in seven steps, and Sir David habitually held his breath as he walked, passing from one conditioned environment to the next with the smallest amount of intrusion by the outside world. He even kept his eyes partly closed, nodding and giving a vague wave in the direction of the driver.

The elevator journey took fifty-three seconds to reach the top floor.

Another deep breath as he left the elevator, which he let out when he saw that his administrative assistant's desk was empty. David hoped he was off somewhere having fun.

He opened the heavy door to his private office and slipped inside.

His large office was tastefully plush and void of all character to the point of being sterile. He manoeuvred around expensive pieces of furniture that no one ever sat in and over to a frosted-glass panel. He slid it aside to reveal a large object that, if anything, had far *too much* character than any object should be allowed.

It was a dark cabinet made of very warped, and very old wood. It was covered in very old carvings, some of which had rubbed away in places and others that featured disturbingly sharp images. There were traces here and there of colour where it had been painted or stained, but these were faint and splotchy.

His fingers twitched as he looked at the cabinet. Then he turned and crossed back to his door, checking again that it was locked. He went to his desk and opened the bottom drawer, taking out three green candles, two stones, a tiny bottle of patchouli oil, and a red velvet pouch containing an expensive mixture of herbs that smelled suspiciously like any ordinary household spice drawer.

With anxious fingers he dribbled some of the patchouli oil on the three squat candles and then lit them with the cigar lighter from his jacket pocket. He arranged them into a triangle and then placed the stones in the centre. Then he unbuttoned two of the buttons on his shirt and rubbed some of the oil on his chest. He rebuttoned and then put the pouch up to his nose and mouth and took three deep huffs through it. He closed his eyes and said, aloud, "All obstacles are gone. I draw prosperity toward myself . . ." He opened one eye slightly and squinted at the two rocks, trying to remember which one the shaman had told him was the lodestone. He snatched that with his left hand and continued the ritual.

"I attract gain and increase. I draw abundance to myself . . ." He squinted his eye open again and picked up the other rock—the aventurine stone. "To me now comes the money that is needed, and that to spare."

He tried to visualise the money coming to him. That was always the difficult part for him. Everything was done electronically these days so what was he to do, visualise a bunch of ones and zeroes? He pictured a duffel bag full of money, like on TV, and imagined taking brick-sized bundles of banknotes out of that. Then he repeated the incantation four more times, blew out the candles, and returned all the spell items to the bottom desk drawer.

He went back to the wooden cabinet. He knocked on it three times and then began walking around the office, counterclockwise. He rubbed his nose, trying to ignore the smell of patchouli. After three circuits he arrived back in front of the cabinet and, observing his own personal superstition, he took a deep breath and opened it up.

The noise was the first thing to flood in, and then the smell. He stepped inside and closed the door behind him.

The long corridor was wood-panelled in what looked like oak. It wasn't like the cabinet at all, it was clean with tasteful running boards and looked to have been recently varnished. He walked swiftly down the narrow passage, just wide enough for him to pass without rubbing the shoulders of his expensive suit.

The passage emptied out into an enormous hall. People were milling around and shouting earnestly at each other; it reminded him of the New York Stock Exchange. Except for the massive wooden crossbeams, the trestle tables and benches that everyone sat at, and the iron braziers that lined the walls and lit the windowless hall, it was just like the Stock Exchange. There were even the TV screens and the banks of computers that traders shouted down into.

He walked past those and started studying the businessmen,

almost all of them dressed exactly like himself, allowing for varia-
tions in their ethnicity and glitzy accessories, which denoted
them as German, Japanese, Chinese, Swiss, and so on. The main
of them were seated at the benches, eyes studying the boards in
front of them—boards with grid patterns on them upon which
coins and markers slid. He watched a man lose €5,000 on one of
these and then his eyes turned to the large wheel at the far end of
the hall.

"Fair greeting and much health to you this day, Sir David," a
voice at his shoulder lilted.

"Mm?" he grunted, turning. "Oh, good morning, Mongan."
He recognised the pinch-faced host. "I mean, afternoon."

The thin man bowed, his face radiating pure obsequiousness.
"Is there anything you desire?"

"Yes, bring me three Churchills and three fingers of bourbon
with three ice cubes in it."

"Of course, Sir David. Do you want me to find you a seat at a
board or . . . ?"

"No, thank you, not right now. I'd like to study the wheel for
a while."

"Certainly. Your signature, please, Sir David."

Sir David glanced down at the wood plank that the host held
before him. He took up the reed pen and dipped it into an inkpot
that was set into the board. He inscribed his name at the bottom
of his bank's funds release document and handed the pen back to
Mongan, who slunk silently away.

Walking down the centre of the hall, Sir David gently
moved from side to side as people passed him, his eyes fixed on
the large wheel—*the* wheel—that was slowly spinning at the far
end of the room.

He came to a row of thin benches set before a narrow table.
They were all packed with people, so he just stood and watched.

The giant wheel with its thirty-nine marked partitions was still slowly turning, its thirty-nine pegs lightly tapping against the three pointers that were fixed to the top and either side. The partitions were of variable sizes and all contained symbols that were completely different from each other, as well as carved notches denoting numbers. The wheel finally settled and Sir David automatically did the arithmetic and ratio calculations, faster than it took the host operating the wheel to announce them. Then the other two hosts went to the number table and converted the amounts, delivering the proper totals to the winners.

A very large bald man threw up his hands in disgust and stood up from the bench he was sitting on. He waddled off and Sir David smoothly slid into his spot, the wood beneath him still warm.

The large man had left behind an empty glass that was wet on every side with precipitated water, and an ashtray where a cigar had been left to smoke itself out—a full three inches of it was still *in situ*, the ash making a tightly packed tube up to the cigar's tip. He stared at this for some moments, the wheel having lost fascination for him.

That's all we are now, he thought to himself. *All of us, altogether. The cigar has been smoked out, and we are the ashes. It holds together for now, but the slightest tap will cause all of it to fall completely, irrevocably apart.*

He was still deep in contemplation when a fast hand snaked out and removed the ashtray and empty glass. His bourbon with three ice cubes appeared before him and three large cigars were held before his face. "Thank you, Mongan," he said without turning. He pocketed two of the cigars and stuck the third in his mouth. A second pair of hands hefted a bowl full of gold coins in front of him.

He took his time lighting his cigar and then fished two of the ice cubes out of his drink and threw them on the floor in front of him. Then he settled in and studied the giant wooden wheel as it spun on its axis. It was going to talk to him, it was going to communicate with him, it was going to tell him where to put his money—his bank's money, his customers' money—so that it would grow and multiply.

"Time to go to work," he said.

IV

Daniel held on to the Gold Rider with both arms. He felt his own essence stretched across the plain—his shoulders were the north and the south, his legs were the foundation of the earth, his body the air, and his head the sky that the sun beat mercilessly down upon. Occasionally a cloud would drift by and his dissipated body would refract the rays throughout his essence. He was moving further and further apart from himself. He wasn't feeling pain anymore, he was feeling numb, which was ever more disturbing.

He could feel things passing through him. Just as Ealdstan had used him as a portal, others were now using him. He knew this, but couldn't see what these things were. Air blew straight through him, the climates of two different worlds mixing—small creatures wandering through, one to the other.

The horizons spread on either side. The sun was now setting, throwing an electric orange luminescence into the atmosphere. Daniel was frantic. *Robbin-a-Bobbin, Robbin-a-Bobbin, Robbin-a-Bobbin* . . . He kept repeating this in his mind, a mantra, trying to keep himself from flying apart.

The Riders stood on either side of him, Gold and Silver, as large and gigantic as he was, but more solid. They had both reached him at the same time, and Daniel tried as much as he could to turn away from the Silver and latch onto the Gold as soon as it came into reach. He could not feel his arms, but he could see the faint outline of them grip the glistening plate armour.

Could anyone see them, towering upon the landscape? If he were in his own world, he would have thought not, but here in Elfland there were different rules, and the elves themselves seemed more spiritually attuned. Would anyone help him?

Daniel looked to the Gold Rider for some sort of comfort. Its visor—the inside as impenetrably dark as midnight—was level with his eyes, but the helmet, which threw reflected light back at him like daggers, and its visor were, of course, impassive.

Twilight came and passed, bringing cold and dark. He had thought the Night might come and whisk him away. He would suffer the usual tortures there, but they would be familiar tortures. And maybe they would override Ealdstan's spell, or whatever it was he had done. But the only night that arrived was that which was the absence of the sun.

Speak to me, he said, or tried to say, to the Gold Rider. Just as he did not know or understand the state of his body, he did not know if his words were formed or if they were even heard. *Say something. Tell me what you want. Say anything.*

The Gold Rider spoke. Its words vibrated through the night, as if the sky itself were talking.

VICTORY IN DEATH.

Its gold armour shimmered into a bright white—for a moment it looked almost exactly like the Silver Rider.

Daniel recoiled. *No,* he thought. *I can still win. I can still make it through.*

RELEASE YOURSELF.

I won't give up. There's no one who can handle all this except me. I won't let go. I won't let myself die.

DIE TO LIFE, AND YOU WILL BE DESTROYED. DIE *FOR* LIFE, AND YOU WILL BE SET FREE.

No! Daniel tried even harder to keep himself together. He focussed, trying to push his mind through the numbness, to feel the pain again—to feel anything.

Day came. It grew and lengthened and then passed. Night fell, and then that too passed. Day into night, night into day, Daniel fought to keep hold of himself and the Gold Rider.

"Hello? Is there someone there?" a voice asked on the sixth day.

The words did not come from the riders. It was a voice that he recognised, speaking below him. *Who is it?* Daniel asked himself, tried to ask.

"This essence feels familiar. Do you have a name?"

. . . I . . . am . . . Daniel . . . Daniel Tully.

"Ah. We were wondering what had happened to you."

He tried to search out the sound of the voice and saw Prince Filliu, sitting on the distant mountain. He was cross-legged, as if meditating. There was a large crowd of elves around him. Their anxious mood filled the air like a toxic cloud. They were terrified, all of them.

His lips barely moved, but Daniel heard his voice.

Can you see me? he asked. *How?*

"The soul of a king is housed in his land as much as his body—they are one. He can feel its wounds."

This gateway—it is pulling me apart.

"And it is pulling this world apart as well. Your spirit is anchored to both this world and yours. It is pulling them toward each other, and therefore pulling them apart. The worlds will come closer and closer until they overlap—they will collide unless you help me stop them."

How do I help you?

"Daniel, you have already helped us bring peace to this land. I am king now, as is right."

Daniel could see the usurper prince Kione Traast kneeling

some distance behind Filliu, as well as the brass chains that bound him.

"This cataclysm you are trapped in—it was brought about by a sorcerer from your world. He made an agreement with the usurper Traast. His help in ascending the throne in exchange for troops to your world to help in *his* ascendency. But it was a sword with a poisoned handle, for that act would have destroyed both worlds—yours and mine."

I don't understand. What are you saying?

"It will be a new age, Daniel. And hopefully a kinder one. Once we have united the other five lands. Even now my armies march forward, the Battle Scryers have divined a perfect strategy. Soon there will be complete order in the land—my order—once all the traitors and pretenders to my throne are found and killed."

I am willing to help. Tell me how. Is there a way you can help me?

"We are all of us truly appreciative. This whole land owes you an honour debt of gratitude."

Filliu, tell me what to do. Help me fix this.

"Daniel . . . I'm sorry."

No. No. What do you mean?

"Daniel, the debt we owe will never be repaid to you in this world—or in yours."

Please, don't.

"Daniel, you must let go."

I can't.

"You and the gateway are one now. If you are destroyed—it is destroyed."

I won't.

"I would walk that path instead of you if I could. I would walk alongside you if I were allowed, but you must embrace death.

"I know what you see. I too have seen the Silver Rider. It

stalks all of us. Sometimes it is just a glimmer in the corner of your sight, but it always runs behind us, until the last when it overtakes us."

But if I kill myself—I will be damned.

"You are not dying to end one life—you are dying to save hundreds of thousands. I . . . I can make it easier for you, however. I can sing a song of release—of letting go. Would you like that?"

Daniel sent a single, grateful, thought. *Yes.*

Filliu closed his eyes and spread out his arms, hands open and palms skyward.

> *I know what loss is victory, what's won after defeat,*
> *What is weak when it is strong, and strong when it is*
> *weak.*
>
> *For those who daily die to life will find no life in death,*
> *Nor will they open up their eyes, when is spent their final*
> *breath.*
>
> *But those who live each day new-born are older than they*
> *know*
> *And seeds must burst the shell around so what's inside*
> *may grow.*
>
> *So may destruction save a man? Shall breaking make him*
> *whole?*
> *And will you fight to save your life, but not to save your*
> *soul?*
>
> *When you dream when you're awake, and not when*
> *you're asleep,*
> *You're not a fool to give away what you can never keep."*

Thank you, Filliu, Daniel said, dread now falling over him like a shadow. *I'm sorry I made such a mess of things. I was only trying to help.*

"I know, Daniel, thank you. You've done well—you are going to save the world. Our worlds. If it was not you, it would not have been possible."

With a cry, Daniel swung his arms forward and embraced the Silver Rider.

V

Most of the children had now been herded into the Langtorr, but more were coming by the hour. Talking to many of them, Freya found vastly common elements in all of their experiences: they had almost all of them faced some sort of conflict with mystical creatures on the surface world, in their normal lives, and they had all heard an audible voice calling them to some sort of battle within the sound of the Great Carnyx.

What was Ealdstan thinking when he enchanted that stupid horn? And, looking back on it now, why had she ever thought it was a good idea to blow it? She had wanted to force a futile situation to some sort of resolution, but she wouldn't have touched it if she knew that she would be putting the lives of *children* at risk—children younger than she had been when she first came here. Talking to them, each set of eyes she looked into reminded her of herself or Daniel, some glimmer of one of them was reflected back at her—either scared, apprehensive, unsure, or excited, anticipatory, heroic.

The knights, for their part, were predominately standoffish—they were as disturbed by the children as she was, she could tell. A few of them would bend to answer a young person's question or to carry them over rough terrain, but in most cases they would actively avoid being around the children. Those looking for them in the tunnels would find the children, bring them back, and gratefully drop them off at the Langtorr to be looked after before heading out to find more. It was like running some sort of bizarre day care.

Task one was to find out who needed food and drink and supply it. But pretty soon that was all of them, and she organised them to arrange the tables and benches in the feast hall. The food stores of Niðergeard were remarkably vast and she didn't hesitate to plunder them—mouths needed to be fed.

The feast hall was by no means large enough for even half of the children to be in and so she kept the others busy by getting the rooms in Niðergeard in order, and that was task two. The bedding and the mattresses that were already on the beds were fetid and rotting, but clean and dry, if musty, blankets were found in a couple closets and some metal trunks. The old beds were stripped, the mattresses carried out of the tower, and the empty, metal bed frames carried into the halls. Then a blanket and a space on the floor were given to each child. A few of them slept, but the majority just sat, nibbling at the cracker bread and dry meat, talking quietly to each other or just looking around expectantly. Expecting what? Something.

She would pass Vivienne on the stairs and in the passageways, as both of them scurried to provide for the hundreds and hundreds of children.

"We can't keep running around like this," Freya said at one of these passings. "We all have to get together and find out how to get these children back—not just to make them comfortable while they're here."

"I agree," said Vivienne. "There's a map room down this corridor. Shall I spread the word and have everyone meet there in an hour?"

"That would be perfect."

Freya turned and started going up the stairs of the Langtorr. She took them two at a time, setting an even, swift pace. Time was tight and she needed to check something first. She went along the floors where a busy noise of activity and chatter made the tower seem alien to her once more—she had never heard such a noise in this place and she found it oddly pleasant—comfortable in an indefinable way. The idea of a weird school came back to her again.

She passed Ealdstan's rooms, feeling her stomach clench involuntarily as she passed the door that stood off its hinges. She went higher, where the walls became rough and the rope handrail stopped. Round and round, as fast as she could go; she became dizzy and out of breath. It was cold and she could see every exhalation billow out in front of her in the cold beam of her flashlight.

She reached the top of the stairs and was faced with a blank stone wall. She was by no means certain that she could get all of them back to the surface world purely by breaking through. That left the option of trying to get through another way—using its enchantment. But she'd never been clear about how that worked; she'd never been able to predict or activate it like Ecgbryt or Alex seemed to be able to. The whole "right person at the right time" principle wasn't one she'd managed to make work for her. But she knew that she didn't need to go through a portal—she had dug her way out of this place the first time she was here, and she was prepared to dig her way out again if she had to. However, that first exit had been through soft earth, and this was solid stone. She didn't know exactly what would be involved in trying to drill through it, or even how far they would have to dig, but she knew that it would be almost impossible to do so. Assuming they could even find the tools they needed—pickaxes, hammers, and chisels, as well as the people who knew how to use them—she doubted they could break through in anything like days, or even months.

She laid her flashlight on the ground, put her hands on the cold stone and leant into it. She pictured home and thought of herself moving through the rock, or seeing it vanish from beneath her hands. She allowed herself to feel how badly she wanted to go home and tried to let that feeling pull her through the solid rock.

Several minutes later she was still pressing herself against the stone, which had not shifted a micron. She took a step back. What were her other options now? Luckily Ecgbryt and Alex were back, maybe they could explain how to do this. And they had a lot of knights and a lot of tunnels . . . she would march them all out of here under armed escort. That was the best plan.

Freya looked at her watch. It was time to head back down the stairs and into the map room.

CHAPTER TWO

The Council of Niðergeard

---------------------------------- I ----------------------------------

Freya decided to check on Daniel first. He had been placed on the long stone table adjacent to Ealdstan's study, and there was a guard outside the door and another one inside it. She recognised both as having come to Niðergeard in Alex's band, and she didn't know their names. Both raised their hands to their heads, tugged at their forelocks, and greeted her.

At first sight Daniel looked dead—laid out as if to be dressed for his coffin. The table was made of the same stone as the stone slabs in the *Slæpereshus* beneath the Langtorr where the fallen knights lay dead and decaying. She dried off his moist brow with her shirt cuff and pulled up a chair. A mix of feelings swirled inside of her, no single one of them coming to the fore. But years of cognitive behavioural therapy came to her aid and she ran through a mental exercise—naming the separate emotions: regret, frustration, pity, sadness, annoyance. He had caused, or at least was involved in, the complete emotional disintegration of her life, starting from when she was a little girl. But she never would have wished this living death on him. He only ever tried to do what he saw was right, and even though she had nearly always disagreed with what the right thing was, she did admire him for that. It was misguided, idiotic courage, but it was courage nonetheless, and it was enviable. It was more than she'd ever had.

Leaning forward, she whispered in his ear, "Come back to us, we need you." She rose, the iron chair screeching terribly on the stone floor. She thanked both the guards as she left and descended to the map room. There was no one else there and Freya sat in the small, circular room, studying the wrought-iron table in front of her where an animal skin with the map of Niðergeard etched on it lay.

Vivienne arrived, looking flustered. "I told the others. They won't be long, I'm sure."

"I checked on Daniel."

"Oh? How is he?"

"The same."

Vivienne tutted and shook her head. "That boy. A tragedy. Perhaps we're all better off with him out of the way, however."

Freya studied Vivienne. "You know—I keep forgetting. I keep forgetting that you have a ruthless, impersonal streak in you. Nobody's well-being matters to you, so long as you get where you want to go."

The older woman received these words impassively, her eyebrows slightly raised. When Freya didn't go on, she lowered them and leant forward. "Now look here, missy," she started, but cut herself off when Ecgbryt arrived with Alex behind him.

The large knight looked uncertainly around the room and then slid along the stone ledge on Freya's side. Alex, carrying the dragonhelm in his hand, smiled faintly and sat down wearily next to his aunt.

"I was just saying that I've been to see Daniel," Freya said, her eyes on Vivienne, who was now silently fuming. "He's still unconscious."

Alex nodded and Ecgbryt folded his arms.

Then Godmund arrived. Freya was surprised that he had turned up—either Vivienne invited him or he had followed Ecgbryt and Alex. The haggard warrior drifted into the doorway as if pulled by invisible threads—unconscious of his own will. Frithfroth shuffled in behind him as if tethered at the waist to him, looking even more tattered and dissociated than Godmund. They sat against the wall next to Ecgbryt, empty, gaunt gazes boring through the table before them.

"Okay, so I should start . . . ," Freya said, her voice sounding thin and weak to her in the small room. A movement drew her eye to the door and she saw one of the children, Benjamin, standing in the doorway, smiling nervously at everyone.

"I'm sorry," Freya said. "This meeting is just for adults."

"I asked him to come," Vivienne said, still glowering at Freya. "I thought it would be a good idea to have one of the children tell us how they got here. Come on in," she said to Benjamin. "Sit next to me." Benjamin closed the door behind him and hopped up beside her, his feet knocking against the stone bench.

"Okay. Thanks for coming, everyone," Freya said, clearing her throat, trying to force out what she needed to say. "This shouldn't take long. I thought it was important to bring together a, um, sort of council in order—"

"Hold. I am uncomfortable holding any sort of meeting or conference without Modwyn present."

All eyes turned to Ecgbryt.

"It is not right and meet that she should be locked away," he explained. "We have need of her wisdom and counsel."

Freya's jaw flexed and she nodded. "Yes, let's talk about that first. Modwyn is not a prisoner."

"I did not say prisoner." Ecgbryt folded his arms.

"No, of course. I just wanted to say . . . she's not a prisoner. She's just out of the way. Safe, and out of the way."

"I do not understand why she must be 'out of the way' at all."

"I also share Ecgbryt's concern," Alex said. "The lady Modwyn is the best and most reliable source of information that we have available to us, in terms of the lay of the land, of resources. She has had a continuity of rule in this city spanning hundreds of years."

"We have Godmund and Frithfroth here for that," Freya said, trying to throw conviction into her words and not looking at the two men, who looked far from reliable in any sense of the word.

"I agree with Alex," Vivienne said sharply. "As the actual ruler of the city, Modwyn would certainly have been privy to Ealdstan's intents and—"

"You and I both know," Freya said, "that she's spent the last decade with a knife in her chest—and she did that because Ealdstan sold her, sold this entire city, in fact, out to Gád and his minions."

"But she protected the city, the tower at least. She doesn't deserve to be shut—"

"Her time here has made her lose perspective, I feel. I think she's putting the . . . the perpetuation of this city above the purpose it was designed for."

Vivienne leant farther in, her upper lip pulled back to show her incisors. "Still and all—"

"Let's not argue about this," Freya said. "Let's move on."

"Stop cutting me off!"

"*Both* of you stop!" Alex said, standing. "I don't know what's between you, but if you want your own space to fight, then we can leave you two alone."

The silence of the room rang in their ears.

"Let's move on," Alex said, sitting.

"Okay," Freya said, trying to catch her breath, aware that her face was flushed. "The most important thing for us to do is to get these kids home. That's priority one, it must happen as soon as possible. Between us we need to decide what's the fastest way to do that. As I see it— Yes, Alex?"

"Sorry, Freya, sorry," Alex said. He had leant forward and was signalling her. "Don't mean to interrupt, but are we actually agreed that this is what needs to happen?"

Freya blinked and opened her mouth to protest, to say that of course it needed to happen.

"I'm just raising the question," Alex said. "I mean, sure, I actually agree with you, on the face of it, yes, they need to go home. It seems obvious. However, they're here for some reason—it's either a good reason or a bad reason—and I think it's worth discussing. For instance, let's say that they're here because they're actually going to be safer here than where they would be elsewhere. What if they were brought here in order for us to protect them? Maybe something else happened when the horn blew. I don't know what, maybe the sky started falling, the seas are boiling, it could be anything. What do other people think? Anyone? Any ideas?"

"It is a question like this," Ecgbryt said, "that Modwyn would be ideally placed to answer."

"Godmund? Frithfroth?" Freya asked. "What has the horn done? What was it designed to do?"

The warchief, who had been sitting against the wall, arms folded, head bowed, opened his eyes and fixed a penetrating glare at Freya. "It was designed by Ealdstan to summon the next army—the army that would fight the battle at the end of time. The greatest warriors of the age."

"Okay," said Alex. "We got those, but we got the children as well."

"Wait, I would like to challenge Godmund's point," Vivienne broke in. "All we got were the ancient knights—and just the ones that you rounded up. We did not, for instance, get any modern armed forces. The SAS, say, is notably missing."

"Perhaps we were given the right kind of warriors for the battle we have to fight," Alex responded. "Perhaps the children can fight a fight the knights cannot."

"No, I don't think—" Freya began.

"That makes a kind of sense," Vivienne said. "And that's the reason I asked Benjamin here, to tell us his story. Ben, would you do us the honour? Start with what you encountered before you came here. Start with the brownie."

II

"I thought it was an elf or a pixie at first," Benjamin said, nervous at first, but gradually warming to his tale. "My sister and I learnt afterward that it was a brownie. We got a book out of the library.

"Um, it would come at night. My sister noticed it first, hanging around the bottom of the garden. She actually thought it was an imaginary friend of hers. She started leaving food out for it, as a game. She introduced me to it one day, thinking I wouldn't be able to see it. She was quite surprised when she saw how surprised I was! It was a little person, all dressed in leaves, he even had a little belt made out of a root and everything.

"My sister wanted to make it some proper clothes, though. She made it some little trousers out of sewing scraps. It took her a week—she did an all right job. She put them out on the doorstep and the next morning they were gone. Not only that, but the house was completely tidy—all dusted, hoovered, and everything. Then my sister made it a shirt. It took her another week and she left it on the windowsill of our bedroom. She wanted to try to see it put it on, but she fell asleep. The next morning it was gone and our homework was done. All of it, in every workbook, start to finish—math, chemistry, biology, English, geography—all of it. That might have been fine, but we could barely read any of what it wrote; there was just this cramped, tiny scrawl right across every page. We had to buy new exercise books out of our own pocket money so our parents wouldn't find out.

"We decided not to make it any more clothes, but by then it wouldn't leave us alone. It started doing our dad's work for him, the stuff that he was bringing home. That didn't go any better and he got really angry. He yelled at us and punished us because he thought we had done it. That brownie was really hard to get rid of. It was my idea how to do it though."

"What did you do?"

Benjamin smiled. "We put some plans on the kitchen table for a tunnel that needed to be dug at the bottom of our garden— out by the trees where nobody goes. To China. When we woke up the next morning there was a big, dark hole and a massive pile of rocks and earth. It was Sunday and we spent the entire morning filling the hole back in. We got back absolutely filthy and had to take two baths apiece. Mum was less than thrilled, but we never had a problem with the brownie after that.

"And then last night—sorry, all of that took place a couple weeks ago—and last night my sister and I were both in bed," Benjamin continued. "We share bunk beds in the little room, me and my sister. I was just about to fall asleep when I saw someone in front of me. He wasn't literally in front of me, but with my eyes closed it was like he was. And he had a sword—he was like this big, hairy warrior person—and he raised his sword and held out his hand and said, 'You of the next army—I summon you!' I woke up immediately and nearly fell out of bed. My sister has the lower bunk, and I could hear her crying.

"I said, 'Did you hear that?'

"She said, 'I don't want to go. Don't follow it, Benji.'

"I didn't know what she meant at first, but then I felt it as well. It was like there was a hook in my chest that was connected by an invisible string, and every few seconds I'd get a strong tug on it. I got out of bed and started getting dressed and Elidh said, 'Don't go.'

"'I have to,' I said. 'Don't you want to come too?' She said that she was so scared she couldn't even move.

"I sneaked out of the house and started walking down the street. It was nighttime, but the sky was a little brighter than it normally is. I think it was that way. Or maybe I could just see better somehow. There were a couple other kids walking down the street, and we were all headed in the same direction, all of us following that sort of tugging thing in the chest. It led me down the street and into a part of the town where I hadn't really been before, where there was a sort of forest. There were more of us by now, maybe twelve other boys and girls, and you could see in their faces that some were excited, some were scared, but mostly I think we were all relieved, I know I was, that we weren't just alone—that we weren't crazy, there was something else going on.

"In the middle of the forest, there was a large hole, big enough so that you could walk right into it. I mean, you had to hop down into it and then it just sloped down. It wasn't freshly dug or anything, it was like it had always been there. There was grass growing around the edges. All of us jumped in and started going down. We could see in the dark because of these bright torches that lined the walls. We didn't know who put them there, but they were comforting because *someone* put them there, didn't they?

"At the start I was wondering if it had something to do with the brownie we had gotten rid of, and if I was responsible for all these others who were with me, that we might get buried or something, in revenge, but then we started talking between ourselves about what was going on. Because we weren't in a trance, you know, we were all fully aware of what was happening, we were all just following the tug inside of ourselves.

"Well, we started talking and found that we all had run-ins with monsters—just like what you've heard.

"Um . . . we kept on walking for a long time. We got tired, but kept on walking, most of us. Some had to rest, and they just sat down by themselves for a while and then got up and kept walking. I did that a couple times. There started to be lots of tunnels, instead of just one big one, and other kids were arriving from other directions as well. But we all knew where we were going, because of the pull.

"And that led us here."

III

Benjamin marked the end of his story by folding his hands in front of him.

"So in answer to my question," Alex said. "About getting the army we need—apparently the children were the right warriors for the kind of battle that we have to fight. The way Benjamin here dealt with the brownie—that kind of creativity—I don't think that many adults would have, *could* have come up with that sort of solution. And if the war we're going to be fighting is against these sort of things, then we'll need their kind of thinking. And not necessarily Ealdstan's . . . which is to say the conventional sort of army with weapons and tanks and all that."

"But it *is* Ealdstan's thinking!" Freya insisted. "*He's* the one who enchanted that horn; who programmed it, if you like."

"All the more reason to trust him, as I see it," said Ecgbryt. "Much of our circumstances are Ealdstan's doing, it is true, but only he had the foresight to take such long precaution against the final hour. I and the others who slumbered for him are bound in strong bands of trust, which I as yet have not sufficient reason to doubt the good and true purpose of. It is not right that our first assumption should be of betrayal. But rather he has fallen afoul of some circumstance, and he needs our aid."

"Well, Vivienne and I happen to know differently. I—we used that thing she brought. The . . . the synatheauraliser. I saw him myself setting fire to books, and . . . and . . . he met with Hitler, of all people."

"Is that true?" Alex asked Vivienne.

Vivienne nodded her head. "Apparently he did, but what was discussed is unclear. Pages were missing from that account."

"Viv, it was *Hitler.*"

"I do not know this Hitler," Ecgbryt said firmly. "But were he the devil himself, Ealdstan may have just reasons for meeting with him."

Freya's jaw was clenched and her lips pressed together in a thin line. "So what's the answer?" she snapped at him, sharper than she liked.

"I would stay the course. I would trust the wisdom of Ealdstan as I have done these ten centuries past. I would be a fool to flinch at the last moment."

"Also, brownies and sprites and whatever are all very well, taken in isolation, but what about a whole army of those things? Or the yfelgópes? Or the dragon I encountered?" Alex said, becoming heated. "Are we going to ask children to go up against those?"

"That's a very good point," Freya said emphatically. "I'm all for the empowerment of the youth, but I don't think that both sides scale equally. An army of children against an army of mystical creatures? Does anybody here really, *seriously* think that is the best course of action?"

"What other course is there?"

The abrupt and gravelly voice startled just about all of them.

All eyes turned to Godmund. "March the children into the drag-ons' mouths . . . perhaps they'll choke on the bones," he said.

Freya held in a deep breath; she felt she had lost control of the meeting. She tried to rally her mental strength, but before she could speak the door creaked open and a small face poked out from behind it. It registered surprise for the smallest of moments and then disappeared. "They're in here," they heard a voice say.

"Is *she* in there?"

"I think so." The door opened again and the face reappeared and vanished again. "Yeah, she's in there."

"So go in."

"I don't need to. You go in."

Alex went to the door and opened it. There were five children there—Fergus, Gemma, and three others Freya couldn't remem-ber the names of. "Can we help you?"

"Yes, sir, sorry, sir," Gemma said, her back straightening. "We didn't want to interrupt, but we thought you should know."

"What?" Alex, closest to the door, said.

"My brother's been taken," Fergus said.

"Taken by whom?"

"He's been captured by . . . by goblins, I think, or something."

"Where?" asked Vivienne. "From inside the tower?"

"No, we, um . . ." Fergus took two steps into the room and nervously addressed them. "Rian and I were exploring—I know you said not to, but, um, we were, and we found a building just outside this tower, outside the big wall, that has a tunnel that goes down . . ."

"He speaks of the path that leads to the Wild Caves," Ecgbryt said.

"Yeah, um, so we went down it, and we were careful to go quietly, and we came to this big area, as big as this place, this niðer-plain—"

"Bigger," said the boy behind him. "There's this massive, wide pit down there."

"That is the *Slæpismere*," Ecgbryt said. "We found it drained—Daniel, Freya, and I—when we set forth on our quest against Gád."

"Well, inside it we saw this massive camp," said Fergus, speaking faster and faster. "Where all these creatures were, like giants and big lumpy people made out of rock, I think witches were there, there were these things with heads like skulls, and there were animals and lots of other things. Rian and I were hiding and so we got a good look at them . . ."

"Hold. You saw all this . . . this army, *under* the *city*?" Ecgbryt said, leaning forward anxiously. Everyone in the room was reacting to the news in different ways. Freya, bent forward, gripped the edge of the stone table with bloodless fingertips. Vivienne stood and clutched Alex's shoulder as Benjamin looked on with wide eyes. Godmund began muttering to himself and Frithfroth just continued staring into nothing.

"Yes. We were hiding, watching them all, we were hiding, and that's why—" Fergus's face flushed and his voice became tight. "And that's why Kieran didn't see us. He must have come looking for us or followed us down. We tried to get his attention, but we didn't want to make so much noise. Rian threw some pebbles at him, but he kept going, he didn't hear us. He looked over the edge of the pit. I was about to go and run get him, but Rian pulled me back."

Fergus looked like he might cry. The boy behind him put a hand on his shoulder. "I grabbed him because I saw some monsters coming out of the shadows. They were short little tattooed men. They put a bag over Fergus's brother—over Kieran, over his head and shoulders, down to his waist. Then they tied him up and carried him off. Fergus wanted to run after them, but I kept holding him. He wanted to shout, but my hand was over his mouth. I knew that we couldn't go after them. I knew that the best thing was to come back here and tell everyone."

"You absolutely did the right thing," Alex said, now crouching before Fergus, whose face was flushed.

"We have to go and rescue him," he said. "He's my brother, we have to save him!"

"We must do more than that," Ecgbryt said. "The army of the opposition beneath our feet even now?" His voice grew louder with each word. "Action must be taken, and quick!"

"You're right," Alex said, wringing his hands uncertainly. "We must—we need to get the knights all together. We need to—"

"We need to get everyone out of here," Freya said, finding her voice. "I'm sorry, am I mad or do we need to get all the knights and children together, plot a route, and get everyone to safety?"

"Yes, yes, of course we do," Vivienne said. "You're right."

"Come on," Alex said. "This is exactly what we were just discussing. We said that the children are needed in this conflict. That they were brought here for a reason. That there is a *purpose* to their being here."

"But if that purpose is something that Ealdstan cooked up," Freya countered, "then I'm sorry, I don't trust that. Ealdstan is a psychopath who has sent children—who knows how many children—to their death, Daniel and I included! You know that— you've seen the evidence for it. Ecgbryt knows it's happened, and Modwyn was complicit. If there is a reason, then I don't trust that."

"It sounds as if your mind is already made up. You didn't bring us here to discuss what to do next, you brought us here to tell us what to do next—but you're out-voted. Psychopath? That's a strong word. It seems particularly arrogant of you to question a man as brilliant and as wise as Ealdstan is."

"Am I wrong? Does anyone doubt it?" Freya asked, trying not to sound frantic. "Daniel and I escaped by the skin of our teeth—Swiðgar wasn't so lucky, Ecgbryt. What do you think he'd say if he were here?"

Ecgbryt's already grim face darkened even further. "I do not see that he would say different than he did when we were in this situation last. This evil must be fought with the tools we have been given—then it was you and the boy. Unhappy though you may be, you were what was most needful at the time. We had need of mortal hands against an immortal foe. Now, with a greater army, our need is greater."

"The only thing that is similar is that children are in danger again. But there's no quest here, Ecgbryt. We have other options. We had other options then as well—more than we were presented with at the time. I knew that, but I didn't have the courage to say it. And the few times I did manage to, I wasn't listened to—I was shouted down. It's not the either/or situation that you think it is. We can *get* a mortal army—a proper one! We take these children back to the surface world right now, with these knights, and I guarantee—soldiers, machine guns, bombs, and grenades—they'll level this place. Absolutely *level* it. How is that not clearly the best option? Why are we even discussing this?"

Freya's heart was racing and her arms and legs were quivering. She could feel sweat breaking out on her face. She wasn't suited well to this sort of confrontation—arguing her points like this—but lives were at stake. Children would die if she backed down, and it seemed as if she was the only one who was really trying to help them.

"This is not normal warfare," Alex said in a low, strained voice. "That is why we are discussing this."

"Alex, come on," Freya appealed. "You know I'm right."

Alex twisted his hands around the crown that he still held, his eyes darting from Vivienne to Freya and back. "I think just because we don't know how this is going to turn out in the end, that doesn't mean what we're doing isn't right."

"There are children here," Ecgbryt said. "Let us ask them what they wish. Benjamin Brownie-Slayer, would you return home or continue the fight?"

"I think . . ." He looked over to Freya, his eyebrows crinkling his forehead. "I think I do want to fight. I want to help defeat whatever's underneath here, whatever Fergus and Rian saw. I think it's important."

"He shouldn't get to—he shouldn't *have* to decide whether he's going to go into battle or not. He—"

"Shush, Freya, now," Vivienne said. "You've had your say, now let them have theirs."

"No! This is—"

"We want to fight too!" Rian said.

"Yes, we do. That's why we're here," Gemma agreed.

"I want to get my brother back. I'm not leaving here without him."

Freya looked at their young resolute faces, appalled. "It's not open to a *vote*," she said. "These kids—*all* of these kids—aren't even teenagers yet. They don't know what's best. *I* didn't know when I was their age, Daniel didn't know either."

"You said just now that you *did* know what you wanted to do," Vivienne said. "But you were not listened to, you complain. And now will you not listen to these children? Because it sounds as if they know what they want to do."

"You and Daniel survived," Ecgbryt said. "It was hard, but you won through in the end."

"But we only made things worse!" Freya gasped.

"I would disagree," Ecgbryt said. "As would Swiðgar, as would Daniel."

"Swiðgar's dead and Daniel's in the next room, a heartbeat from death. So things haven't turned out so great for *them*. Can't you see? It just keeps getting worse and worse! We thought back then that we would be solving everything, but here we are again, eight years later, with even more lives in even *greater* danger." Face hot, Freya stood, panting slightly. She felt she had entered a nightmare—a dream state in which she had no will to affect anything or anyone around her and was only a bizarre distortion of itself. She felt the authority she had managed to gather since the city was retaken by Alex and Ecgbryt's knights was slipping through her fingertips.

"I will take what lifiendes will come with me," Ecgbryt said. "Those who want to return may—that is the bargain I shall make with Freya, who has argued well."

"No, that's simply unacceptable. Alex—stop him. Look at this reasonably."

"I don't know," Alex said. "Reasonably, it sounds like a good compromise to me."

"*What?*"

"We're giving them the choice, Freya. The one you didn't get. Don't be a stickler for this. Isn't that what you wanted when you got here?" Alex said. "The option to choose whether you would return or not?"

"What I *wanted* was never to have been put in that position at all. To never have had to make the choice in the first place."

"Well, we must make the choice now, there's no getting around that," Vivienne said. "And that seems to be the fairest thing—to let people decide for themselves, not to force them."

"Okay then," Alex said. "Are we agreed?"

"Agreed," Ecgbryt said.

"I don't like it any more than Freya does," Vivienne said, "but I am agreed."

"Agreed," said Benjamin, and the children in the doorway said, "Agreed."

"No," Freya said, slumping forward. "No . . . no . . ." But she knew she had lost. "Listen to me—we're still playing Ealdstan's game. We have to *stop*—"

A shout from the hallway interrupted Freya. A knight dashed into sight and crowded into the doorway. He scanned the room and then addressed Alex. "*Haefod*," the knight said, "One has arrived—he has returned."

Alex leapt up. "Who has? Kelm? Ecgbryt, quick, we need—"

"No, sir," the knight interrupted. "Not he—it is Ealdstan. Ealdstan the wizard has returned!"

They all leapt to their feet now.

"Hear that, Freya?" Ecgbryt said. "We might even now be saved. The maker of Niðergeard has returned! Where is he?"

"In the courtyard, under view of the throne."

The last fragments of flour fell from beneath Freya's feet.

They bustled out of the room, all except Godmund and Frithfroth, Freya behind all of them. That was it, then. After all the effort, she was just going to get swept along with the tide again. Maybe she never had any power, ever, to change her situation.

"My lords! My ladies!"

This call came from behind them. They all halted and turned. One of the knights who had been posted to look after Daniel was hurrying down the corridor.

"What is it?" Freya asked, rising as anxiety flooded into her. "What's wrong? What's happened?"

"Tugdal?" Alex said. "Answer her."

"It is the boy—Daniel. He is awake."

Freya blinked in surprise as her world took another turn. She turned to the group, her mouth open, but not knowing what to say.

"Go and see to him, Freya," Vivienne said. "We'll meet you outside." Freya turned and followed close behind the knight called Tugdal, taking the steps two at a time.

IV

He felt a sudden sensation of movement, like he'd been blasted out of a cannon, even though there was no cannon, and there was no "him" to be shot out of it. He even understood that there wasn't really anything for him to be blasted through either, but that was the sensation he experienced.

It felt as though there was an electric fire that danced across every nerve of his body. The space around him was streaming with bright blurs as stars in their galaxies coursed past him. Turning his head in the direction he was travelling, he saw the Silver Rider, sitting on its black charger, pulling him along. Looking down at himself, he saw that he was in chains, being dragged through the galaxy, wrists and feet bound. He was confused at this. A moment ago he had been nothing, but now he was very definitely a thing, and in chains that felt very real.

"What . . . was that explosion?" he asked, saying the words before wondering how he could be speaking and how he could be hearing his voice.

"We passed the light barrier," the Silver Rider told him in a voice heard in his head that brought a strange mix of emotions with it—nostalgia, loss, melancholy, comfort, and familiarity. "We have reentered your universe."

"Why am I in chains?"

"This is the way I carry all who travel with me."

"Am I dead? Is this what death is like?"

"You are not, but this is what death is like." They tore through a cluster of stars.

"How can I hear you talking right now?"

"You cannot. I am not talking. This is not even how I appear. This is simply what your mind is telling you in order to rationalise what you are experiencing. To experience the true, unmitigated reality of your situation would destroy you, sending you to the furthest reach of insanity."

"Wonderful. So where am I going, O figment of my imagination?"

"Your soul, flung from the world you just left, is being returned to its house—your body. We shall not meet again until it is time for you to pass through the final gate."

"What's that?"

"It is the gate that few have ever passed through twice."

Before Daniel could speak again they had arrived at their destination. The sensation of movement was replaced by a sudden weightlessness as he hung over the world—his world. It wasn't the earth though; it wasn't a planet as such. What he saw was a web of lights that radiated out from a centre that he felt, intuitively, was his home. He was aware, somehow, that it was a sort of soul map of his world, and he remembered he had seen it before, when he had first been whisked away from here. The continents and land masses were traced in pale smoke, it seemed, and each point of light that made up the complex web was a person's life. Some lights were very dim, some were dark, as if consuming light from those near them, and others very, very bright.

He felt himself falling down toward it—like that first slow movement at the top of a roller coaster, the anticipatory acceleration before the plunge. The web of lights spread out before him and he saw Britain, and at the centre of it a cluster of the brightest lights in the country, painfully dazzling in their intensity.

Underneath was a great dark fog, so thick and noxious that it seemed as if it could completely consume all the light above it.

And below *that* was something else. Far, far deeper than even the Wild Caves was another presence, a winding, twisting flame of black and red. He looked at it and the red part of the flame leapt forward at him, entering him through his eyes, flooding his skull with red light. He heard a voice say, "Come to me."

And then he was back in his body. He knew it was his because it throbbed in pain, but it was so good to feel it. After experiencing so many bizarre sensations not associated with his body, he was now grateful for it, whatever kind of shape it was in.

He coughed and gasped as he rolled over to one side and tears of relief trickled down his face. He was back. He was back. He was back.

"Daniel—Daniel, are you okay?"

He opened his eyes and saw Freya's creamy brown face in front of him, her dark features pressed into concern. "You're sweating, you need to drink something. Here." She held a stone bowl up to his lips and he took a sip of pure, cool water. It was the most glorious liquid he ever remembered tasting and as he swallowed, he felt it soothe his sore throat and rest, cool, calming, in his stomach. "And take these. Viv brought a lot of painkillers. There's a bottle over there. Do you want something to eat?"

Daniel took the pills and leant forward to drink from the bowl again. He bit a strip off the hard meat and chewed it, letting it become soft in his mouth.

"What happened to you? Were you captured by Kelm? Did he torture you?" Freya gently touched the side of Daniel's bruised face, pulling her hand back when he winced. "Sorry."

"It's okay. I'm happy to feel anything right now." He tried to swallow and was mostly successful. "No, Kelm didn't actually need to do that at all, in the end. How long . . . have I been out?"

"Well, apparently it's been more than a week since you left Vivienne and me."

"Uhn. So I've probably been out a few days. Still, feels longer."

"What happened to you?"

"I was back in Elfland. But, like, my spirit was. To me it

seemed like months again. I think it was my soul that got pulled back because . . . of something that I'd done there the first time. It was a sort of punishment . . . a kind of hell, really. And then there was . . ." He thought of the Silver and Gold Riders and of falling through the cosmos. More of it was coming back to him now. "I don't know, maybe it was a dream or a hallucination." He thought of Prince Filliu's poem, the words that still felt fresh in his ears. "Maybe. I think something was going on." He bit off another shard of meat. "What's happening here?"

"The short version? Vivienne and I found out a lot about Ealdstan. We found Modwyn—she was in this tower all along, keeping people out by some sort of . . . sorcery, I guess, that I don't really understand. She stabbed herself and her spirit was trapped in the Langtorr, keeping people out. She showed us where the Great Carnyx was—Godmund was guarding it, and I—well, I used it. I wish I hadn't. Alex and Ecgbryt arrived with the army of knights they managed to raise and they chased the yfelgópes out of Niðergeard—just like we needed, and like what was planned for, but then these children started showing up, all these twelve- and thirteen-year-olds—the age that we were when we first came, and younger. It seems this is what was meant by the next army. I don't know if I summoned them too soon, or if we need children to fight this war, or if this is another part of Ealdstan's perverted plan. We were just arguing about that, in fact, when— What is it?"

At Ealdstan's name Daniel's eyes went wide and he started to gasp for air as a sudden panic choked him. "Ealdstan—I remember now. I saw him in Elfland . . . he did something to me. He's not on our side, Freya!"

"I know."

"No, I mean, he's got some bigger plan, something that he's not telling. He . . ."

"I *know*. That's what I've been trying to tell people—you, Alex,

Vivienne, *everyone*. I've been saying that since I first met him. Idiot."

"Hang on, wait. I'm sorry, but I'm trying to remember exactly what he did and said . . . he wants to open up portals from this world into other ones. I think he's trying to tear this world apart—I mean literally apart. If we don't close the gates, then I don't know what will happen. We have to stop him. We have to *find* him first."

"That won't—"

"We need to find out all we can about the gates; where they are, how to close them. It's absolutely vital. We—"

"Daniel, stop. He's here. Ealdstan's *here*. He arrived just as you woke up. All the others went to see him, I came to see you."

"We need to get there," Daniel said, rolling forward. He lifted his arm and Freya slipped underneath it. "Do they know about him? Not to trust him?"

"Of course not! They're like you—like you used to be. They think the sun shines out of his arse and he's the answer to all the problems in the world. They're confused and, I think, more than a little afraid, and they're going to go down there now and do whatever he says. Wait, don't get up."

"I have to," Daniel said, straining with everything he had just to sit up. "Ahh! We've got to warn them."

"Well, here, swing your legs like that—there. And just slide forward now . . ."

Daniel's feet hit the ground and before his eyes he saw a heart of flame, resting beneath the lake of black fog, which was beneath the cluster of bright light. And the flaming heart called to him again: *Come to me*.

"Are you okay?"

"I'm fine. Did you hear that?"

"No. What?"

"Uhn. Maybe I just stood up too fast. Let's keep going."

After a few initial failed attempts Daniel's muscles started to loosen up and they found he could move fairly easily. Freya didn't need to help him much more than steady him occasionally. It was a long way down the staircase to the ground floor though, and Daniel had to take frequent rests. During these he told Freya what happened to him with Kelm, and most of what he remembered of his second, most recent trip to Elfland. They ran into several groups of children who lined the stairs and studied Daniel quizzically, not knowing what to make of him. Freya told them to go back into their rooms but very few of them even made a pretence of doing what she said.

"You're good with them," Daniel said.

"The kids? Yeah, I'm a natural."

Finally reaching the ground floor, they crossed to the Langtorr doorway. It was standing ajar, and through it they could see no one and hear nothing. They walked through it and the Langtorr courtyard in quiet apprehension.

Suddenly, Daniel couldn't breathe. He stumbled forward and fell to all fours. A deep, rumbling hiss sounded in his ears. *So may destruction save a man? Shall battles make him whole?*

"What was that?" Daniel gasped, his breath exploding.

"What was what? Are you okay?" Freya was at his side.

"Those were the words that Filliu sang to me in Elfland. I remember them now . . ."

"What words?"

Daniel couldn't breath again; his spent lungs couldn't draw air. *And will you fight to save your life . . .* A flame bloomed before Daniel's vision. *But not to save your soul?*

Flame beneath darkness beneath a pillar of light. *Come to me,* the voice said from the flames.

"I have to go," Daniel said, gasping for air. "I can't stay—I won't see Ealdstan—I've got to go and find—" He stumbled.

"But what about telling everyone about Ealdstan—what he's done and doing?"

"I can't. I have to go somewhere else. Haven't you ever had that before? The very strong feeling that you were supposed to do something but you didn't know why?"

"No. This was a mistake. I'm taking you back to the tower." Freya started to turn him around.

"Stop! I'm okay. But I need to be somewhere—I'm being called. I have to go."

"Where?"

"Down into the Wild Caves again. I think."

"That is what you *absolutely cannot* do," Freya said. "We've just found out that there's an army down there—not just yfel-gópes, but trolls, giants, and I don't know what else."

"I can slip by them, somehow." Daniel turned back around and his left leg struck resolutely out and down, as if he weren't controlling it. "I need to get farther down. There's something calling me. I don't think I can resist it." He took another involuntary step forward.

"You're half naked! You're shivering, you're bruised, probably concussed, you've just been in a coma—"

"I wasn't in a coma, my spirit was in Elfland!"

Freya had a firm grip on his arm. Trying to shake loose, he found that he was holding as tightly to her, on her wrist and shoulder, as she was to him. He let go and tried to push her away as his feet kept moving underneath him.

"You're not thinking straight."

"I'm thinking fine. Trust me, this is important, I need to do this."

"Like you needed to kill Kelm?"

"No, I was wrong to try to do that. I'm sorry about that."

The apology brought Freya up short.

"I'm . . . rethinking things right now. I think I was wrong to do that, I think I was wrong to do a lot of stuff. You may have been right about going after Gád, even. I'm sorry. I think you're right about Ealdstan. That's why you have to warn them. And something's calling to me in the Wild Caves—something that knows what someone said to me in Elfland. That's why I've got to go."

"Daniel, why do you keep doing this? You're always so absolutely *certain* of whatever you're doing. And when anybody argues against you, you only say that this time you're even more certain than you were all the other times before! It's so infuriating!"

"I'm sorry. It's always true, though."

"But you're always wrong."

"I won't be this time."

"You always say that!"

Daniel didn't respond, his feet just kept moving underneath him.

"Are you listening to me? To yourself?" Still he said nothing. "I'll come with you," Freya said. "I can help you get there."

"I'm sorry." Daniel started to hobble off to the entrance to the Wild Caves. "I don't know what else to say except, I'm sorry."

"What if it's Ealdstan, or Gád down there who is trying to tempt you out?"

"It couldn't be. The words—they were some of the words that helped me out of Elfland when Ealdstan wanted to keep me there. It couldn't be . . ."

Daniel was aware that Freya had stopped walking alongside him. He turned his head to call over his shoulder. "I'm sorry, Freya. Good-bye."

She didn't answer him, but only watched him hobble slowly away between the stones of the partially ruined bunker that had once housed the Great Carnyx, the entrance to the Wild Caves, and disappear.

V

Godmund wandered out of the map room, Frithfroth at his side. The news of Ealdstan's return brought no change to their pallid, morose faces. Guards in the hallway behind them said something and the girl Freya turned and pushed past them.

They continued slowly down the corridor, those ahead leaving the two ancient men trailing farther behind. Godmund and Frithfroth descended the stairs, the noise of excited children rankling them.

"Ever since Niðergeard was created," Frithfroth said, "never such a sound was heard in it."

The central hall of the Langtorr was emptying as the children followed after Vivienne, Ecgbryt, and Alex, curious to see what was going on and why the adults were looking so anxious.

Godmund and Frithfroth also left the Langtorr, the children streaming around them, but stopped just inside the outer gate.

They stood for a long time, their hollow eyes gazing despondently out at the semi-destroyed city.

"I had not forgot the ruination these buildings, this fortress, had faced, but to see it again hurts like a newly opened wound."

Frithfroth said nothing. Spittle was collecting heavily around his mouth.

"What was that rhyme of old that spoke of the passing of beautiful things?"

> *Bright were they: the buildings and bridges, the walls,*
> *Hallowed and high hung the arches.*
> *Mightiest among all men the mead-benches were filled,*
> *Singing lusty songs of swords; but fate,*
> *Worker of wyrds, wrought an end to that.*
> *Now empty are the eating places, ale-horns lie splintered.*

The battlefields are barren, bodiless and cold.
The city of the sleepers is steeped in silence.
Bright cornices and crenellations crumble to the ground.
Smiths and stonewrights this site have abandoned.
What workers will repair the ruined walls
Decayed into dust, lying in the dirt?
Gone a long time has been any giver of gifts in
Niðergeard, the nothing—the neglected, the nowhere,
                                    The Ruin.

"Aye, that is enough like it," Godmund said after a time. "Thank you."

And then everything began to shake.

CHAPTER THREE

Wargames

---------------------------------- I ----------------------------------

Whitehall

The permanent under secretary of state for defence sprang through the corridors of the Ministry of Defence with a swift and purposeful bounce. This was a day that would be long talked about for untold years to come—the hand of the future would write this day as its history, and it would not find him a man wanting in strength and resolution.

He tapped on a heavy oak door and walked in without waiting for a reply. He scanned the room. There were maybe half a dozen junior servants, four other under secretaries, the press secretary and his assistant, and three cabinet ministers, including his superior, the secretary of state, as well as the secretary of state's personal staff. They were sitting, standing, or leaning nervously, crowding the large office. Their faces were pallid and gaunt, and those who talked did so in low, hushed voices.

"Ladies, gentlemen, deputy commissioner, sir," the permanent under secretary said, nodding deferentially, fixing his eyes finally upon his boss—the secretary of state for defence, the head of defence for the British Isles—who was seated behind a large teak desk. Timothy Edward "Ted" Towne, member of Parliament for Crawley, West Sussex. The permanent under secretary had found no strong feeling for his political superior. As a civil servant he was immune from the intrigues and power plays of those forced to stand election, and Ted Towne was the typical slimy bastard who was able to work his way up the ladder through guile and evasion. He had started out in the cabinet as secretary of state for works and pensions briefly before taking over as secretary of state for defence when his predecessor developed health problems. He was not a hard worker, but was a very good delegator, which the permanent under secretary much preferred. Things just ran more smoothly when the politicians stayed out of the way. The machine of government ran smoothest when left on its own. Were he to stay the course and not create any waves, there was undoubtedly a barony, or at the very least a knighthood, waiting for him at the end of his career.

"Come in!" Ted Towne waved the permanent under secretary of state for defence in. "Sit or stand where you like." His head tilted forward and he consulted a handwritten list. "We're still waiting on a few more, but as you're here, I think we may as well begin and the rest will have to catch as catch can. Right. First, I want to thank those of you who came in early this morning, and for the work you have already done. You were not obliged to do so, but it is very much appreciated, and so is the hard work you will undoubtedly be doing in the coming days." Ted Towne gave a smile of camaraderie to all of those arrayed before him.

"Next item of business," he said, plucking the reading glasses from his nose. "What the hell has happened?"

There was a little uneasy shifting, but no answer. The permanent under secretary averted his eyes by looking down to the folders he was carrying, as if consulting a note, but there was nothing there.

"I don't mean *how* or *why* it happened, I mean just what I said: *What* has happened? What do we know? Can we even articulate the situation? Come on, out with it. What do we *know*?"

"Children have gone missing," said one of the minister's secretaries.

"Good, thank you. What else? Come on, no reason to feel silly. Let's try to state this in the most basic words possible."

"Not *all* of the children have gone missing," volunteered a junior civil servant.

"Good. Many, but not all. Do we have any idea how many? Clive?"

The deputy commissioner of police of the metropolis of London leant forward in his seat. "The reports are coming in faster than we can record and file them. So far . . ." He consulted a sheet of paper. "Eight hundred children from the London area are reported missing. From other parts of the country . . . the number is ten times that, at least. Other districts are just as swamped as we are."

"Is it terrorists? Mass hostage takings? Ritual or religious killings? Something like that?"

"It is unlikely, sir."

"*Un*likely?"

"Highly unlikely, sir, in my opinion, sir," the deputy commissioner said, his gruff London working-class tone at odds with Towne's Etonian inflections. "There are about seven hundred confirmed and suspected terrorist cells in the UK. Even if those cells coordinated—which would virtually be impossible since they span the entire spectrum of culture, religion, and ethnic group—even *if* those cells coordinated and mobilised within the same hours of last night, they would have to abduct fourteen children apiece, from all over the country—not just the major urban areas. They would have to do this without anyone seeing them, without any tip-off coming through CID or MI5. And the picture that we're starting to get from these abductions is rather bizarre. Usually only one, or at most two children taken from each household. Not all of them. And of those, only children between the ages of ten and fifteen—the great majority between twelve and fourteen. And it's a clean ethnic and societal slice. No one race or class has been targeted. And all of them are within the British Isles. Not a single abduction of this stripe has been reported from the continent or from Ireland." He dropped the folder he was carrying on the ground and rubbed his hands over his face. "It's completely baffling."

Secretary Towne furrowed his brows. "Has there ever—I'm sorry for asking this, it's a ridiculous question—but has there ever been anything like this recorded anywhere, throughout history?"

The deputy commissioner spread his palms out and shook his head.

"The plagues of Egypt?" said one of the MPs.

"When was that?" Ted asked, his eyebrows rising. "Was that back in the seventies?"

"It was . . . I'm talking about in the Bible. The twelve plagues of Egypt."

"Weren't there ten plagues?" said an administrative assistant.

"No, twelve."

"I thought it was ten."

"I'm certain it was twelve. The last one—I think it was the last one—was the death of every firstborn."

"It wasn't second born?"

"No."

"Okay, the twelve, possibly ten, plagues of Egypt. It's worth researching. Someone find a Bible from somewhere, make a note, thanks. But biblical apocalypse aside—" the secretary of state said, shifting in his seat. "Leaving that—"

"It wasn't the apocalypse, sir. That's in—"

"*Leaving that aside*, has there ever been a similar situation?"

There was a brief pause before a junior civil servant put up her hand.

"Yes?"

"The Pied Piper of Hamelin?"

"I'll take that as a no, then." The secretary of state for defence rolled his eyes, which was his cue for everyone else in the room to make similar signs and noises of low-key ridicule. "Clive, is there anything else of importance that we need to know? Anything at all?"

"Just this: there could have been more."

"What do you mean?"

"Bear with me, because this is where the tale gets really strange. Those brothers and sisters that were not—that did not go missing, and that were of the ages of early teens, have reported that they heard an audible voice inviting them to join some sort of battle. The exact words they heard, and this is a verbatim quote from forty-three different, uh, witnesses, is this: 'You are the next army, I summon you.' From forty-three different children that we've talked to so far, all pretty much the same words. Some variation, but basically the same."

Silence hung thick in the secretary's office.

"Any idea of what that's about?" Ted Towne asked. "Some sort of mind control? Drugs or some kind of . . . thing?"

"We're looking into that. We're not ruling anything out, but on this scale . . . it could be posthypnotic suggestion."

"Pied Piper isn't sounding so silly now, is it?"

"Hypnotic? From what?"

"From a video game, say. Perhaps a website. It could be in a song, but that's unlikely—not enough information could be coded, I'm told."

"Television? A film?" asked another MP.

"Also unlikely. The BFCC and British Television Standards Committee have a firm lock on subliminal flashes, so it is unlikely to have occurred at the programming level. Possibly at the manufacturing or broadcasting level. There are some large disc-manufacturing plants in India and Pakistan that feed distributors here in the UK. But the problem with that is—"

"Why only that narrow age bracket?" Ted said. "Why not younger brothers and sisters, why not parents?"

"Isn't there a certain sound range that only teenagers can hear? A very high pitch?"

"There is," said Clive, "but you can't *communicate* to them on it. Not unless they knew Morse Code and had pen and paper available."

"So it could still be a terrorist act," a junior minister said.

"It could, but unlike anything we've ever seen," another answered.

"It's *obviously* a terrorist act."

"It may not be."

"How *could* it not be? It is *literally* an act of terror."

People began to debate openly. The meeting was starting to get out of control. "People, people, people! Please!" Ted Towne banged an open palm down on the table. "Let's stay calm, yes? Just calling it this or that doesn't actually solve anything. Clive, you may—did you have anything else to add?"

The deputy commissioner of the Met had been starting to fidget nervously. He shook his head. "No, sir."

"Very good. You may leave if you like. I'm sure that you have a lot of pressing demands to see to."

"Thank you, sir. I think I will be off." He rose and left by a side door.

"Leaving the causes of the crisis to one side for now, the next item of business is to discuss the *public* face that we will put on this crisis. How to address the media, what message to send, how to shape it, spin it, that sort of thing. Everyone will be looking to us to lead. What can we do to show them that we are?"

"Can we get the press into some barracks? See the soldiers ready to mobilise? Get an interview with one of them?"

The minister frowned. "I don't think that would go. Official secrets, and all that."

"Perhaps actually deploy some of them, then. Get pictures out of armed guards outside—I don't know—an inner-city school or something."

"Yes, that could work. What if . . ."

The permanent under secretary tuned out the talk of how to play the media—strictly the purview of the press secretary and his assistants and civil servants. He surreptitiously slipped a hand into his jacket pocket and checked his secret phone. This one looked identical, but it had a red tinted graphic on its screen so he could tell the difference. There were no messages.

He felt a hand grip his upper arm. He looked up and found the room giving him their full attention, and Ted Towne looking at him expectantly. "I'm sorry, sir?"

"I said, do we have a status on the prime minister?"

"Pardon me, I was just reading an e-mail from his secretary," he lied. "He's still locked in deliberations with the rest of the cabinet at Number 10."

"He hasn't sent for me?"

"He believes that you are of best service where you are," the permanent under secretary of defence said before judiciously adding, ". . . no doubt."

"Very good, thank you," said Ted Towne. "All right, that's all we need to discuss for now. I'm going to order you all to clear out now and get busy. Could I ask my personal and the civil staff to remain behind, however."

People started filing out of the now warm and stuffy room. The permanent under secretary and other members of the defence office staff shuffled into the seats and chairs vacated by the more senior officials. The door clicked behind the last person to leave.

"Now, onto more specific matters. In approximately fourteen and a half minutes I have meetings with the heads and deputies of the Defence Council. What I want you lot to do in the meantime is to run figures on military commitments and see how fast we can mobilise what we have, and where we can get it once we do."

This was typical of the minister's usually vague instructions. "Did the minister have any idea where he would deploy said British forces?" a staff member asked.

"Oh, the usual Middle Eastern and Eurasian hotspots. Print those up. I just want something I can flap in front of the PM this afternoon when he starts getting, ah, 'up in my grill.' Also find out which countries we can rely on for further manpower when pressed. He'll want to know that. Ring the US embassy or whomever you know in Washington. Sound the Americans out. What with that, and whatever the DC chaps say, we should all squeak by this matter without too much bother. Thank God my kids are in uni. I should call Carol. Thank you, that is all. Bugger off now, like good little lambs." With a wave of his hand he dismissed them.

The permanent under secretary closed the door and stepped into the hallway. He put his work phone in his pocket and drew out his secret phone. As he thumbed a number into it, he swiped his identity card and entered from one secure area into another. These halls were not recorded by CCTV and were safer than his office to talk in if there were no one around.

"This is Gád," he said. "Send word to Kelm—ready the troops.

The horn may have been sounded earlier than anticipated, but all is chaos and disorder up here. Niðergeard must be crushed, first and foremost, and then we can move forward from there. Tell him to await my signal. What passes in the city? Has *he* returned?"

Gád listened as a report was made. He glanced up at a colleague who was approaching from the other end of the hall.

"Do so, and do it quickly," Gád said menacingly, "or I'll have your head on a plate and your entrails for afters." He nodded to his colleague and gave her a charismatic smile, rolling his eyes. His colleague gave him a chiding, you're-naughty purse of her lips.

The permanent under secretary for defence ended the call and replaced his phone, stalking back to his office.

II

Each step felt surer and firmer. It was as if the ground itself was reaching up and grabbing his foot, holding it until it was time to take the next. Daniel felt that he could close his eyes and just let his feet walk automatically. Was it his mind being controlled, or his body? Which was worse? The argument he'd had with Freya kept circulating around in his head. Was this a part of Ealdstan's power? Or Gád's? But how would they know about Filliu's verses from Elfland? Snatches of it replayed in his mind, and to try to forget about what he was doing and its reasons, he tried to reconstruct them as he kept moving.

> *I know what loss is victory, what's won after defeat,*
> *What is weak when it is strong, and strong when it is*
> *weak.*

It was poetic, certainly, but did it have any meaning? Or was it just a trick of rhetoric? That was the sort of thing he heard people say—like those African street preachers and Islamic proselytisers who peppered Oxford's Cornmarket Street on summer mornings. It was new age sophistry. Chinese calendar wisdom—so obtuse and nonspecific it could be taken any way that fit. It reminded him of the elaborate riddles that Swiðgar and Ecgbryt had shared with him and Freya, but those were more straightforward at least. Strength was strength and weakness was weakness. That's what he'd learnt in the army. But sometimes it was better to *appear* weak. Was that what the poem meant?

He felt a pang when he thought of Swiðgar again. He missed that knight, who was by far the wisest person he had ever known, now that Ealdstan had turned out to be up to no good. He wished Swiðgar were here, with his twinkling eyes and thoughtful pauses. He would know what to do.

He moved silently down the sloping tunnel that led from the Carnyx's fortress to the Wild Caves below. He cautiously tried to slow his compulsive footsteps, remembering what Freya said about an enemy army beneath them. He could hear or see nothing yet, but it made sense. What with Ealdstan roaming through different worlds or dimensions, opening portals, allowing things to roam through . . . there would have to be someone on this side to catch them and bring them here when they appeared. Gád and the yfelgópes were probably well placed for that. In eight years, what could they assemble? Alex and Ecgbryt said they had noticed a boost in mystical beasts that they had been hunting, but that was only in the last year or so. They thought it was circumstantial—but now, knowing that this wasn't a coincidence, that the bleed through from different planes was part of a concerted effort involving Ealdstan and possibly others . . . That meant Alex and Ecgbryt had only been dealing with the creatures that spilled out of wherever they were being gathered, not a higher number that were leaking through.

There were footsteps in the rock dust that lay on the floor of the tunnel; small, like children's shoes. It looked like there was more than one type of shoe both coming and going, but that was as much as he could tell.

The first sign of the enemy camp he noticed was the smell of burning coal. It was a dirty and musty smell, mixed with the smell of grease and sweat.

His automatic footsteps took him to the end of the tunnel and the start of the uncharted, treacherous maze that was the Wild Caves. This started with the *Slæpismere*—a dark, underground lake that was now long dry. Daniel cast his mind back eight years to when he had first been here with the knights. The place was almost completely changed.

The dry lakebed was no longer empty and dark. It was crowded, absolutely filled with the enemy army encampment. There were tents and fires spread out across the expanse. Yfelgópes wandered here and there, to the metallic din of blacksmiths forging and tempering weapons and beasts crying out. Hasty, irregular tents had been erected wherever there was space—or nearly enough space, packed in tight next to each other and the rock walls that lined the shallow depression. There were areas that looked like a zoo more than anything else. Enclosures made of thick stone walls held the more savage and untamed beasts. He saw large furry shapes—bears, perhaps?—corralled in a central pen, huddled together for warmth. There were large wolves that prowled along the walls that fenced them in and fought each other for splintered bones that fetched up alongside them. Against the far right-hand side of the cavern were large, seated forms that looked to be giants—their heads bowed on their drawn-up knees in the despondent manner of the homeless, trying to stay out of the way in a crowded place. Large casks were resting beside them and the front of their shirts were soaked. They obviously had been allowed to drink themselves into mindless stupors. Daniel was able to pick out the shapes of the rock-skinned trolls littered throughout the camp as though they were some sort of grotesque statuary. The right side of his body twinged with the memory of the last time he had mistaken one of those for an inanimate chunk of stone.

The camp was getting ready to mobilise. Daniel knew this instinctively, through his time in the military. Everyone was moving with a nervous, anticipatory energy. Items were being packed up, ready to carry out or stow out of the way. Unable to stop his feet, unable to turn around to run back and tell Niðergeard about its impending attack, Daniel said a silent prayer that they would be ready in time anyhow. He was moving around the encampment—to the left, along a sloping, rocky edge where there was piled debris, garbage, and a stinging, rancid smell that suggested cesspits of some sort. Absolutely nobody was here and he was able to pick his way through the uneven tip completely unobserved.

It was long and hard work. His feet knew where they were going, but not the rest of him, and he often had to lunge or pull himself suddenly in different directions in order to steady himself. But as he padded across a torn tent canvas, he was out of the rubbish heap and onto clear, open ground again. The light from the camp was dim here, and it would have to be very sharp eyes indeed that saw him, a grey shadow moving across a black wall. The walls of the cavern were narrowing now and the ceiling was lowering. Ahead of him he could see a series of upright stones, higher than he was, and at least a dozen bent forms of yfelgópes slouching against them.

He held his breath as he crept closer and closer, wondering how he would manage through. His hand went reflexively for his sword, which was not there. He swallowed hard and looked harder at the slumped figures. It was then that he noticed the manacles they wore; flat, metal clasps screwed down on their wrists, attached to iron chains fastened to metal brackets sunk into the standing stones. And they weren't yfelgópes crouched beneath the stones—they were children. As he moved around the stones he saw there were at least a hundred of them, all quietly huddled. Many of them were bruised, crying quietly, trying not to make any sound; others were sleeping or pretending to, or just trying to wait out the situation. One of the particularly sharp-eyed children noticed him and nudged his neighbour, pointing out Daniel with a finger drawn close to his chest. Daniel held a finger of his own up to his lips and shook his head. The two boys mimicked him, smiling private smiles, excited at the prospect of escape. Daniel smiled and continued on, a profound pity in his chest. *They think I'm going to rescue them,* he thought. *I hope I'll be able to, sometime.*

He moved on, leaving the encampment behind. He was now heading into darkness, and he felt a cold chill. He was still exhausted and he could feel his legs wobbling, trembling wildly at his knees, so violently, in fact, that his teeth started chattering. Then he realised it wasn't him that was shaking—it was the ground beneath him. It suddenly gave a roll like it was the deck of a ship in a storm, throwing Daniel forward. An incredible rumbling and crashing followed, sounding like twenty thunderstorms all at once.

Daniel felt himself smack repeatedly against the stone floor. He curled up and put his arms up to protect his head. It felt as though the world were ending already, as if the hand of God were repeatedly beating down on the earth.

And then it was over, all except for the throbbing of new bruises on his body and the loud ringing in his ears and the thunderous echoes that continued many long moments afterward. He looked around and saw that everything was darker than before, and he was a good deal farther away from the camp. He had been bounced a hundred feet or more, and although he would sooner have not been bounced along like a ping-pong ball, it was just as well that he had since the camp was now buzzing with the renewed activity of an angry wasps' nest. Orders were shouted and animals or lower creatures bellowed in pain and confusion.

It hadn't been an explosion—or even a series of them, it had to have been an earthquake. "What's happening up there?" Daniel asked himself out loud, more to hear his own voice than anything as he went deeper and deeper into the darkness and the Wild Caves.

III

Permanent Under Secretary of State for Defence Alexander Simpson flashed his badge at the gate to Number 10 Downing Street. Two police officers inspected it, made a log on a digital pad, and then buzzed him through. He made the walk down the street itself, which seemed more like a movie set than a street, being spotlessly clean, no more than about fifty feet wide, and filled chock-a-block with video cameras along one side. Reporters were busy nattering away, giving reports and updates on a situation no one knew anything about. Except for him, of course. He managed to twist his superior smile into a frown of resolution and concern as he made his way up the stone steps to the building that housed the seat of the ruling authority of the nation. The reporters would, no doubt, be speculating on his identity, so he made a brief show of fumbling for his distinctively coloured civil service ID badge as he handed it to the guard on the door. Then he was allowed in.

The building was almost dead silent. There was another security checkpoint just inside the door, but the two policemen there did not even stand to clear him through—the larger of the two only flapped a lazy arm at him and went back to moving his stubby finger across his smart phone.

Gád navigated the hallways to the Cabinet Room. There was a

privately contracted guard outside this room. He nodded at Gád, giving a small, private smile. Gád's eyes went up to the thick lintel of the door as the guard's back was turned. He recognised the small stick—no wider or thicker than a wooden ruler, but half as long—that he had carved his runic spell onto and placed there just days ago.

The door clicked and swung open and the guard stepped aside to let him pass, allowing entry into the long, high-ceilinged room with chandeliers, pillared entryway, and large Georgian windows with two vistas over the garden. In sharp contrast with the rest of the building this room was very noisy and active. Most of the cabinet was crammed inside, milling around and standing above the long conference table—there was no room to sit. The busy, wavelike hubbub of their voices was driven by a current of urgency and the occasional cry of triumph. The table was the focus of all their attention. Just about every inch of the polished mahogany surface was crammed with maps, reference cards, and plastic miniatures symbolising troops and armies. Gád located the prime minister toward the centre of one side of the table, surrounded by three aides who were all on mobile phones, talking into them in low voices. The PM had one hand cradling his chin and the other gripping the opposite elbow in what had become a stereotypic stance for this particular world leader.

"Excuse me, sir," Gád said, drawing near.

The prime minister looked up. "Oh, Simpson. Good to see you. Bringing work, no doubt. No rest for the wicked, eh? Stand here. Take a look at this board and tell me what you think."

Gád looked down at the board, not giving it more than a cursory glance. "What colour are you?"

"Blue."

"It seems to me as though you are in a tight spot."

The prime minister bent his head and grimaced at the map.

He was in the middle of a painful decision. "But if we move most of our forces from Iceland to Scandinavia, then all we need to break through is Ukraine and all of Asia is open to us."

Gád felt a small but powerful hand push against his upper leg, shoving him back slightly to make way for a small creature with a bald head and large, exaggerated features. Its skin was leathery and shiny, with a dark green hue.

"Fool of a general!" the thing barked in a belligerent, nasal whine. "It would then be straight shooting for the Reds to get all the way up to Greenland from North Africa. Why would you even attempt to try for Asia without defending Europe?"

The prime minister chewed his lip. "I don't know, I don't know." He turned to the aide at his left. "It's Stephen here, he really has us all over a barrel." The PM raised his eyes and glowered at the minister for education. "What are you up to, you fiend?"

The minister returned an enigmatic smile.

One of the PM's aides leant in toward him. "Sir, if I may . . . ?"

"Go ahead. There are no bad ideas in this room. Bad moves, yes. But no bad ideas."

"Sir, the minister for health is entrenched in Australia—she has been for some time, and she's only been adding reinforcements to Indonesia. Black is absolutely ready to explode, so any action on Asia would only help them further down the line."

"But they have South America as well."

The aide rolled his eyes. "*Pff!* South America! Ahem, sorry, sir. Yes, they do, but they've only got three armies on each country."

"Sweep Europe!" the short dwarf said, hopping up onto one of the plush chairs and shaking his fist in the prime minister's face. "Iceland! Scandinavia! Great Britain! Northern Europe! Western Europe! Ukraine! Southern Europe! Your armies *must* finish in Southern Europe so that you may reinforce Western Europe as your final act. The threat will come from North Africa, when it comes."

"Yes," the prime minister said slowly. "Yes, you're right, of course you are. You always are."

"Sir," said the minister for health, "I feel I must protest at how much help you seem to be getting in terms of strategy from not just your aides, but also—" She waved a hand at the little leathery hominid.

"Rank has its privileges," the PM stated bluntly, swiftly picking up the three red dice in front of him. "All right, Backhouse, are you ready to go?"

The minister for education nodded.

"Okay, Greenland to Iceland."

The two men leant forward and each picked up some dice. Staring into each other's eyes, they shook the dice and then let them fall. There was a second of silence as they compared the amounts.

"Ha! Lose two armies! Let's go again." They rolled and compared amounts again. "Ah, lose one each. Okay, again. And . . . yes! I win." The prime minister gave a short cheer and bent over to shift some of his plastic pieces across the board.

"Sir," said Gád. "If I might take this opportunity to get your signature on a few documents?" He opened the file folder he was carrying and placed some documents under the prime minister's hand, holding out a pen.

"Hmm? Oh." He bent over just far enough to jot his name on the lines Gád pointed at.

"Thank you very much, sir."

"Not at all, not at all."

"How goes the war on other fronts?" Gád said, waving a hand at the other maps on the table that the rest of the cabinet was engaged in playing on.

"We're still in early stages of the tournament," he said. "I haven't really been keeping an eye on the others. Edward?" The prime minister looked to the aide on his right and raised an eyebrow.

"Well, Minister Deasy seems to be doing well on board two," the aide replied. "Sir Luke is holding pretty tenaciously onto the Middle East. But it's Burdett—sorry, sir, it's the secretary for transport who is the one to look out for in the future. He's positively running board four over there. Really knocking them all for six—only a few more turns left on it, I expect."

"Well . . . we'll burn that bridge when we come to it. Now, what was I going to do next?"

"Iceland to Scandinavia!" the imp at his waist barked.

"Ah yes. Going again." He started to shake the dice again.

"Sir . . . if that is all?" Gád said.

"Oh, certainly, Simpson."

The dice rolled again as Gád turned to go.

"Oh, Simpson!"

"Yes, sir?" he said, halting and looking back over his shoulder.

"By the way . . . ," he said slowly, as if his thoughts were coming from a long way off. "How's all that . . . how's all that other stuff coming along? The children and all . . . ?"

"Nothing to report yet, sir. You'll know as soon as there is." Gád fixed the imp at the prime minister's side with a sharp look.

The creature immediately reached a hand up and grabbed the front of the prime minister's jacket. "Focus! This is the most crucial turn for you on this board!"

"Of course, of course. Just wanted to . . . Where was I? I'd just moved all these armies, hadn't I?"

Gád carried on to the door, knocked on it, and waited for it to be unlocked.

IV

Freya strode through the empty streets of Niðergeard. There was a . . . hubbub, it was best described as, coming from the central courtyard. Coming closer to it, she saw a large gathering of knights and children. *They shouldn't be out of the Langtorr,* she thought. *And who's guarding* that *if so many knights are here?*

They were all standing around the hero's throne, which she had not seen up close before—only at a far distance from the Langtorr's windows. Up close she could see the stone pile it sat upon was made from the rubble of the collapsed buildings nearby. Particularly skilled and well-crafted designs and carvings had been selected to face outward, making it a mess of design and sculpture, defaced by being broken and shoved together in an undignified mess. The magical silver lamps that illuminated the city had been sunken into it, casting everything in an unnatural and irregular light.

Standing around the stone pile were between thirty and forty tall, white-faced men in dark robes trimmed with sinister patterns in gold thread. Their faces were angular and there was something cruel about the set of their mouths and arched eyebrows. They stood to a loose sort of attention, shifting their weight and moving their heads in a reptilian manner, sending dark tongues out every so often to lick their red lips. Their features and mannerisms seemed familiar to Freya and it took her a moment to place them—they put her in mind of Nemain, the elf boy they had encountered on their first quest in Niðergeard. Ealdstan had somewhere picked up a band of elfin bodyguards. She bit her lip as she remembered how quickly just one of them had disarmed and incapacitated Ecgbryt, and that one had not even been armed. Each one of these elves held long, thin swords with intricately wrought handguards in silver and gold. The blades were long, flat, and a rich copper colour. They shifted and shimmered in the semidark as if impatient for something to cut into. Freya shivered. There was nothing about the strange warriors that wasn't menacing.

And on the top of the stone pile, on the chair made by slabs of masonry pillaged from the walls of the ruined buildings around it, was Ealdstan. He had seated himself on the throne, his elbows propped gently on the armrests. His long white beard cascaded down his chest and his red, gold-hemmed robe, to coil on his lap. He looked just as old and belligerent as when Freya had first seen him and was speaking into the crowd.

Everyone before him was dead silent—barely breathing—straining to hear his words, which were issued in a thin, high voice that split the silence with a sharp edge.

"—for you or any here to question the extent of my plans. Plans that are literally hundreds of years in the planning and execution. Plans that have been conferred with kings, queens, and ministers throughout the history of this nation. You had faith in me at the start—all of you who were laid to sleep by me had faith enough to put not just your lives but your deaths in my hands. As did the people of this city, who had faith at the start. Would you abandon that faith now, when all that we have prepared for is about to descend upon us? Continue that faith now. The time is coming that you were prepared for. Do not value your long years of obedience as nought. Do not stop at so short a distance from the land of your destination."

Freya quietly pushed her way through the crowd of knights and children, trying to get to the front. Her heart was pounding like a jackhammer. A voice was answering Ealdstan's—a quiet voice speaking in even tones. Freya recognised the voice and was angry. Who gave *her* permission to be here? Whatever illusions she'd still entertained about being in control of the situation, they evaporated now.

Modwyn's hands were bound in front of her, but her posture was anything but meek. Her chin jutted defiantly forward and her brows were set in determination. She was apparently going toe-to-toe with the old man in the chair of rubble. She called up to him in a challenging voice. "You left this city in a time of great need, and have stayed gone these past eight years. Many have died, the city itself is in ruins, its citizens fled, dispirited, or killed. And now you return without word of where you have been, or instruction to us in how to prepare for the enemy we have just informed you is on our doorstep—beneath it, in fact."

Ealdstan's scowl deepened as the silence after Modwyn's words grew. Freya spied Ecgbryt, Alex, and Vivienne in the crowd, standing together among the assembled knights, not quite to the fore of the group, but near Modwyn. Children were here as well, at least a hundred of them—they were not easy to spot between the massive figures of the knights. Their eyes were wide and most of their mouths hung open. She couldn't see Godmund or Frithfroth anywhere.

"I know where he's been," Freya said, taking care to make her voice loud and clear. Those around her parted and she was able to make her way to stand next to Modwyn. "Daniel Tully—a servant and knight of this city, as well as a friend of mine—has seen what Ealdstan's been up to. A mission that he was on took him to the Faerie Otherworld, Elfland, where he saw Ealdstan making deals to bring an army here to destroy our world. In order to return back here, Ealdstan tricked him, made him a living sacrifice in order to prop open the portal between this world and that. He—"

In a flash of movement, Ealdstan was up from his chair, flying from the throne to the base of the pile in a single leap. His band of warriors separated to give him space. He landed before Modwyn and Freya.

"I am accountable to neither of you," Ealdstan bellowed wrathfully. "Neither to this servant woman," he said, looking at Modwyn, "nor this dark-skinned foreigner." He turned to Freya. "You have no authority or stake in this country!"

Freya was nearly paralysed in the face of this anger and abuse. She fought to find her voice. "D-Daniel Tully—"

"Yes, where is the boy Daniel? I would be interested to know if his perception of events is what you claim."

"He's being protected. He's somewhere safe. Somewhere where you cannot harm him."

"I doubt that very much."

Ealdstan began to pace very slowly before the two women, his manner taking on something wolfish. His eyes went from Freya to Modwyn and back again, several times. He stopped his prowl as he moved back in front of Freya.

"*Where* is he?"

"He—he's not here. He's left this city."

Ealdstan's lips compressed into a thin white line before he spoke. "He has gone to the surface?"

"He didn't tell me."

Ealdstan's head dipped and he stroked his beard. "It would be possible to divine his path if needed . . . ," he murmured and then drifted into silence.

Freya felt the weight of the attention of all those behind her, still quietly straining to hear all of what passed. "You are not in power here anymore, Ealdstan," she said, barely even able to force the words out of her throat. It was unlikely that anyone but Modwyn or Ealdstan even heard her, but the old man's eyes flared with renewed rage. She saw anger, spite, and disgust in those hard eyes and she immediately wondered what she had ever done to justify such a look. What had she done to deserve what this man had done to her, apart from being young, frightened, and vulnerable? She felt a door open inside of her and found anger enough to match that which Ealdstan was even now displaying.

"You're not in power here anymore, Ealdstan!" she shouted, raising an accusatory finger. "You may be the architect of this place, but you are not its defender! You have returned only after it was saved by these knights, the ones led by Ecgbryt and Alex Simpson. You are no longer this city's defender, you are no longer its ruler!"

Face flushed, panting, Freya matched the power of Ealdstan's gaze with equal intensity. She felt as if she were hovering above herself, above Ealdstan, above them all. She seemed just to speak the words she wanted automatically.

"Are you ready for the path you will walk?" Ealdstan asked in a low voice.

The air seemed to change—a perceptible drop in the pressure, it seemed. In the edge of Freya's vision, she saw a hunched figure in dark clothes move to the front of the circle of people around her. It was an old woman whose eyes were puckered in a sightless squint—one of the old ladies from the island in the dry lake underneath the Niðerplane. She turned her head and saw more of them, moving into the circle around them. *Where have they come from?* Freya wondered. *Is this moment really so important that they've felt compelled to witness it?*

Ealdstan followed her gaze and also noticed the appearance of the old women, but he seemed to be the only one. His anger dimmed and he said in a low, confidential tone, "It appears you *are* ready to walk it. Tempered by cold and fire. I have done well in strengthening you."

"I strengthened myself."

"Do you really believe that?"

"I do."

Ealdstan moved forward, causing many in the crowd to take a step back. He went straight to Alex and stopped in front of him. Alex's hand was on his sword, but he was nearly paralysed with fear. Ealdstan's hand shot out at his face as fast as a cobra and his fingers clenched on the dragonhelm, tearing it off Alex's head.

Alex staggered back, drawing his sword instinctively, unsure of exactly what had just happened. By the time his sword was out of its sheath and levelled in front of him, Ealdstan had already turned and was moving away.

Passing Freya, he brought the helm down on her head, not quite with violence, but certainly without much consideration.

"All hail the new ruler of Niðergeard!" Ealdstan called out in a deep, booming voice, an ironic smile twisting the left corner of his mouth.

Freya was not sure what Ealdstan was trying to do with all of this, and everyone else around her shared her confusion. As Ealdstan moved past her his hand shot out again, and this time it gripped Modwyn around her throat.

"No!" Freya shouted. Modwyn's eyes bulged and her legs went from underneath her—she opened her mouth but couldn't even gasp. Her hands clawed at her throat as she tried to pry Ealdstan's fingers from around her neck. Freya dived in and tried to help her. But before she could even get her fingertips on the old man's hands, Ealdstan gave a mighty leap and pulled Modwyn with him. Freya fell to the ground. The old wizard alighted at the top of the hero's throne again, the body of Modwyn flapping beside him like it was a rag doll, his talonlike hand still gripping her alabaster throat.

Alex was already moving forward, sword at the ready, but the mob of elf guards closed ranks and raised their weapons. He ducked in one direction and lunged in the other, swinging his sword. His motion was stopped completely dead, however, and he was caught trying to fight through three different defenders. Ecgbryt fared better, throwing his weight behind his axe, knocking two of the red-robed warriors to the ground, but soon he was swarmed, his feet just at the base of the loose stone pile.

"People of Niðergeard!" Ealdstan bellowed. "The night is

ended! Your time of sleep is over! Join those already now awake! I break all my enchantments—all my curses."

Alex's knights were rushing to his aid, passing close to Freya. Alex had been disarmed, his sword flung to the ground beside him, but the red-cloaked warriors apparently were not intent on killing him. They only kept him back, threatening him with the tips of their swords.

Ecgbryt meanwhile was pulling himself swiftly upward with powerful arms, at least two of the red elves hanging off of him. He was within reaching distance of Ealdstan when the old man dipped down and struck him on the face with a motion that was almost too fast to see. The massive knight flipped backward and tumbled down the pile of stone to where the elf warriors allowed him to hit the ground and then kicked him until he rolled back beyond their perimeter, near to where Alex and his knights were being held at bay.

"Let there be light!" Ealdstan called out. His hand jerked and he pulled a knife from somewhere beneath his robes. It had a curved, black blade. He gave another jerk, his shoulders twisted just slightly, and an ugly, red gash appeared at Modwyn's neck. She was not able even to utter a sigh as blood burbled out of her pure white neck. Freya and all those behind her watched in horror as Ealdstan continued to make strokes and new cuts opened on Modwyn's chest and throat. Freya had to turn away, crouching into a ball, shutting the world out, fighting for breath—the Fear was back and it overwhelmed her. A few short seconds ago she was as large as a mountain, right now she was as small as a grain of sand at the bottom of a deep and cold ocean. The earth began trembling beneath her feet, rolling in deep waves. She unbalanced and fell to her side. Opening her eyes, she saw that the movement was not just in her head—everyone was staggering and trying to stay upright in an earthquake that was rocking the underground world. A low rumble built from a sound almost too low to be heard to a huge boom.

And then the ceiling split open, breaking apart in awful, great chunks of stone and earth acres wide and high. They fell slowly, it seemed, their descent illuminated by spears of pure white brilliant light, and for the first time since the forming of the earth, daylight was seen in the hidden realm beneath England.

CHAPTER FOUR

The Snake in the Mind

I

The noise and confusion were left behind him, and Daniel's footsteps went from a hasty shuffle to a regular stride. Every step he took was a step away from the army, and he found out now how much he had been sweating. His skin was cold and damp, chilled by the icy air. He wished that he had been better prepared for this trip. He had taken no supplies, no provisions—not even one of the silver lamps. How would he see? But his feet continued to fall firmly and surely, and he figured he probably wouldn't need to.

The enemy camp was steadily and surely left behind him, along with its smell and its noise. All was now pitch-black around him, but he kept walking automatically. Would he tire? His feet were getting weary and hot. Would he be allowed to rest? He was constantly afraid he would walk into something or that his steps would lead him into a pit, a rock slide, or even just a low ceiling or outcropping, so he kept his hands in front of him and his chest and stomach muscles tight, quickly making his movements drain-ing, exhausting.

He had a lot of time to think and reflect. His thoughts carried him far and wide and he entered a near hypnotic state. Images and scenes drifted before his mind's eye like elements of a dream. The faces of the rebellious yfelgópes—the *léafléas* they called themselves—who had rescued him rose from the darkness, as if surfacing from a black pool to appear for a moment or two before him and then sink back into oblivion again. He could not in all honesty tell one from the other, but their names came to him also. Ridiculous names for anyone to have, but rather poignant in the circumstances. Certain Doubt, Argument, Judicious Speculation, Informed Dissent—improbable, hilarious names, but names of lives he had ended—names with voices he had silenced, which would never speak again.

Why had he done it? He had been overwhelmingly tired, he remembered. He hadn't slept at all for . . . nearly two weeks at that point? He remembered feeling paranoid, feeling detached from his body. Yet, oddly, he felt that he was in control—on top of the situation, like he was running on top of a ball or a barrel in one of those old silent movies—his movements and the world around him just slightly faster than real, slightly jerky and frenetic. If he kept running fast enough, he'd keep up. But where was he run-ning to? To kill Kelm and Gád and end the war.

Daniel wished his feet would stop moving, partially so he could take a rest, but also just so that he could have some time to think without wondering where he was going. He rubbed his tired and aching face with his hands. So much had happened in the last few weeks—weeks that impossibly included many months in Elfland. He had pushed his body past its breaking point. He felt not only physically and mentally drained but also . . . what? Spiritually drained? Was that a thing that could happen? He had never before thought of himself having a soul. He had a body, certainly, and a mind as well, but awareness and consciousness were by-products of an organic brain—electrical impulses that fired in particular patterns or rhythms. That's what most people seemed to believe.

But if he was going to be honest with himself—that's not what it *felt* like. It didn't feel like his mind was an organic computer, as he'd been taught in school. What it felt like was that his mind was only tethered to his body, but largely free to roam. It could look into the past by remembering, it could look into the future by predicting, it could enter into another body by empathising. He remembered once when he was begging on St. Giles, back in Oxford. A little girl, about seven, got into a disagreement with her mother. She shouted and then pulled away from her violently, losing her footing on the pavement and then tumbling into the street, her hands out in front of her. Even though he was down the street a little, he immediately felt as though he were falling right along with her, and when her hands scraped on the road, ripping through layers of skin and quickly becoming bloodied, his own palms twinged as well. As she cried his heart went out to her, and still hours later he found his hands unconsciously pressed together to quell the tingling sensation. Even now, thinking about that time, they tickled.

It could still be chemical side effects or primal conditioning reinforced so frequently and often that it was hard-wired into the biological structure of the *homo sapiens* brain. There could be solid, scientific reasons for how the pain of another made him feel. And what if he hadn't been looking in her direction at the time of the fall? Would he still have felt as he did? He didn't believe so.

But that didn't mean that something else wasn't going on. If there was something as a soul—which all cultures that believed in it insisted was connected only loosely at best to the material world—then it very probably could leave echoes of movement in the organic structure that it was connected to. Science had no explanation for it, but there was a lot that science had no explanation for yet.

And if everything was really just electricity and chemicals, then there was no morality. What would be the point? The preservation and creation of human life would just mean that there were more bio-computers walking around on the face of a warm, spinning rock in a solar system in a distant corner of the universe. And the neuron firings of one brain were just as allowable as the firings of another—the conditions that made them fire, or the end results of those firings, were as arbitrary as their firing at all. There was nothing to say that the conclusions of one were right or wrong when compared to the other. Even if a million brains reached one conclusion and only one reached another—if it was just chemicals and biomass, what was the difference? In biological terms, there was no right or wrong, just active and inactive.

His foot splashed into cool water and then pulled back. The spell he had been travelling under left him suddenly, and he nearly gasped at the sensation of freedom. He lowered himself into a crouch and curled into a ball, his shins and forearms pressing against the cold stone ground. He heard the soft hush of water as it moved in an undisturbed flow along a quiet course. Then, gathering his strength, he inched himself up to the still invisible stream and took his shoes and socks off. They were sweaty and stinky, and his feet were hot from moving inside them. Rolling up the cuffs of his trousers, he placed his feet into the stream in front of him and then leant forward and splashed water up into his face, washing and refreshing it. Then he took some sips of the cold water and hung his head between his knees.

But there *was* a morality, there definitely was a morality. Ask any soldier that, and he would say there was. A crusty old professor might say different, but he had the luxury of doubt, the comfort of no responsibility in society. A soldier knew different—to a soldier, mind and body were one, just as thought and action were one. And that act was good or that act was bad; it depended what resulted from it, more than the intent. There were those who believed that action in and of itself was the only morality—that might made right, that the enforcing of a will on the world to change it was the highest morality. History was littered with those who thought that, just as the Nazis famously had, and absurdly those people who believed only in the power of their own will were never strong enough to keep hold of it for long.

But true moral right still demanded the strength of will to commit conviction to action, and that is what Daniel had prided himself on throughout his life. Not only did he know what was right, but he had the strength within himself to follow those convictions and enact good on the world—whether it was moving one scraggly yfelgóp from this world into the next, or it was assassinating a massive oppressor. Daniel had been in basic training with a lot of new recruits who kept knocking up against that—they thought they could do certain actions, but found the connection between thought and action weak when it came to combat and facing enemy fire. Daniel found it easy to face combat—and a gun was more abstracted than a sword, after all.

Daniel had only been resting long enough to catch his breath and let his heart settle into a slower rhythm when he felt the pull to continue walking. He was fairly relieved since he would much rather be walking in the darkness than sitting down in it, directionless. He found his socks and shoes and put them on, continuing this time along the stream.

No, combat wasn't a problem for him—it was the orders. It was his inability to accept the morality of his superiors when the limitations of their perception of the world were taken into account. They just didn't know the realities of the world like he, Daniel, knew them.

At least, that's what he understood at the time. Now he wasn't so sure. Ealdstan wouldn't have tried to kill him—or do whatever it was he did—unless he, Ealdstan, was evil. Or would he? It depended on what his objectives were, Daniel supposed. But could any really good act ever involve killing or causing pain to someone else? That was part of the Coventry Conundrum, which he had learnt in training. In World War II, Winston Churchill allowed the city of Coventry to be bombed instead of giving the Royal Air Force orders to protect it, which would have let the German High Command know that their encryption codes had been broken. More important coded transmissions were received and decoded in the following weeks and months that aided an end to the war for good. His commanders used that incident to illustrate to the common soldier the need for absolute obedience and trust—don't try to reason out the orders on the ground, just do what you're told— there's a lot more going on in a war than you are allowed to know about, so just follow orders, no matter what, and trust your superiors that you are working for the greater good. Daniel admitted that the reasoning was wholly consistent, but it wasn't good enough for him since he believed that he was privy to an even bigger picture than they were. He couldn't take what his commanders told him on trust because he knew there was more going on than even they knew—what with the hidden world that he had been sucked into. But now he realised that even through his caution, he had taken far too much on trust—there was even more going on than he had first thought. Why had he accepted everything Ealdstan told him without questioning it like Freya had? It humiliated him to think about it. He questioned the value of even a single training march in the army, but blithely ran along on a transcendental assassination attempt in a dark cave underneath the ground.

Now, for the first time since he was thirteen, he was having the opportunity to reevaluate what was most fundamental to his beliefs. Why had he not found cause to in the past eight years? Surely doubt and reconsideration should have been a process he was continually undergoing. How responsible was he being not to do so? He believed, at age thirteen, he had seen the world as it really was and since that time he had not changed his view. And if Ealdstan then turned out to be a monster . . .

Or was he? Was, in fact, Ealdstan really privy to a larger picture himself, or was he another Hitler? And would even Ealdstan know if he was a Hitler? What made the bad men of history so bad? Physically, mentally, they were sound—physically capable, in other words, but where did the wrongness come from? Were their spirits warped? Instead of being physically disabled, or mentally handicapped, were they suffering from some sort of spiritual disability? A lack of empathy or ability to attain spiritual satisfaction? Were they spiritually too weak to do good and yet mentally and physically able to do anything they wished? Were their outward actions only compensations for crippled souls?

He repeated the words of Filliu. *And will you fight to save your life, but not to save your soul?* And he suddenly remembered that Alex had said those words once. He hadn't given it much thought at the time, but now it whizzed around and around in his mind. Why didn't people fight to save their souls? If he was supposing correctly, and souls really did exist, and if they were eternal as nearly any religion claimed—then what was more important than saving that? What was the point of living even ten more extra years if it meant that you had decapitated the part of you that was going to live past those ten extra years? And again—why were these thoughts he was only thinking *now*? Why hadn't he asked himself these questions before? Why hadn't *anybody* asked him these questions? Why had he never even heard anyone ask each other these questions?

The way continued, lonely and dark. His mind tired of its philosophical meanderings, which it was ill-equipped to sort through, and retreated into more comfortable thoughts. He thought back again to the first time he had passed this way—with Ecgbryt, who at the end had pushed him away, and Swiðgar, who he still missed. He figured he must be in the area where there were all those large, dark puddles. But was that before or after the incidents in the gnome camp? It was hard to remember now. But maybe he had already passed through where the gnomes were, and just couldn't see them, wrapped as he was in complete blackness, which was worse than even a blindfold. He might be more apprehensive about what was going on around him, but it was so silent, apart from the sound of his footsteps, that the outer peace entered into him, and he felt as much a part of the dark underworld as he would feel a part of the stream he had left behind if he were a leaf floating on that. And with that idea in mind, he entered into a sleeplike state, the steps of his feet falling between the beats of his heart. And in a near unconscious trance, he walked on.

II

Something was after him.

With a snap of his head, he became more fully awake. His feet still moving, he was not able to sleep fully but was walking drowsily, for how long he didn't know. In a confused moment, he worked out where he was and what he was doing, his mind replaying the incidents that led him here. Doing this, he then tried to convince himself that he was still dreaming, but he was unsuccessful.

And the feeling that something was following him persisted. He kept trying to push that to the back of his mind, as a fragment of a waking dream—after all, he couldn't hear anything but his own movements, and everything was complete darkness around him—but the feeling kept rising to the top, making his breath quick and shallow, his heartbeat fast.

It was becoming warmer. The faint outline of the world he was walking through could be made out, illumined in a faint orange highlight. At first he thought the hallucinations were returning, but the colours shifted in synch with his movements. He could see where he was again. He could see the wall to his right rise steeply, tilting inward at an angle as it rose higher and higher. To his left the ridge plunged straight downward, running out of sight.

He skated along this ledge as quickly as he dared, the idea that something was after him—something reptilian and cold— still weighing on him.

And then, with growing realisation he found he knew where he was. He had passed this way before, with Swiðgar and Ecgbryt. He had gone over nearly every step on that journey in his mind a hundred times since, and remembered they had passed a sort of bridge over a heat vent at one point.

And sure enough, after about ten more minutes of walking, he passed the large stone wall and turned into a large cavernous space that was windy with the movement of hot, heavy air that rose from two vents on either side of him. He estimated these vents to be about fifty feet across and curved at the far end, bow- ing out roughly fifteen more feet. They also emitted a dim orange light, which, after Daniel's journey through absolute darkness, made the cavern seem like a well-lit room. The rocks around here were bulbous and hard, with sparkly flecks in them. Abruptly, he whipped his head around. He knew, just *knew* something was following him—he could sense it, silent and slithering, tracking his movement. He urged himself forward, not even slowing as he entered, and walked to the end of one vent. Then, eyes wide with apprehension, feeling like a passenger in his own body, he lowered himself into the corner of it.

Barely even breathing, he descended. The crevice was so tight he couldn't even tilt his head to see where he was going. His arms gripped along ridges and rough surfaces as he tried to lower himself down, desperately trying to keep up with his feet, which found footholds he couldn't see. He went from holding his breath to gasping at each foot of descent. Many times there wasn't anything to hold on to, or his hands would slip in their haste and he feared falling, but his feet always held. He came to ridges and ledges and virtually vaulted over them as his entire body obeyed the near-instinctive movements that were controlling him. It was getting hotter and hotter. He was sweating and his back was being baked by the hot air that rushed upward.

And then, after who knew how many frantic and heart-stopping minutes, his feet both smacked onto flat ground and he realised he was finally at the bottom. He held his raw and scraped palms to his chest, brushing them slowly to get rid of the dust and gravel that had been embedded into them. Then he blew on them to cool them and looked around, trying to figure out where he was. But the bulbous rock with crystalline flecks created a series of corners and crevices that made it impossible to see more than a couple feet in any direction.

It was bright—the glittering flecks in the rocks reflected a light from somewhere. He couldn't see what might be creating it, but he imagined it must be coming from a stream of lava or something. But molten rock had to be incredibly hot—how close could he get to it and not be completely roasted alive? Even now it was almost too hot to breathe, and he couldn't even see it anywhere. What if he was being led somewhere that he was incapable of surviving? Would he just fall over dead? Would his dead body be compelled to keep walking? Would his spirit?

"What the hell is going on?" he asked out loud, and then regretted his choice of words.

There was a ledge, over which the orange, ambient light was strongest. Heat waves rose and distorted the wall opposite, making the bright flecks embedded in it twinkle like stars.

He raised his arm to shield his face from the thick, hot air, dazed by its intensity. His feet were planted now at the cusp of the ledge.

After several moments he still had not moved and he began to lower his arm, fighting to keep his eyes open in the thermal vent. Whatever had brought him here must want him to see something.

Far, far below him he could see the churning brightness of magma, the superheated rock that illuminated everything before and around him. For a time he just squinted into the shifting colours, mesmerised. And then he found there were different shapes writhing amongst the waves of molten rock. They looked like tree trunks at first, but that didn't make sense—the largest tree in the world would be cinders within seconds in that heat. Rock, then? Rock that could not be melted in that heat?

One of the logs twitched and flexed, rising upward, lifting a giant set of talons, long claws ending each one. They scrunched together and then spread out again in horrific slow motion.

And then the thing that had been chasing Daniel caught up to him.

III

Andrew Philip Richmond hated going to the office. He positively loathed it. But it was so vital for his well-being that he only did so when he could absolutely *not* bear to not go in. It was a frustratingly contrary state for his emotions to be in, and he suffered it like an ache. He needed to do the thing he hated to keep doing the thing he loved. His beasties needed to be fed.

The time he spent in his lush office was torture. He paced, he sweated, he looked out the window, and then paced some more. He picked leaves off the plants, looked out the window again, and when he could stand the tension no longer he looked at the office clock. Only twelve minutes had passed since he first walked in to the blasted place—he searched around the easy chairs placed around a small coffee table for something to read, but there was nothing. It was just as well. The news was depressing these days; dispiriting even to glance at. There always seemed to be a woman crying on the front page next to some child's photograph. It was always, invariably, some tragedy involving dead or missing children. What was happening to this country, and who was to blame? He shook his head. Society had already collapsed, it just hadn't hit the ground yet—everybody was trapped in free fall.

He felt chest pains and sat down, trying to wipe all the sweat off his face with his palms. He opened his desk drawer and took different items out and arranged them on the wide, polished surface. Then he put them back. He checked the time again. Eight minutes had passed. He sat and watched the second hand sweep along the brushed metal faceplate. He watched it do a complete circuit and then stood up. That would be enough time, surely. He was in the office, and that's what people would remember, even if they didn't know exactly how long. He'd try to make a trip in another few days.

He cracked open the door and listened. He could not hear Edward, his effeminate personal secretary, and, opening it wider, saw that he was not at his desk. He dashed down the hallway and to an elevator with no call button—only a silver keyhole. This elevator went to only one floor—the basement.

He called it and waited in agony as it came up to meet him. A security guard rode in it at all times, a thick, burly man with an expensive white shirt and a gun. Smiling in what he assumed was an amiable and chummy fashion, he entered the car and waited for the doors to close.

"Going down to the vault again, Mr. Richmond?" the security guard asked, completely unnecessarily.

Andrew gave his smile a twitch and turned to face the doors as they closed. He counted forty-seven seconds this time before the elevator reached the very lower level, set deep into the foundations of the bank.

Heart racing, he waited eagerly for the doors to open, stepping out immediately once they had done so. He was now in a vestibule—concrete walls painted white, with two low walls behind which were two empty desks and two more security guards. On the ceiling and every wall were visible cameras and, Andrew knew, just as many cameras that could not be seen by the naked eye. Ahead of him was the vault door. He wiped away perspiration again and approached the guard.

"Good evening, Mr. Richmond—you're early this week," he said in a languid, yet respectful tone. "Get you the usual?" He started tapping on the keyboard in front of him.

Andrew nodded and stood before the guard—whose name he had once asked and almost immediately forgotten—trying to look calm, collected, and in no way anxious or distracted.

Forty minutes later he emerged with a wad of banknotes in a carrier bag. Forty minutes was too long. The security checks shouldn't take that long—almost half an hour. The guards didn't need to be so thorough with him. They didn't need to be so inefficiently flippant. They didn't need to put limits on what he could withdraw within a certain period.

As he drove back home he reflected on his actions. It was his money—it was *his own* money, he kept reassuring himself. He wasn't doing anything wrong, he only ever took his own money. Of course, that didn't stop him from being tempted to take more, but who wouldn't be? That didn't stop him from trying to think of ways to get the rest, naturally. He had so far been able to make all the right noises to the board in order to give him an exceptionally large bonus, and he would continue to make those same noises in order to get another one this next year. He certainly deserved it. The director of the second largest building society in London was entitled to a handsome bonus to perform his very skilled tasks. Anyone who had the ability to earn as much money as he did certainly deserved to have it. It stood to reason.

And so, following that logic, if anyone has the ability to steal a great amount of money, then why *not* steal it? Stealing was only another way of working for it.

It would be a question for another day. Right now he just had to get home as soon as possible. Of course he would pick the busiest time of day to make the journey back and forth. His eyes were drawn to the crisp notes in the plastic bag sitting on the passenger's seat.

They were beautiful—just beautiful. There was no work of art superior to what was printed on a banknote. The rose-red fifty-pound notes, the majestically purpled twenty-pound notes, the sunshine and hay–coloured tens, the dappled blue and green fives, all of them were bright and beaming in his hands, the colours of summer and glory—but better than those, these would never fade. They glittered like fragments from a stained glass window, each one reflecting back a mood and emotion. They contained so many possibilities. These little glorious leaves of currency could be seats at the theatre, sumptuous meals with a bottle brimming with bubbly champagne or a glass of velvety-smooth red wine. They could be rare operatic recordings, volumes of leather-bound books, or even a woman. They were his car, his house, his villa, his driver, the jewels for his wife. They were his drugs, his days and nights in dark, windowless pleasure rooms. They were his bribes, his payoffs, his rewards.

He was caressing one of the smallest of the notes, a five, between his thumb and forefinger, feeling its thickness, its

softness. The very words *hard currency* contained primal poten-
tiality. He lifted it to his face and held it beneath his nose. As he
let its odour penetrate his lungs where it was distributed through
his bloodstream, the surface tickled his lip. He leant closer in and
let its surface wander along the contours of his face, its coolness
warmed by his skin, its crispness broken by his oily sweat.

He let it fall, spent, onto the seat next to him and peeled another
small note from the bound block in his lap. This one he raised to
his mouth where it fluttered and danced. He parted his lips and felt
it run across his teeth, which also gave way slightly, and then came
back down in a tender, tentative nibble. He tilted his head and the
money strained and grew taut until it finally tore.

He drew the corner of currency farther into his mouth and let
it become warm and wet with saliva. He swirled it around, moving it from cheek to cheek, and then tilted his head back as it slid
down his gullet. Delicious. He imagined it entering his tummy,
where it would be digested and burnt as food, as energy. Money
was now his fuel. He was literally powered by money, and it felt
divine. The Americans put "In God We Trust" on their money,
and he desperately wanted to eat one of their notes. He wanted to
feel God inside him.

The traffic jam up ahead finally broke—somebody had
jumped off a building and into the street, it seemed, the inconsid-
erate so-and-so. Police diverted the traffic around a bloody stain
in the road.

Twenty minutes later he was pulling into his private garage.
He quickly chewed and swallowed what was still in his mouth,
then gathered the rest of the money, stuffed it in the bag, and
lurched out of the car. He fumbled in his pocket for his keys and
opened the door that went straight into his private home office.
His practised actions were swift; it was the work of a moment to
have the door opened and shut and himself on the other side of it.

"It's back!" cried a gruff, croaking voice. There were nasty cheers.

"Has it brought its allowance?" wheedled a nasal voice.

"If it hasn't, it shall be whipped!"

Andrew Richmond smiled. He knew the belligerent tones were meant only in jest. "It's right here, my beasties!" he called as he pulled the banknotes from the bag and waved them above his head. He tore off the paper strip around the tens and was about to throw them into the air when they were snatched from his fingertips.

"Give me those!"

Andrew Richmond looked abjectly down at the short, greenish-grey, warty figure before him. It held the notes under its large nose and sniffed them, not lovingly as he had done, but officiously, peremptorily.

"What? No coins?" it said, and snatched the rest of the notes from him.

"No coins?" wailed another voice as two more of the naked beasties appeared. "Coins are the only things that matter! I'm sick of paper! Paper's not metal!"

"It's fine, it's fine," Andrew told them calmly. "I'll get coins next week. Coins always take longer to get. I'll get them next week." Good lord, an entire week without more cash? How would he survive?

The green creatures took turns snorting derisively at him. Flecks of mucus briefly became airborne.

"Hey, wait a minnit! There's one missing!"

Andrew emulated surprise. "Really? I don't—that's odd. I could check the car . . ."

"He's been at it again! Check his teeth!"

"Smell his breath!"

Giggling, Andrew Richmond was pulled onto all fours by the stumpy creatures and his mouth was forced open. Sharp fingers probed his cheeks and under his tongue before picking at his teeth.

"Aha! Found it! Look at it, my darlings!" A damp triangle of chewed banknote was waved in the air. "It has! It has! It's been *eating* them again!"

"Get him!"

The little things all leapt on him, their little fists smacking him ineffectually, tickling him in some places as he rolled on the ground. "Stop! Stop!" he protested between laughs.

"Take him to the money room!"

Hilarity overtaking him, Andrew scrabbled to his feet and allowed his beasties to chase him into his den, where money was spread on the floor, pooling and piled into small drifts. There they chased him around, stripped him down, and smeared banknotes and coins on his bare skin.

He couldn't remember ever being happier.

IV

Daniel was instantly racked with pain. The chasing thing must have leapt at him, catching him in the neck. He could feel it burrowing into him. He clapped his hands to where it made its entrance, piercing his skin with burning cold, and he couldn't find anything there. But he could *feel* it. It was now inside him, wet and snaking up the inside of his neck—not his throat, but his *neck*. It was burrowing its way past the base of his head and into his brain—worming its way to the front, and then biting into it with needlelike teeth.

He was on the ground, rolling in agony. The pain subsided, leaving him panting, his stomach heaving but expelling nothing from it. "Whuh—" Daniel's speech disintegrated into a fit of coughing. "What happened?"

Hello, Daniel.

"Who said that? What just happened?"

I have awakened the wyrm within your mind, so that we may speak.

His head ached as the words were formed. The voice was his own—at least, it was what he heard in his head when he thought his own thoughts to himself, but there was a low, tingling sensation, which he felt down the centre of his spinal column. There was a reptilian coldness in the voice that he heard that, even though he knew it as his own, made it seem alien.

A part of you remembers what it is like to be like me—when I had more of a grip on your kind.

"And who are you?"

I am below you.

Daniel crawled back to the edge of the crevice and looked down. He watched the enormous limbs move languidly in the luminous liquid rock. He marvelled at them, trying to calculate how far away they were and how massive they must therefore be. The tips of the claws were submerged again, but he could see the leg they belonged to, and the knee that was attached to it, and the thigh, and farther away than these he also saw what looked to be part of a wing. Against such a bright sea, these all looked black to him, but with a dark green tinge.

"Are you that . . . thing down there?"

Thing? There is more than one "thing" down there. Look closer. Or rather, look larger.

Daniel kept looking, his eyes sweeping along the sight. Then the whole lava field shuddered and Daniel saw the creature emerge with a lurch. It rose up and Daniel could see a reptilian figure, its head curled beneath it, its talons flexed, gripping tighter to something beneath it—gripping large triangular objects. Daniel looked at these shapes—a field of regular, overlapping triangles—puzzled, and then he understood the creature was latched onto a creature like itself, but much, much larger than itself.

"What are you?"

I am Britain's brother since the time we were born of the same fire rising from the sea. I am Britain's grandsire as I watched it arrive in infancy from foreign shores. I watched it in its young and vital days and I watch it in its dying. I am Britain's priest and I watched as it died when all of what was this earth was blown away like a pile of dust.

I am this island's breath and its flame. I am the authority by which its kings rule and I am the strength by which its warriors defend it. I am the image on the crown and the blazon on the shield. I am remembered when women and men are young and I am forgotten when they are old. I am alive in what is youthful because I am kin to what is most ancient.

You know the answer to that. You tell me what I am.

"You're a dragon!"

I am the dragon—the white dragon of this realm. I fought with all contenders over many centuries—and I am dying.

"Is that other dragon killing you?" Daniel said, trying for the moment not to think about how strange it was to be talking aloud to a voice inside his head. Stranger things had happened to him recently, but this was still unsettling.

It already has. I am in my death throes. Once I was magnificent. The shadow that fell upon the earth when I extended my wings reached to the furthest end of this worldsrealm, where dragons are revered and worshipped.

I was proud in those days.

At that time I welcomed battles against all comers, but this . . . leech has wormed its way insidiously inside of me, finding the cracks and burrowing into them. It has no honour, it has no poise or composure. It just sucks and sucks, hoarding all that it drains.

It is a dark dragon that rules this age, now that my time is passed. It is not a dragon of pride and strength, but of greed and spite.

Daniel laid himself down on the flat stone, his head jutting over the edge of the chasm. "Why did you bring me here?" Daniel asked, his voice coming out in a murmur that even he barely heard.

I watched you when you were a boy. I saw you through a window as you scratched in a notebook a picture of an archway. I watched as you grew, shedding the dead skin of your former self as you grew into the world around you. I watched as you studied me in an old book. I watched you sleep on cold steps in dark doorways. I have witnessed your violent acts, when the snake in your mind ruled over your body. I watched as you were pushed out of this world and into another. I watched you return and then get pulled back again, as though snagged on the talons of a falcon.

"But you weren't there. How were you able to see all of that?"

My eyes are not mortal eyes—they have seen mountains raised up and worn down by aeons of wind and rain. My eyes have seen the earth covered with water, and the sky when it was on fire. They have seen rock transformed by ice and eroded by the sea. My eyes see not just the present but the past. They strip what is before them to the core—layer by layer of skin and muscle and bone. My eyes see you at your birth—at your first step—at your first fight—your greatest triumph and your deepest shame. My eyes see your first and your last.

"Why me?"

The darkness in your thoughts illumines them to me. Through your life you have felt that you have seen underneath the layers that cushion humanity against the hard factuality of existence— the thick and comfortable lies that they wrap around themselves against the cold wind of reality.

Although in total darkness, Daniel blinked in surprise. That was exactly what he thought, and in words he might have said himself.

Peeling back the layers, and peeling back the layers . . . just as you have been stripped back and stripped down. What do you expect to find, Daniel Tully?

"Truth?"

There was a noise in Daniel's head that sent shivers down his spine and into his bowels. Was it laughter?

Is there truth at the centre of an onion?

"You mean . . . maybe the layers are all there are?"

Breathe my breath.

A wind rose up and suddenly the air around him was thick and smelled sharp. His nose tingled and his eyes watered; he held his breath instinctively but was forced eventually to let it out and then he breathed in deep and felt a warm, sweet, and intoxicating air enter into him. His vision suddenly filled with colours that swirled, it seemed, actually inside his eyes.

Suddenly, the top of the cavern was torn off to reveal a golden dome—the dome of heaven that appeared over the garden when God went looking for Adam and Eve. It was blinding for the first moment, but when his eyes cleared, he saw he was now standing in the garden. Then the plants all withered in the blink of an eye, the flames were around him and animals were fleeing, charging along the ground or flying overhead. And not just animals, but large mystical creatures as well, rising from the flames with enormous wings and horned heads. The dragons had entered the world.

They began to fight. Their passion for destruction was bottomless. They fought each other with irrational, passionate hate, clawing eyes out and splitting bodies, committing wholesale slaughter and genocide in their battle for possession. Their viciousness knew no bounds of decency or dignity; they abased themselves in unrestrained aggression, exulting at the terror they had caused. They fought until just a fraction of them remained and the vast multitude of species was obliterated. Many of them died before they tired and found places on the world to sleep. And where they slept, land formed around them, millennia passed, and they were buried deeper and deeper. But although they slept, their aggression did not dissipate. It circled the world entirely, and Daniel saw it as though it, too, were a beast, a serpent that surrounded the earth, winding its way among the seabeds, growing longer and longer until it doubled on itself, forced to place its tail in its mouth, devouring itself to feed itself.

It seeped from their scales and into the ground around them, into the mud and clay. Man arose, tainted with the dragon's blood. They had attained a capacity for rape and destruction that they elevated to an art. They hunted down and extinguished every creature they came across, everything that was different from themselves they killed. And then they started finding differences among each other, drawing the lines against who looked what way, who spoke like what, who believed what, who acted and thought like what—and then they hounded and tortured each other because of those perceived differences.

But then a light of creation descended onto the planet to try to extinguish the darkness and kindle a fire against the cold hate. It started to spread, slowly, from one heart to the next.

And the people of the planet raced each other to destroy it.

Daniel wept—he saw the massive futility of trying to stop or even slow an engine, the entire purpose of which was set upon self-destruction. The only thing that seemed to keep it running was its prodigious ability to procreate faster—often only just faster—than it was able to destroy itself. And as the living organism that was all of humanity spread and became larger, it drew more and more from the land it was living on to sustain it and quickly moved from a state of symbiosis to parasitism. Daniel wondered what would happen first—would the beast kill itself, or would it destroy the only thing that could sustain it?

The serpent devours its tail.

"What's the point?" Daniel asked. "Why are we here?"

I know not. But we are here nonetheless.

"So we're just here to die? To kill or be killed?"

We all carry our deaths with us to be offered up at the time when demanded of us. The question is how you will use yours, Daniel. Are you going to go down fighting?

That decided him. "I know what I'm going to do, now. Send me back."

CHAPTER FIVE

Letting in the Light

I

Vivienne took her hands away from her ears and opened her eyes. She and every other inhabitant of the underground realm looked up to the sky, amazed they were still alive.

Rocks and boulders were still settling, sending *basso profundo* shockwaves through the bones of everyone gathered, making the ground tremble like the head of a drum. Rock dust was swirling thick in the air; rays of light, made dim and brown by the refraction, circled in a spiralling dance as the dust clouds billowed outward, mushrooming into the clear British sky. The unreal light seemed to flow in waves around them.

Above them, the large, dark rocks of the underground realms still hung in the sky, as if supported by a miracle. But it was soon clear the city of Niðergeard had been preserved by six mighty stalactite pillars, of which the Langtorr was the central. They now held up a roof of stone like the legs of a table as earth and debris settled around it. This meant everyone in the city was still very far away from the open air. The closest of the debris from the fallout was still a good hundred feet away from the edge of the city.

Vivienne didn't know what it was exactly—the attraction of the light, the thought of escape, or what—but some of the children started running toward the light, and then a herd mentality started to take over and all of them started to run toward it. They had to be stopped.

"Go after them!" Vivienne commanded the knights. "Alex!" she shouted as he turned to her. "They have to protect the children."

Alex started shouting orders to his knights to go after the children who were racing to the light like a stampede. Both he and Vivienne started after them, calling them back, but nobody was listening. Their feet moved quickly over a ground that they could now see fairly clearly in the ambient light, and it was only a few minutes before they were all lined up along the edge of the flat plain. Vivienne joined them as knight and child alike spread out to inspect the fallen earth and look up at the daylight. The rock pile created a steep ridge around them, and the sky was starting to poke through as the dust dissipated or settled.

Crooking her head, Vivienne tried to see how widespread the collapse had been. It was impossible to say—it could have been miles in each direction. And what exactly had been above them? Clumps of what appeared to be grass and twisted limbs of trees protruded from the top of the pile of stone in front of her. But were there roads, motorways, or cities that had been caught in the collapse? The pile of collapsed rubble was still shifting and settling. "Stand well back, everyone," she called. "It's not safe yet—everyone stay back!"

Vivienne started to take stock. She turned and pushed her way out from the crowd around her, looking for familiar faces.

She saw Ecgbryt first, being the easiest to spot among the tallest of the knights, and Alex was not too far from him.

But Freya . . . where was she?

Vivienne turned to look back at the city behind her. She could not make out the details of what lay beneath the silhouette of Niðergeard's skyline. It actually had a skyline now, she realised, which seemed odd and unfamiliar to her, jarring with the one that she had assembled in her mind.

"Alex!" she called out, raising her voice to try to pierce the excited hubbub of the children and knights who were starting to explore the debris. "Alex!"

They made their way toward each other. "We need to round them up again—get them together. It's not safe for them to be here, but—" A thought occurred to her, and Alex finished it.

"—But it might be easier to get them out of this place if we *can* find a safe way up all of this."

Vivienne nodded emphatically. "I think I'm taking Freya's case now—after what Ealdstan did to Modwyn . . . and what he said . . . I have no more faith in the man. We must get them all back home."

Alex's lips compressed into a thin, white line before he answered. "Yes, I agree. Plus, the lid's come off this one, literally. The whole country's going to get drawn into it, some way or another. Let's make the safety of the children our first priority."

Ecgbryt was lumbering toward them. "Should we take them back to the city?" Vivienne asked.

"I'm not certain . . . ," Alex said.

"I still believe Ealdstan should be trusted," said Ecgbryt. "Even . . . even after what he has just done. We should return to the city."

"Maybe we should. Most of the children are still in the city. It would be easier to protect them all together."

"But this supposed army that awaits beneath us," Vivienne said with a grim face. "If anything was to draw them out, it would be this. More so if this was some sort of prearranged sign given by Ealdstan. In that case—"

"It may already be happening," Ecgbryt said.

"Alex, take all the knights with you back to the tower immediately. We'll follow behind you."

"We'll go together—it's too dangerous to go back on your own."

"There's a hidden tunnel through the beacon. I've used it before, we'll go through that," Vivienne explained.

"I don't know . . . ," Alex said, rubbing his chin.

"Speed is what we have on our side at the moment," Vivienne urged. "That and the fact that the enemy does not yet know where we are. Let's use those things to our advantage."

Alex's eyes flicked around him uncertainly, taking in Vivienne and the children.

"We are agreed," Ecgbryt stated. "We regroup in the Langtorr. Defend ourselves until we can mount an attack?"

Alex nodded, resigned. "Very well. It shall be done," he said.

"Wonderful," Vivienne said, turning. "I shall bring this lot to order and go there directly. We should already be there by the time you arrive."

"I'll leave a few knights with you, Aunt Viv," Alex said. "I'm going to insist on that point."

"Very well."

"Listen up, everyone!" Alex called out, and began giving orders first to the children and then to the knights. It took less than a minute for Alex and Ecgbryt to assemble the knights, only about forty of them, and start them on a march back into the city. Vivienne then looked around at the children who were there— about fifty of them who had now turned their attention away from the rocks and boulders and looked to her, the only remaining adult, for direction.

Vivienne had just opened her mouth to tell them the plan when she heard someone fairly distant call out.

"Hey! You down there! We need help! Can you help us?"

Her stomach plunging, she looked up. A figure was waving to them from about thirty feet above her head. "What . . . what do you need?" Vivienne shouted back.

"This . . . this earthquake! The entire village is buried! Everything's collapsed. I was lucky, but—people are buried! I can hear them shouting for help! Please! Can you help us?"

—— ‖ ——

Everything around Freya was a blur. People were running, yelling, pushing. Light seemed to be all around her and whenever she opened her eyes it stabbed into her skull. A voice was shouting. She turned to it and saw Ealdstan on top of the heap of stone, his arms outstretched, bellowing, "Go!" at the top of his lungs.

The noise and confusion swirled around her and echoed in her ears. And then everything became calm and still and she opened her eyes and straightened up. She was standing in the middle of a very small crowd now, beside her was a clutch of scared-looking girls, and around them all were the hooded women—the old ladies.

And above them Ealdstan still sat on the throne of rubble with his elven guards. Freya looked up. Relaxed, his weight shifted slightly to one side, his elbow crooked at a right angle on the chair's arm, forcing his shoulder up to his ear. His eyes tracked her as she moved to stand forward of the chair but out of reach of the elf warriors. He made no movement to address or speak to her. He seemed to just be waiting, his legs stretched comfortably in front of him, resting carelessly on a rock above Modwyn's muti-lated body.

Modwyn . . . her skin was cut apart, the flesh of her body exposed, and even in the surreal, brown light it seemed a bright, almost cartoon-like red. She had fallen back and lay upside down, inverted, her arms above her head as if about to embrace some-thing or someone. Freya felt woozy and the world took a spin as she lost her balance and let herself collapse by stages to the ground, coming to rest on her hands and knees. She could no longer con-trol herself and she vomited, her stomach muscles tightening to a painful fist.

Working saliva around her mouth to clear it out, she spat sev-eral times and made herself stand. She was aware of the ladies and the children who had stayed standing in a cluster, standing behind her, keeping her between them and the throne.

She turned to the girls. "It's okay," she said in a calm, quiet voice. "Just stay together and stay with me."

"What's going on?" one of them asked, large wet eyes blinking.

"I'm finding that out," Freya said. "Just stay here and stay calm—don't panic or go anywhere. You should be safe." The words nearly caught in Freya's throat; they were openly untrue, but if saying them meant that they really would stay calm so they ran less risk of hurting themselves or wandering into some other danger, then it was worth the lie.

Neither Ealdstan nor the elves seemed to be overly concerned at, let alone threatened by, her presence. It seemed she had an opportunity to try to find out some answers. Freya turned to one of the ladies, realising that something had changed since the ceil-ing collapse. A few paces from the woman Freya stopped to study her. The dark robe she was dressed in now looked to be of a deep royal blue. It was not threadbare as Freya remembered it, but thick and full and covered all of the woman's form. Her head was draped with a large and wide hood, but what she glimpsed beneath it was no longer old and decrepit, but mature and strong. White, flawless skin and a straight chin jutted forward, and she could just see full, dark pink lips before the rest of the face disappeared in the rich, heavy fabric. Coming closer, Freya became uneasy and found that she did not want to see the full face of the woman.

"Do you remember me?" Freya asked eventually.

The lady raised her head, showing strong features—an angular jaw, a straight nose, full lips, and a high forehead. Their eyes locked and Freya looked instantly away. "We do remember you."

"What . . . what are you all doing here?"

For a moment Freya thought that she wouldn't get a reply, but then the lady's lips parted and she answered.

"We have come to bear witness to the starting of this age."

"Or the ending of it," the lady some ten feet to her right added.

"You look different," Freya said. "Younger."

"There are some who have called us the Norns—of the ageless and nearly eternal."

"We are this new time's protectors—"

"Its spirits—"

"Its messengers—"

"And so are we young."

"We are the midwives," the lady in front of Freya said. "We are to witness this age as it is born—"

"Or stillborn."

"What do I have to do with it?" Freya asked. "What do I have to do with this new age?"

"That remains to be seen."

"But you remember me, right? You told me—one of you told me—that I was a strong thread in the tapestry. Was that, like, a prophecy? Do you know what's going to happen here?" Freya thought of the images of herself that she had seen in the enchanted mirrors in the Langtorr and she asked herself the question she had asked a hundred times before. Were they real or were they only possibilities?

"What you were told was a true-speaking, but made no claim on what might one day pass. A fabric has a hue and colour, a weave and pattern, but even the strongest thread will be cut easily by a knife. One fabric may be sewn to another, or left to unravel completely."

Freya closed her eyes and rubbed her forehead. "That's interesting," she said, "but not very helpful." She turned and walked back to Ealdstan, looking up at him past the mutilated body of Modwyn, trying to push even the thought of it to the back of her head; but just seeing her again made Freya dizzy and she could feel her pulse pound in her temples.

"What's going on here, Ealdstan?" Freya called up. "What's the plan?"

She mostly expected him to remain silent, ignoring her, but he rocked forward in the throne and bent his elbows to his knees in a conversational position—he looked like a school librarian about to tell a story to a young child. "Do your parents love you?" he asked in a clear, level voice.

"Yes," Freya said after a moment, raising an eyebrow.

"I am glad. I would hope that they do. My own parents . . . I can barely remember them. Some days I think I cannot remember them at all, I just remember that they must have been there. Other days . . .

"I have had the memory of them far, far longer than I have had the experience of them, and the lights of remembrance die just as all flames eventually die. It is only with the greatest concentration that I can recall them at all, and their voices and their faces have been lost to me for centuries now. Perhaps they will one day be lost to me forever. And I am the last to know them—after me there will exist no trace of their existence within this world. No name in a book, or carved on a slab of stone—nothing. Imagine that, dead not just in life, but in memory—a second death."

Ealdstan raised his hand to his domed forehead and stroked it. Some of Modwyn's blood that was still sticky-wet on his fingertips transferred to it in a grotesque smear.

"Of course those whose spirits live again will not die. And as for me, I have not died yet. I have watched brave men die in battle—I have personally sent brave men to die. And not just men, yes, children also, which I know you find reprehensible. I watched them walk before me to complete their fates on this earth and move past the curtain of mortality. Yet no less significant than their sacrifices is mine. To die for a just cause is to be applauded, but to live your life for one—to be a continual sacrifice is to burn a longer light, and I am that light, the burning ember that fires the fuse. If I were to lose my light and heat, what hope would there be for the world to continue when all the heroes have died? Who would inspire them when the valiant are forgotten?"

Freya glared at him.

"I'm trying to understand," she said, "but what does this have to do with you collapsing the roof and whether my parents love me or not?"

Ealdstan sucked in a breath and drew himself up, now flattening his shoulders against the throne's back. His eyes sparkled down at her like distant stars. "It was never my own wisdom that governed my acts, or so I believed. My own vanity and purpose were never at issue. I was happy enough to hide myself in the ground and in the shadows of the night in order to serve a larger purpose—to serve God's purpose, my heavenly parent, and to work every day for His glory and not my own."

He paused and looked down at his hands, seeming to notice the blood on them for the first time. He rubbed them together, idly trying to brush it off.

"So what went wrong?" Freya asked.

Ealdstan looked down at her and smiled pitifully. "I do not know. The years passed and at the turn of each new one I believed that very soon the time would come when I would rouse all my knights and lead a righteous host into the gap at the mouth of hell to fight back the flames and close its terrible gate finally and for all time. But the years continued unrelenting. Had the moments I waited been grains of sand, entire beaches would have issued through the hourglass of my waiting life. I have seen this world—the nation above me, its people—start badly and continue worse and worse. Godless, faithless, without noble action, thought, or even impulse. They steal, rape, kill, and hate more and more with every passing day. They war not with the stranger in the street, or the outsider in their neighbourhood; they save the worst atrocities up for those that are nearest them and the young, the most vulnerable.

"And they do it to themselves. They are suffocating themselves with their machines of laziness, turning the planet into a hostile force against them, against future generations. They know what they do—they are told repeatedly, but they do not care if they smother themselves tomorrow for comfort today. Simply to kill them would be kindness enough. A merciful act.

"All this I have watched not just in these recent years, but all the hundreds of years before now. And God does not feel it worth His while to stir His mighty hand and use me against this determined march into destructive fire that you all are making. What must happen before I am made use of? How complete must the destruction of your souls, your bodies, your planet be before the Almighty Creator intercedes, before He intervenes? Your parents love you and that is good. But what loving parent sees two of his children fighting, cutting each other, drawing blood, even to the point of death . . . and does nothing?"

Ealdstan spread himself out on the throne with an air of satisfaction at his point so strongly and elegantly made.

Freya looked at the elven guards for a moment and then back up to Ealdstan. "That's why you're doing this?" she said. "You've lost your faith and belief in God?"

Ealdstan tensed and leant forward. "I still believe in God," he said sharply. "But I have lost my faith in Him, certainly. At one time I felt His love, His attention—I thought I did. But it has been many a long year, a long, cold year from that time to this. God has abandoned me, abandoned you and all of us—but I aim to make Him remember what was started in His name. All of this will be destroyed—the island itself and perhaps the world will tear itself apart unless He steps forward to prevent it."

"You'd destroy everything you've made—you'd let people die—just to prove a point to God? But what *is* your point?"

"Not to prove a point, to try to rouse Him out of His apathy. What hope have any of us to live in this world much longer if He does not move Himself? I am forcing His hand before it is too late for Him to act."

"What if you make God angry and He comes after you?"

Ealdstan gave a slight shrug. "The most He could do is move me from one hell to another."

"Well, thanks for making so many important decisions for all of us," Freya said, turning away from Ealdstan. "I appreciate that. I'm sure Modwyn does . . . did—would—" Freya could not finish the sentence. "All of these children would thank you as well, no doubt, if they were all here and trying not to escape."

Ealdstan's face did not change; it remained clear of any emotion except a patient carelessness.

"Your frustration makes sense, but does any of that mean that you had to *kill* her? *Why?* What possible reason did you have?"

Ealdstan grinned and pointed a finger upward. Freya looked

to where he gestured and then flinched, her legs buckling. "What is that?"

A dark, swirling cloud hung in the air above them. Smoky tendrils slowly extended, flexed, and then recoiled into the inky mass. Every few seconds something shadowy and fluttering would flit out of the centre of the mist and fly upward.

"That is what remains of Modwyn—I have used her soul to open a gate into another world, one that should never have been connected to this. Do you see those things that are flying out of it? I have no idea what those are, but each one of them is dragging our world closer to the one they come from, cementing the bridge. It is one more anchor pulling this world in another direction, and I have made many of them—I made our friend Daniel into one of them, in fact. Gád has been using these—using what comes out of them, rather—to create an army, a mystical invasion force. I think it needlessly raises the stakes, but we shall see. What he scarcely understands is that even if he conquers the world, it shall soon be destroyed. Perhaps he doesn't care—perhaps he believes he has a plan to stop the planet from rocking apart as it sways on its axis, which is technically what will happen. It is of little consequence. The ends of these actions are that this world is now in the ultimate physical and spiritual peril. If anyone has the ability to stop me, they must. But my course is set and cannot be altered now."

"The ladies say that this may be the start of a new age."

"Yes. I find that possibility rather exciting, don't you? Either way, what happens next will be an entertainment rare to be seen."

Freya just looked at him with cold eyes and then snorted. "Crazy old man. Whatever you've done, I'm going to dedicate my life to stopping it, and then to stamping out every trace of you on this planet."

Ealdstan smiled. "You don't know how encouraged I am to hear you say that," he said, closing his eyes and spreading his lips apart to show his teeth. She even thought she saw him shiver briefly with pleasure.

And so, her mouth contorted with disgust, Freya walked forward to get Modwyn's body and take it away from him.

Suddenly an elf was in front of her and she was flying backward, her chest smarting. She hadn't even seen the blow that struck her and she hit the stone floor with a tooth-rattling impact. The elf who had attacked her leapt forward and stood over her, his sword wavering near her face as Freya desperately fought to catch her breath. She rubbed the area above her breastbone; the elf must have hit her with his open palm. She scooted herself back with her heels as the elf shifted his weight to move forward—

Then there was a flash of light and for a fraction of a second Freya saw a towering form stand before her. It appeared to be about twenty feet tall, wrapped in bright clothes and shining armour. Long, black silken hair flowed down its back and although Freya could not see the face, being turned away from her, she knew it was fearfully beautiful.

The world dimmed as darkness rushed back in. Not just the elf that had attacked her, but all the others behind him were lying on the floor, rolling onto their sides, trying to stand up. Between Freya, who was now picking herself up, and the elves was one of the Norns, standing cloaked and still, unmoving.

Ealdstan leant forward in his chair as the other six women slowly walked forward and came to stand around Freya and the three other girls.

"Fascinating," he said.

III

Bent forward on a hand-carved, plushly cushioned chair, Alexander Robert Simpson, permanent under secretary for defence, also known as Gád Grístgrenner to certain acquaintances, rested elbows sleeved in a very expensive and highly tailored suit jacket upon knees wrapped in equally expensive matching trousers. His hands held nothing and so were clasped lightly together, his head bent to one side to better read the papers in the file that Secretary of Defence Timothy Edward "Ted" Towne MP was agitatedly holding. Actually he was only pretending to read; papers weren't going to be very important any more, he had recently decided. The minister was also sitting forward in his seat, talking about the papers that he had even less intention of reading

The minister was mostly preoccupied with how he might best raise his political profile where at all possible, and, secondary to that, his public profile. The worst-case scenario was predicated on what could be done to minimise his perceived involvement; but this was all in the event that "circumstances deteriorate irretrievably," as he put it. He apparently had endless views on the topic, and he exposed Gád to all of them. It seemed important to an obsessive degree that he, Ted Towne, was to be seen to be "in control of the situation." To be called upon to resign was the penalty he would pay for any misstep he took from here on out, a blunder that could range from a single unfortunate turn of phrase in an interview to a full-scale bungling of the situation in the eyes of the merciless public. The consequences would not be fatal to his career, but every pitfall was to be avoided. The consequences of such would range from being sorted to the bottom of the deck to await the next cabinet reshuffle, or to be forced to withdraw from the public forum and turn to the private sector. Which wasn't the worst that could happen, of course. There was a lot of money in the Middle East for consultants of his political calibre, and that so often went to the Americans and their grey suits, jets, and security entourages.

Would it be worth getting a security entourage? the minister asked his permanent under secretary. No, no, probably not. He didn't want to seem weak. In fact, perhaps he could even take off his jacket and appear just in shirtsleeves and tie—he would look vital, busy, unconcerned with appearances in the face of this tragedy. He wanted to manage public opinion without *looking* like that's what he was doing—or at the very least, in this cynical age, to leave people with a reasonable doubt as to whether he was doing so or not.

The compounding layers of irony were not lost on the permanent under secretary, especially that of the two people in the room, there was one who was actually in charge of the situation.

And so he waited, counting off the minutes and answering the minister's facile and inconsequential questions. He listened uninterrupted, indulging Ted Towne with his attention as he segued from inane musing to rambling anecdote and back again, seemingly lost in the train of his own seminar. And yet, between the odd pauses for breath or to clear his mouth, the permanent under secretary sensed a man fully conscious of the situation but powerless. Who was merely stalling for time until the next piece of news came in and he was called upon to act. He was talking to fill time, to affirm contact with another human being so as not to feel lost during a profoundly disturbing and confusing tragedy. And, it serving his purpose, Gád let him talk on.

Abruptly, Ted Towne stopped. Gád thought that he stopped in the middle of a sentence but since he was not actually following what Towne was saying, he wasn't sure.

"What's going on these days, Alexander?"

The permanent under secretary raised an eyebrow. The minister rarely used his first name—and certainly never when he was sober.

"It's not just the children—that is a shock, but hardly a

surprise. Things in this country, this planet, have been getting worse. Don't you feel it?" Towne caught his eye. "Name an aspect of society. The political: wars, binge spending, financial bubbles and meltdowns—constant recessions due to unchecked money racketeering. The environmental: droughts in the summer, flooding in the winter, everyone racing each other to drain the world of everything it can give us to burn—they know time is running out. Are we truly surprised that the populace is jaded? Cynical? Depressed? Suicidal? So we give them pills and pop stars and reality TV. Bread and circuses, Alexander, pills and TV. The opiate of the people is self-indulgence. We, the government, let them dope themselves into a stupor and when they complain we offer them a painkiller to fix a broken leg. And it stings when we slap it on and they hate us for it. No, they revile us. The people have us over a barrel. The political minefield—ha! Never a truer word spoken. Every year, it seems, we are given a more and more unreasonable political gauntlet to run and one misstep, one faltering, and they demand our blood. And they complain there are no visionaries, no statesmen. Anyone with any intelligence or integrity would be mad to subject themselves to such unreasonable sadism. They tear themselves apart. And anyone who intervenes, who challenges the status quo, who disagrees with the populace, who tries to save them, is thrown to the lions. You know, in the gladiatorial ring, it was the audience who decided if the defeated would live or die. Mob rule; no one man is as bloodthirsty as the collective. No dictator is more monstrous than the people he governs. We get the government we deserve. And yet we're the ones they revile. The electorate uses more fuel every year, they use more electricity, they take out more and more loans, they buy more and more inexpensive crap from third-world countries that they dispose of more and more into their rubbish heaps. They leave their wives and their children, they tear down the churches, they burn the libraries—they put the nooses around each others' necks and they cry for us to save them. All of it will end in fire—assuming we don't use up all the oxygen first, in which case we'll just smoulder out of existence. A world of corpses on a smoking spheroid lurching giddily through the cosmos. I go home every night and I wonder if there's any point in carrying on—if I'm just perpetuating a cycle of suffering for me and everyone else. I can only go to sleep after I've resigned myself to keep going, but the best reason that I can think of for doing so is the fact that I don't think there's anything else to be done.

"Tell me—tell me just one thing—do you think it's too late?"

"I think—" Gád paused. He was taken aback by this sudden and uncharacteristic rush of honesty. His instinct was to reward it in kind, but at the same time he knew it was unwise to share anything of his true aspect. Honesty and trust were so quickly forgotten, after all. "I think we all may have one more chance. But we have to act quickly. And it won't come from us—it will have to come from everyone. They will have to rise from their stupor—they will have to wake up and chase all that is foul and wrong and evil to the very shores of the island and into the sea—" Gád choked himself off, biting the inside of his cheeks to prevent himself from speaking. He tilted his face down and pretended to study the paper in front of him. He had started to say too much, and he hoped it would be forgotten, along with the rest of Ted Towne's sudden lucidity.

There was a tap at the door. Gád watched the minister as the spell was broken and the mask of self-confidence slid back into place.

Ted Towne gestured to Gád to open the door. There was a young, frenzied-looking man in a light suit fidgeting nervously on the other side. A look at the man's face told Gád all he needed to know—that Ealdstan had finished his tasks, the stage was now

Gád's to do with as he would. He stepped aside and gave a jerk of his head, summoning the man inside.

"I'm from Number 10, sir," the aide said. "Something—something's *happened*." The aide held up a computer tablet that he had brought with him. He taped twice on its screen and then angled it toward the minister. Gád came to stand behind the minister's chair to get a better view, catching the aide's eyes, who gave a smirk and a stiff nod while the minister's attention was transfixed by what was playing on the screen. Gád frowned at this theatricality.

On the screen was a brown skyline, a column of what Gád knew to be rock dust slowly rising into the air and dispersing, looking for all the world like a tower of smoke or a pillar of cloud. The labels on the video and the scrolling news feed identified the station as the BBC and the location as being "near Chipping Campden, Gloucestershire." The image was shaky and pixelated, obviously sent in on someone's phone.

"Turn on the sound," the minister said.

The aide fiddled with the pad and the low, even tones of a newscaster's commentary filled the room.

". . . less than twenty minutes ago." The image switched to the news anchor in the studio, his face appropriately grave and sullen. "And I'm told we can switch live now to an image from the sky above the site." The picture immediately cut to an aerial view of the Gloucestershire countryside, where the enormous crater of collapsed land could be seen. For all appearances, it was as if a meteorite had struck down. "Ian Lally is there—Ian, can you tell us what you see?"

The image slowly panned around as the helicopter drifted to the side and then jerked as the camera adjusted to try to take in more of the view. The raised and distorted voice of a man talking through a helicopter's communication equipment accompanied the image. "It's quite simply incredible, Hugh. The site looks as if it was hit, impacted by something, or perhaps there was some explosion, but experts are saying that this wasn't the case, that what we are witnessing here is merely subsidence, on a massive scale. I am told that there have been no reports or records of the micro tremors that forecast any sort of tectonic movement or resettlement, so what exactly caused this collapse remains shrouded in mystery."

The newscaster reappeared on the screen. "Thank you, Ian. Never in the history of the nation has there been a more terrifying day than today. To remind viewers of our top story—"

A woman crying to the camera in a busy London street was shown.

"—Two thousand, six hundred and thirty-eight children are now confirmed as missing. If you have reports of missing children yourself, or even sightings of them, then please do not hesitate to call the number—"

"That's enough," Ted Towne said, standing abruptly and then realising he wasn't sure where to go or what to do next. He buttoned his suit jacket and then pursed his lips and leant over his desk, shifting a couple items around with his fingertips.

"Does the prime minister have any special instructions?" Ted Towne asked.

"Yes, sir," the aide said. "The PM wants a presence on the site of the . . . the geographical incident. He says our government needs to be a visible presence. I think he's—he didn't say this—but I think that he's frustrated about the *other* incident—the children—and the speculation and rumours, the media just going crazy, just going—well, you've seen them. It seems that with all the, uh, tumult, and all the coverage that this new—I don't know, I suppose it's a new development—all the coverage, the visual coverage that is, that this new development is getting, he wants someone on the ground, as it were. With the authorities, to talk to the press, do the sound bites—that sort of thing."

The secretary for defence frowned. The aide's eyes flicked to Gád, who gave him a nod, allowing him to make his exit.

"It's an important job," Gád said. "Very high profile."

"Yes, yes, it is," Ted Towne said quickly. "A lot of responsibility. A lot of responsibility." He frowned. "And the area will be secure. There will be . . . people to see to it, no doubt. The danger—"

"Of course, it's very busy here," Gád said.

Ted Towne MP looked up at him, an eyebrow raised.

"I could go up myself, initially, on your behalf, until you've wrapped everything up on this end."

"Hmm. You know, I think that could work. Yes, why don't you do that? Keep an eye on things. Report back. I won't be long here and then I'll just pop up and relieve you." Ted Towne's leg bent and he sank gratefully back into his plush office chair.

"I'll just need your signature on this document . . . ," Gád said, making a show of hunting for and fishing out a sheet of paper that he had been brushing with his fingertips through the conversation.

Ted Towne held it up in his fingers, eyeing it sceptically. "And this is . . . ?"

"A transfer of powers. I am not elected, as you know. It's a formality, a common document. You'll have signed one before, of course. Many times, in fact, I'm sure."

"Is this really necessary?"

"Strictly speaking, yes. But if it would be simpler for me to stay here and *you* to—"

"No, no," Ted said hurriedly. He flattened the sheet of paper on his desk and moved his pen in a swift, almost desperate, scrawl. "It's only a signature, isn't it? The work of a moment. There. It's done." He swept the document up again and held it out.

"Before I go, however, I made you an appointment." Gád opened the door and three very tall, very thin men entered. They were immaculately dressed but Ted Towne noticed there was something wrong with their faces—he couldn't quite make out any features. One of them stretched out a long, slender arm and held out what appeared to be . . . a suit.

"They've got some items they would like to show you—would like to see you in."

Ted Towne stood, a wary smile creeping across his lips, his enthusiasm piqued. "Yes," he said. "Yes, that would be just the thing." The three tall men surrounded him, holding up different fabrics for him to admire. Gád, whose vision was not being enchanted, saw nothing, of course.

"I shall leave you in their capable hands," said Gád, partway out of the door.

"Yes, yes," the minister said. "Off you trot."

"Be seeing you."

As the door closed behind him, Gád reached inside his jacket pocket and took out another rune stick. He placed this one on the lintel above the secretary's door and then turned and walked briskly down the hall and out of the building for the last time.

CHAPTER SIX

The First Attack

I

Gád descended from the afternoon sun. The enormous crater before him grew larger until it filled his whole vision, opening below like the maw of an enormous beast. A large section of the A44 had been swallowed by the fall-in. Most of the section known locally as Five Mile Drive had effectively been erased from existence, and a long line of cars were parked along it, pointing at a roped-off area that was made black with densely packed people. From his dwindling altitude he was able to mentally sort the crowd—there were the reporters, there were the local spectators, and there were the policemen and military commanders. As he let his eyes wander around the circumference of the site, he saw soldiers spaced regularly along the rough oblong; even from his height he could see that they shifted uneasily. And dotted at certain points on the landscape there were more clusters of people looking down on the proceedings, witnessing from the green country hills of England.

The pit was filled with large chunks of boulders, rocks, and fresh soil that was a deep charcoal black, having never been exposed to light. Only small patches of green dotted here and there gave indication to what was above the ground before it collapsed; otherwise everything had been completely churned up and all landmarks—roads, signs, or villages—were obliterated or buried. Gád scanned the debris looking for a particular detail and found it near the centre of the bedlam, which he estimated must still be a few miles away. It was a rounded tuft of green at a higher elevation than the rest of the rubble. That was where Niðergeard would be, that was where the entrance to the Wild Caves was, and where his army awaited his signal.

The speed of the helicopter's approach was checked and it descended sharply downward toward the roped-off area. With a lurch, the craft swooped and landed a safe distance away. Gád waited until the roar of the helicopter's rotors stopped before thanking the pilot and throwing open the canopy door. He sniffed the air, which smelled musty and dirty. The cloud of dust caused by the collapse had dispersed into the air and was settling on the meadows and trees of the countryside, coating them with a light tan dusting where it gathered the thickest. The particles of dust still in the air gave the light a muted, sepia-brown tint.

A sergeant constable strode toward him, meeting Gád midway in his walk to the crater's edge.

"Good afternoon, sir," he said deferentially. "What can I do for you?"

Gád presented him with a copy of the letter Ted Towne, MP, had signed less than an hour ago. "This order temporarily but completely transfers the powers of the elected minister for defence to me for the duration of my time here. You are going to want to phone Whitehall before anything else, in order to verify what I tell you is true. You may keep the order—I brought several copies with me. Once you've done that, join me; I shall be talking to the internal defence commander on the ground, I assume he's that well-decorated gentleman over there."

The police sergeant was reading the sheet Gád had given him. He bent his head to his shoulder radio and began to relay information back to base. He peeled off from the group and stood a short distance away while Gád addressed a man dressed in a British Army uniform with a major's insignia.

"Hello, sir," the man addressed him cheerfully. "I got notice you were arriving. How can I assist you?"

"I saw on my way here," Gád said, "that you have created a perimeter around the site. How many men have you got on that detail?"

"Eighty-six. They're on a fifteen-minute staggered radio-in cycle. Nobody's getting through there."

"Good, that's good," Gád said. He went to the hood of the major's military-grade Land Rover, which had a map spread out on top of it. There was a pencilled outline that was shaded in with rough, broad strokes where the caved-in area was. "I want to extend the cordon by a mile." Gád pulled out a fountain pen and uncapped it, starting to trace another, bolder line around the demarcated area. "Everything and everyone inside this new area is to be evacuated. Everything in the airspace—commercial and private air transport—is banned. Also military—keep everyone away from this, even our people. After one official warning, all trespassers are to be fired upon. And all commercial satellites with imaging capabilities are to be blocked or otherwise deactivated under the Emergency Powers Act of 2002. The relevant paperwork is still being processed. Do you understand these instructions as I have given them, Commander?"

"I do, sir."

"I will paraphrase in any case, so that there is no misunderstanding. In short, I want a complete blackout on this site—the press media, casual observers, *everyone*."

"Yes, sir."

"Even our own eyes. Do you follow? Once the area is secure—the perimeter secured—I want our own cameras and monitoring equipment turned off. Is that clear?"

This made the major pause for a moment. But before Gád could reiterate himself, he choked out a final, "Yes, sir."

Gád looked at his watch and did a rapid calculation. It was ten fifteen in the morning just now. Most broadcasters updated the news on the hour; if he gave the stations fifteen minutes to edit his statement down, and if he talked for ten minutes . . . "I shall give a press briefing at ten thirty-five."

The police sergeant had rejoined them by this stage. "What about the rescue teams, sir?" he asked with a face expressionless except for a furrowed brow.

Nearly imperceptibly, Gád's shoulders stiffened. "There are teams already in the area?"

"No, sir, they are still being assembled, but rescue 'copters are already en route—the big boys, being flown in from the coast, and some of the mountain rescue teams from up north."

"Thank you for telling me that. They are to land . . ." Gád's eyes scanned the map. "Here." He hovered a long finger over a suitably vacant area to the northeast. "Here, outside of Evesham—which is going to be evacuated, isn't it, Major?"

"As you say, sir."

"Thank you."

"But, sir, we estimate that as many as—"

"Police sergeant, job one right now is to control the situation. Without control there is chaos and no security, wouldn't you agree?"

The sergeant blinked his eyes.

"Why don't you help the commander here clear the innocent bystanders from the area and then you can come find me and we can discuss the matter further, yes?"

"Sir—"

"The quicker you finish, the quicker we can get on to other matters."

"But I must insist—"

"So must I. I am only enforcing—passing on, really—what my superiors have commanded me to pass on. We are all wheels in a machine—let's just focus on running smoothly at the moment. Issue the orders, do the work, and we'll hopefully all get through this to see brighter days." Gád pulled his phone out and thumbed a number. "And remember your orders come from me, not the military. Now, if you'll excuse me," he said, putting the phone to his ear and walking away. "It's me," he said in a low voice. Turning slightly, he saw the commander and the lieutenant begin barking frantic orders into their radios. "Assure Kelm that I am ensuring no outside interference.

"And then tell him to give the order to invade."

II

Vivienne strained to make her way over and around the chunks of rock and soil. She cursed her ageing body and weakening limbs as she struggled to keep up with the woman from the village. The two knights behind her were some of the new ones Alex had found in his travels. For some reason—their dress or the cast of their faces, perhaps—she believed they were Slavic in origin. Although she hadn't had an actual conversation with them, they seemed to understand her, stepping forward instantly when she asked for volunteers among the knights to accompany her.

It had taken them nearly half an hour just to find a route to climb up to meet the woman, and they had found that the ground was still settling and subsiding and they had to be very careful where they put their feet. Sometimes the ground would support the weight of a foot but not a whole body, and then the world would take another sudden, nightmarish lurch.

The woman's name was Helen. She was bleeding along the side of her face and supported most of her weight on one leg. She only looked at the knights for a moment, her eyes flicking up and down their tall, powerful, anachronistic forms, and then turned back to Vivienne. "Thanks so much—it's not far, follow me." And then she turned and led them away.

The children had been left with the other four knights, but it gave Vivienne a twinge in her already tight and anxious stomach each time she thought of this fact. She needed to get to this ruined village, help however she could, and then back to the children as quickly as possible. Wild scenarios raced through her mind, what she would do in different circumstances—what if the children were attacked? Would they be able to elude them? Could they hide in the rubble, or find a route through it? What if they weren't fast enough? Would it have been best if they stayed with her here? Should she go back and get them? What if there were further earthquakes? How would they avoid those? What if there were rescue teams already helping out the villagers? What if . . . ? What if . . . ? What if . . . ?

The questions whizzed around her head, spinning her around into knots.

She had been concentrating . . . but when Vivienne's nose began to sting at an acrid burning smell, like burning tires or plastic, she looked up and gasped in surprise at the sight of the ruined village. Houses were now no more than piles of masonry and splintered wood, cars were crushed, and streets were warped and broken. All objects of modern living had been completely junked. Clambering over a ridge, Vivienne found that she was walking along the side of a tarmacked road, now nothing more than ruined clumps of back tar and stone with a line painted on one flat side.

Listening, she could hear whines, groans, and voices calling out in pain and agony. Vivienne clamped her hand over her mouth, aghast, not knowing exactly what to do or say, surveying immeasurable damage. She could see maybe fourteen or fifteen people who had managed to escape being trapped. Each of them was extremely battered, and had divided into about three groups. They were trying to lift roofs, walls, and rubble off collapsed buildings to get to the people underneath. Vivienne was suddenly struck by a new human aspect to the tragedy. Lives had now been lost as a direct result of Ealdstan's actions.

Helen had moved to a pile of rubble and was pulling boards away, trying to shift some of the wreckage. "One of my children is in here, with her sister," she explained, trancelike, to no one in particular.

"One of your children's sister?"

"Yes, one of the children from my class, and her sister. I'm a teacher. At the school. The school. The school was closed today—because of the disappearances. Where did they go? One lady I talked to said they had been whisked away, up into heaven. I thought that was dreadful to say at the time, but now I kind of hope they were. The mad old bat. I haven't seen her since . . ."

Helen the schoolteacher had paused while she was talking, her hands gripping a rough wooden beam that was sticking up out of the ground. Vivienne motioned to the two knights to take over and start to clear away what they could. Then she herself approached Helen and pulled her away. "You should have a sit-down, my dear," she said.

"Hello!" a man's voice called. "Do you need help?"

Vivienne turned to see a middle-aged man picking his way among the wreckage. He was dressed in a suit, but the left-arm sleeve was missing and his shirt had been slit from top to bottom. He wore a bright, clean bandage on his bare arm and carried a brown leather satchel. "I'm a doctor. Do you need help?"

"No, I'm fine—but take a look at this one. I fear she may have a concussion."

The doctor made his way to the woman with difficulty. Placing his bag beside him, he bent down and gently started feeling her head. Helen seemed oblivious to him, but passive to his instructions; her attention was intently trained on the knights digging into the house, it seemed to Vivienne, or else she was in a world of her own.

"How—?" Vivienne paused and took a moment to evaluate the doctor. Although rather banged up, he seemed to be in control of himself and relatively calm. She hoped he really was as competent as he seemed, and not suffering from some form of shock himself. "What's your name?" she asked.

"Sarraf. Sanjay Sarraf," he said in a low and calming voice. "I'm not a GP, I'm actually a surgeon. I don't practise here, but . . ."

"How many are . . . ?" She didn't know how to phrase the question, or even what she herself was asking. "What I mean is, how many . . . ?"

"I've been seeing as many as I can," said Dr. Sarraf, now rocking Helen's head slowly back and forward, a slow nod. "So far I have seen thirty. Eighteen were dead."

"Eighteen out of . . . ?"

He frowned. "Well over two hundred. I'm not sure. My practice isn't here. I'm a surgeon, in Reading. Yes, a couple hundred. But fewer, I suppose, since some of the children went. Follow my finger, please," he said softly to Helen. "That's excellent. And now here? Thank you. Tilt your head back."

Vivienne felt a hand on her shoulder. She turned to find one of the knights, who beckoned her to follow. They both joined the other who was staring into a dark hole in the ground. His hand was almost casually propping up a large chunk of building—brick on one side and wood and plaster on the other. Rounding it, and peering into what it had been lying on top of, she stifled a scream, clapping a hand to her mouth. Tears welled in her eyes and she blinked them away, forcing herself to look at the bodies of a woman with greying dark-brown hair and a young girl who could not have been more than eight years old. Only the upper parts of their bodies were visible—they were dead; had been crushed, their skin discoloured in bright and deep hues of red and purple fading into black. The woman's arm was cradling her daughter's head.

Vivienne felt her legs shake and she reached out a hand and grabbed the shoulder of one of the knights to support herself. Finally, she could look no more and she turned away. *Ealdstan did this. He's responsible for all of this,* she told herself.

"Clear the rest of it away," she said softly. "And there—see that? That's a shower curtain. Use it to cover their bodies, for now."

Vivienne returned to the doctor, who was finishing his examination of the schoolteacher. "You appear to have a slight concussion," he said. "But you are only bruised rather than broken. I still want you to sit and rest—do not exert yourself. Do not try to move any buildings, and you should be right as rain. I'm going to clean you up a little now." He opened his bag, took out a sterile pad and a white bottle. He uncapped the bottle and squirted some clear, stringent liquid onto the pad and started dabbing at Helen's face. "You're number thirteen," he told her. "One of the survivors. And you," he said, his eyes flicking to Vivienne, "are number fourteen."

"Oh no, no I'm not," Vivienne said. There were shouts from farther up and she saw one of the groups of men scampering wildly, trying to get out of the way of a roof that was collapsing beneath them. "This is worse than a war zone," she said under her breath. "I'm not number fourteen," Vivienne said, turning back to the doctor. "I'm not from here."

"You're not? Then who are you, exactly? But you're not one of a rescue team, are you?"

She turned at a scrabbling noise. Four men were approaching, carrying between them an elderly woman who Vivienne honestly couldn't tell was alive or dead.

"I'm Vivienne. I—"

The doctor touched her arm. "Well, then?"

"What?"

"Who are you? Where are you from?"

"I'm not from here, I wasn't in the village. I'm . . . I . . ."

"Just passing by, perhaps?"

Against the odds, the old lady actually did seem to be alive and was responding to the doctor's tests.

"No . . ." Vivienne bit her lip. How best to explain? She took a deep breath. "I was beneath the ground when this started. I was with the person who caused it—this tragedy." The faces around her all looked at her in confusion, puzzled at what she was saying.

A distant moaning bark sounded, creating distant and ghostly echoes. Everyone tensed at its sound.

". . . *eeeeeeaaauuuuggggghhh—gyungh—gyungh—gyungh* . . ."

"What was that?" Helen asked.

"It's . . . a lot to explain," Vivienne said, continuing. "But this is also connected with the children going missing." Behind her, the two knights stalked out of the shadows and stood, looming behind her. The villagers' eyes widened in astonishment.

"And you're in danger—even more danger than you already know." All eyes turned to her again. "We need to rescue as many people as possible, as quickly as possible, and you all need to come with me if you want to have even a *chance* of survival."

III

"What are we going to do?"

Gretchen felt all eyes on her, whether by virtue of the fact that she was the tallest or the closest to the door, she didn't know. Maybe she just looked the oldest.

"We should—I think we should keep waiting."

"But everything's collapsing. Maybe we should get out of here, before we're buried?"

"Yeah, is this place safe? Shouldn't we go out?"

Gretchen was uncomfortable having these questions put to her. She felt her heart racing. "And go where? This tower seems to be most of what's holding what's above us . . . well, above us. I mean, what are our other options?"

"We could make a run for it."

Gretchen turned her head and tried to estimate how far away the horizontal strip of jagged light was. They could make it, probably, only if . . .

"But there are things out there," a boy said from behind her. "I mean, you heard about that guy's brother who got snatched, right? I mean if we can believe—"

"That was my brother." Heads swivelled. Gretchen recognised Fergus. "I saw it happen. There's definitely things out there—it's an army of bad guys and nightmares, hundreds of them. Thousands maybe. Not just one or two at a time."

"If we leave, they could get us," said someone.

"But what if they come here? We're easier to find if we just stay in one spot," said someone else.

"We can keep the doors closed," Gretchen said.

"But for how long?"

"The knights and the grown-ups should be coming back soon," Gretchen said, trying to sound convincing.

"But what until then? Or what if they don't?"

"Look at that," Gretchen said, gesturing to the belt of daylight that separated two spaces of darkness. "*Someone* is going to come because of *that*. We just need to wait until they do."

"We need weapons," said a girl from the back.

"Yeah," someone agreed.

"If we had weapons, we could defend ourselves."

"What kind of weapons?" Gretchen asked. "I don't see a lot of guns or knives around here."

"There are swords and axes though," Fergus said, and the background murmuring dipped slightly. "A massive great pile of them. I've seen them. And shields and helmets and armour too."

"Let's get them. Where are they?"

"They're outside," Fergus said. "In the city." More hush followed this statement. "They're not far though. And they're sitting right out in the open."

"But we can't use swords and spears. We don't know how."

Eventually someone spoke in a low voice that nonetheless carried through the whole room. "It doesn't matter, I'd feel better with *something*. We have to go get them."

"I'm not sure we should."

"We should get them before the enemies do."

"Why would they? They've got their own weapons."

"Well, what should we do instead?"

"We should wait for the adults to come back," Gretchen insisted.

"Why?"

"Because they'll know what to do."

"Why?"

Gretchen tried to see who was asking all the annoying questions. "Because . . . they're adults. They'll know what to do."

Another pause. "I'm getting some weapons." This came from one of the taller boys who had sandy blond hair and was already getting broad in the shoulders. Gretchen had heard someone call him Richard. "Come on, Fergus. Show me where they are."

They came to stand in front of her, as if asking for permission, and she realised that she was standing in the way. A couple more boys fell in behind him, and then a small girl named Jennifer. Gretchen froze, not knowing what to do—let them go, try to stop them? Surely the best thing to do was to wait for the adults to come back. After all . . . after all . . .

After all, what? What were the adults going to do for them? They'd already abandoned them in the tower, perhaps permanently. If they could get weapons, then they should.

"Okay, let's go get them." Face flushed, Gretchen also turned and went through the door, joining the boys and Jennifer.

By the time they got to the gate in the wall around the Langtorr, there were eight of them. They paused briefly to look at each other and then back at the Langtorr.

"It's this way," Fergus said. He darted into the darkness and they followed after him. It was hard to navigate through the streets. The sporadic lighting from odd angles—the silver lamps were all arrayed haphazardly amongst the rubble—often masked potholes and cast shadows that created a disorienting movement of light and darkness.

And then they arrived at it. It almost looked like some sort of a large bushy shrub, but as they moved slowly around it, the jagged-silhouetted mound proved to be a heaped pile of weapons and armour. What looked like branches were spears, many of them bent, and what seemed to be leaves, swords.

"A lot of it is kind of mangled and rusty," Fergus was saying. "But some of it's all right. I'm sure there's stuff we can use. Like look at this—" He gave a grunt and pulled something from inside the pile. "This is mine now. Whoa, look out." The metal subsided in a loud clatter that rattled off the buildings around them. They stood in stock-still silence, holding their breath as the echoes died, their eyes fixed on Fergus, who held a silver helmet clutched between his white-knuckled hands.

Silence descended again and nothing happened. Then all of them started diving in, pulling things out that looked useful or attractive. The metal pile started to shift and subside, but they kept digging into the plunder.

"Careful . . . ," Richard said. "Careful . . . don't pu—*don't push that*! Whoa. That was close. You nearly had my hand off!"

Gretchen found a shiny breastplate that still had all of its straps and a bunch of short swords that ran like a seam through the pile. She started to gather them in her arms, laying them lengthways like firewood. "Try to bring things back for other people," she said as a spear fell toward her. She stepped briskly aside and let it clatter on the ground. It had a metal shaft and wide blade. She bent down and tried to work out how she could juggle it with the rest of her load.

They were all interrupted by a deep moaning that reverberated through the entire city, punctuated with abrupt glottal stops. They froze.

"*EEEEEEEAAAUUUUGGGGHHH—GYUNGH—GYUNGH—GYUNGH!*"

"Hurry, let's get back," Gretchen said in a harsh whisper. "Bring everything you have."

IV

"What are you doing here? Why aren't you with the others?"

Benjamin looked up into Alex's face, studying it. He didn't seem angry, just surprised. "I wanted to go with you. I thought it was okay because I was in the briefing with everyone. I thought you might still need me."

"You should go back."

Benjamin looked behind him. The others were already a small and indistinct cluster around the bright piles of rock. "All by myself?" he said, sure to make his voice sound small. "It would be dangerous to go back on my own."

"You can't stay here. It's going to get a *lot* more dangerous soon."

"Let him stay," Ecgbryt said, his voice gruff. "We shall be wasting good time in debating the matter."

"All right. Just stay next to me if anything happens."

Benjamin hurried to keep up alongside the knights, but he was soon out of breath. Literally half the height of many of the knights, he had to jog to stay apace. Were the knights scared too? he wondered. Their mismatched armour jangled together as they stalked along without speaking. They were all fixed on the same purpose, on getting back to the Langtorr as quickly as possible, intent on getting the job done.

He was starting to lag behind, so he put his head down and concentrated on sprinting.

They reached the city fairly quickly, and that's when Alex broke the silence of their march.

"Slow down, everyone," he said, raising a hand and motioning behind him. *"Dìobair astar,"* he repeated in Gaelic. "Let's take this part slower," he said, eyeing the rubble of collapsed and half-ruined architecture. The sunlight was dimmer here, and the still-shining silver lanterns illuminated walls at odd angles, sometimes making it hard to distinguish the separate planes. "We want to get back as quick as possible, but we don't want to blunder into anything if there *is* enemy movement somewhere." He set the pace, moving slowly around every corner and blind spot.

They hadn't gone more than a few steps when they heard the cry.

"EEEEEEEAAAUUUUGGGGHHH—GYUNGH— GYUNGH—GYUNGH!"

Everyone froze. "Keep moving," Alex commanded. "Quickly."

They had not gone far before they heard another cry, this one human, loud, shrill, and distinct. "Help! Help! Help!"

Benjamin flinched as, at this last call, half of the knights took off running toward the cry.

"Wait!" Alex cried out. "Wait—come back! *Fuirich!*"

None of them did, and by the time Ecgbryt called out, *"Cierren,"* most of them were already out of sight.

───────────────────── **V** ─────────────────────

"They're not back yet," was the first thing someone said as the awful grunting noise died in their ears.

"They might be dead," one of the boys said.

"Who might be dead?" Gemma demanded. This wasn't a time to be frivolous with what was and was not actually happening. "How would you know?"

"Well, how would *you*?" the boy returned, his voice rising higher with anxiety. "We have to get out of here! We have to— we have to get away!" Spittle was flying from his mouth and his eyes were wide, looking as though they were bulging out of their sockets. "Let's run for it. Let's all rush to the nearest part of the big cave-in. Maybe—I mean, some of us might get caught, but they wouldn't get all of us. A lot of us would make it. Probably. We . . . we—can't stay here doing nothing." He rushed forward, making a break for the big iron door. Everyone had been listening to him in rapt silence, and as he made his move those around him tensed. Gemma saw the effect he was having on the crowd—they were all close to being hysterical, just from a noise they didn't understand.

"No!" Gemma shouted, quickly stepping sideways to block his way to the door. "You think they might be dead and so your solution is to run out after them? Yeah, that's real smart. We have to stay calm." Gemma held up one hand, fingers spread. "We don't really know *what's* going on, but we do need to stay safe. We can't just rush out blindly. Our best bet is to stay here in the tower. There's walls around it, big thick doors—"

"We don't know anything about this place!" the boy said. Although he was a foot taller than Gemma, she seemed to be getting through to him, on some level. "We don't know if this is the only door—they could get in from anywhere."

"You're wrong—we *do* know this is the only entrance. Unlike you, some of us have been looking around. There is only one door, and that's this door."

"So let's close it!" Those around the boy nodded and muttered in agreement.

"What's your name?" Gemma asked.

"Malcolm. It's Malcolm."

"Malcolm, we shouldn't close the door until we know we have to. There are some of us still out there who went to get weapons. And if—" Gemma caught herself. "And when the knights come back, then we don't want to shut them out, do we?"

"Fine!" Malcolm said, throwing his hands in the air. "So what do you suggest?"

"This! This is what we're going to do!" Gemma said, raising her voice so that everyone could hear her. "The doors in the wall outside look far too heavy for any of us to move, so we're not going to try to close them yet. Some of us are going to stay here and be lookouts and close the doors as soon as we see any bad guys coming. And if it's the knights, then we let them in. Right?"

"What about the rest of us?" another girl asked.

"Get up into the tower. Just keep climbing the stairs and get as high as you can. That's the best we can do right now. Got it?"

Gemma looked around at all the faces turned to hers. "Anyone have a better idea?" she asked. Nobody said anything.

"Then let's get going."

VI

Gretchen, Fergus, and the others raced back through the streets, sweating and breathing heavily, each of them carrying nearly their own weight's worth of solid metal in the form of weapons and armour. Jennifer was in front of Gretchen, wavering, almost staggering, under the weight of a helmet, two shields, and an armful of spears. At times it looked as if she would run into a wall, either by being overbalanced or blinded by the helmet that wobbled on top of her head.

"Wait, wait," said Matthew. "I just need a second to—" He stopped and they all slowed to a halt.

"We don't have time to catch our breath," said Fergus, turning around. "We can rest when we get back to the tower."

"No, I just need to . . ." Matthew readjusted a short bow that had been dangling around his neck so that it bisected his chest and then hitched up a quiver of arrows that was in eminent risk of shaking its contents onto the floor. "Okay, I'm good," he said, picking up a shield that he had let drop at his feet. "Let's— Look out!"

They all turned to see an yfelgóp glaring at them. He stood nearly an arm's length from Fergus, who yelped and stumbled back. He fell, which saved him from getting a knife in his neck as the yfelgóp lashed out with a quick strike, fast as a snake attack, the dark, scraggy blade passing close to his head. Fergus hit the ground, arms spread wide, flinging his loot around him in a noisy clatter. The yfelgóp advanced another step and drew his arm back for another strike.

But Jennifer had circled around and gave a cry that was a high, shrill shriek: "Help! Help! Help!"

Her voice was so loud and so close that the yfelgóp actually flinched in pain for a moment, and that gave Richard opportunity to charge forward and plant a sword in its chest. In either horror or surprise, the yfelgóp's eyes widened as it threw its shoulder forward and made another slashing motion at Richard's throat. The creature didn't know that its own hand had already dropped its weapon, however, and the action had no effect. As it slumped to the ground, Richard stood over it, looking down on the body, panting and shaking from the adrenaline.

"Yeah! S'what I'm talkin' about," he rasped as Fergus picked himself up from the ground.

"You killed it!" Fergus exclaimed admiringly.

"It was easy. Thanks to Jennifer. Thanks, Jennifer," he said, looking up and smiling. "That's a powerful scream you've got."

Jennifer gave a mock curtsey. "I mostly only use it on my brothers."

"Come on, let's get back to the others quickly," Gretchen said. "There will definitely be more of those about. Especially after all this noise."

VII

They passed a landing that had a doorway set into an alcove. "Stop!" Gemma called. She was near the front, and this caused the three ahead of her to freeze.

"What? What is it?" asked the boy at the front.

"This is far enough,"

"No, there are more stairs. We can keep going."

"Keep going," said someone from below them.

"Wait. We don't know what's up there."

"I think we should stay here. We don't want to get too far away."

"Too far away? I don't think we *can* get too far away from what's happening down there." He started up the stairs again. Gemma paused but people started jostling past her so she stood to the side, on the landing. No one else joined her, they just streamed past, climbing upward, so she set her mouth and rejoined the group, trying to fight back feelings of panic as she went higher and higher.

At the next landing, which felt like a mile from the previous one, their ascent stopped. Evidently, someone had decided that *this* was far enough, even though there were still more stairs going upward, Gemma noted.

The line of children went down a dark passage and into a room behind a silver, reflective door, which was held open by one apprehensive child to the next. It was cold to Gemma's fingers as she touched it on her way through, and caused her to shiver.

They were in a large, dark room. Those who had brought silver lamps flashed them around, finding the walls and corners. Gemma stood in the middle of the room and listened to the voices of the others trying to figure out where they were.

"There's no way out."

"Except the way we came."

"No, there's another room through he— Oh! No, it's a mirror. And— Whoa!"

"What is it?"

"There's someone else there. He— Oh my gosh."

"What? What's going on?"

"That's so weird."

"What *is* it?"

"Oh, that is *so* freaky."

"*What?*"

"Let me see."

"Look, that's me, but it's how I looked when I was little. But it's still a reflection. Look, I can raise my hand like this . . . Oh, wow. That must be you."

"No it's not . . ."

"It is! Wave or something."

"He's right! That's so weird. Crazy."

"Let me see."

"And me." People started to crowd toward the mirror.

"It must be magic. A magic mirror."

"Can it tell us what's going on downstairs?"

"And just how would I know that, exactly?"

"So ask it."

"What?"

"If it's a magic mirror then you should be able to ask it questions. Like in *Snow White*."

There was a moment of silence.

"*You* ask it, then. *I'm* not going to talk to it."

"Mirror. Show us the way out of this tower."

"Is it doing anything?"

"I don't think it worked."

"Try again. Ask it louder."

"Hey, there's another one here. Oh, wow."

"Is it another magic one?"

"Uh—yeah. Yeah, I'd say it was."

"What's it do?"

"I'm pretty sure that's me, but when I'm older. I look, I don't
know, thirty or something."

Gemma went closer to this second mirror and looked into it.

"You're not thirty," she said. "You're like twenty or something.
Here, shift over a bit." She tried to get a better angle to see herself
in. "That's weird."

"What?"

She was aware that more people were clustering toward them.
"I can't see myself."

"Yes, look. There you are." The boy next to her pointed at
the glass and the image of his older self matched his movement
exactly.

Gemma tilted her head. "No, no that's—look, that's that person standing there. That's her. I—I can't . . ." She stepped even closer, looking at the whole room's reflection. A realisation struck her that made her stomach tighten. "We're . . . we're not all here."

"What? What do you mean? What do you mean we're not all here?"

Gemma turned around and looked at all the faces in the room, each one of them looking at her now. "There must be at least forty of us in this room," she said.

"So?"

"So in this mirror—the mirror that shows the future—I can only see"—she paused as she counted—"twelve of us. Only twelve of us have a future reflection."

There was a much longer period of silence.

VIII

"Decide, Alex," Ecgbryt said, his words running together with urgency. "Pursue them, or continue by another route."

"Argh—" Alex swore under his breath. "We can't—" Alex stood tense. "We can't just go running off. Ecgbryt, what should we do?"

"It is not best to have our forces divided," Ecgbryt answered, looking set to chase after the knights already.

"Okay. Okay," Alex said, running a hand over his face. "After them!" he shouted. "Weapons drawn! Forward!"

The knights around Benjamin blurred into action. Unsure what he should do, he felt a hand grip his shoulder. "Stay *very* close to me," Alex said, bending toward him. His custom-designed sword was drawn, its incredibly sharp edge gleaming. "Give me your hand. Don't let go. I'm going to get you somewhere safe and I want you to stay there until I tell you to leave, understand?"

Benjamin said he did but he couldn't hear his own words come out so he nodded his head emphatically.

"Okay, keep up now," Alex said and then they were running. Benjamin tried to keep his feet moving fast enough not to drag or trip himself up, but they were scarcely on the ground. A few times he did stumble, but Alex pulled him along, dangling at his side until he got his feet back underneath him.

They had not yet reached the Langtorr when Benjamin heard shouts and sharp striking noises. The knights all seemed to have their own unique war cries in a variety of languages, and between these he could hear bellows and screeches of whatever it was they were fighting. One roar was so deep it seemed to vibrate in his stomach and there was a high-pitched keening that raked up his spine and put his hair on end. Underneath all of these noises was the clattering and pounding of swords, shields, axes, and spears—of blows taken on armour and bare flesh.

The noises grew louder the closer they got and Benjamin started panting with deep, irregular gasps. Then they turned a corner—his eyes bulged and his jaw dropped.

The first thing he saw were the giants—enormous, bulky rock creatures that stood waist-high in the sea of bodies around them. Two of them were swinging large hands down into the fray, where the knights who had raced ahead of them were already fighting the yfelgópes and the army of mystic creatures. The knights were fighting prodigiously, spears thrusting up through inhuman skulls, sharp swords hacking at limbs and chests.

As Alex and Benjamin entered the battle, he had to remind himself to keep breathing as he ducked out of the way of a creature with a bull's head on a stocky human body, its reptile-clawed hands wielding a sword, its mouth baring wet, needlelike teeth.

Alex jerked Benjamin through a pounding flurry of stamping legs, undulating tails, and swinging weapons. His own broad-bladed sword whipped in tight, deadly arcs and before Benjamin knew it his feet were knocking against the stairs leading to the Langtorr entrance. He looked up, not even aware that they had passed the inner wall, but there they were, at the foot of the crescent-shaped stairs. The knights, for all their disorganised fighting style, had obeyed Alex's command of making it to the Langtorr, their veteran fighting intuition taking the place of expressed tactics. It was a messy melee, but not one without a kind of wild order.

Alex made his way up the steps, hacking at a dense crowd of yfelgópes who were assaulting the door of the Langtorr, pressing in on a giant who looked to be about fifteen feet high. He was pounding at the ancient iron with a war mace the size of a pillarbox, giving a barking grunt at each assault. "Clear the courtyard!" Alex shouted between stabs. "Hold the gate. Don't let them through."

With no sign of acknowledgement except for a redoubling of effort, the knights did as he commanded. More knights joined Alex to clear the attackers around the Langtorr entrance. The yfelgópes tried to put up a fight, but they were hemmed in by their own forces. In such a tight space, their own numbers were working against them. Not that this made them any less cautious fighting, but it meant that as often as not they got in their own way and the more skilful knights were able to make short work of them. Alex himself hung back with Benjamin and they scanned the scene, wary of any threats. Benjamin noticed for the first time fallen knights mixed in amongst the bodies of the enemies that they had killed, bloodless faces gaping and pale hands clutching at wounds that dark blood seeped from.

"Okay, everyone's in!" Alex shouted, turning around. "Shut the outer gates!" Benjamin turned to look at the two massive stone doors, completely banded with steel, which started to swing closed as five knights apiece put their shoulders to the gates. The rest of the knights were then divided into three groups, one to keep more attackers from entering through the doors before they closed, one to clear the rest of the courtyard, and one to deal with the giant pounding at the doors to the Langtorr.

The giant with the club turned on them. Seeing himself surrounded, he gave a howl and uttered a very human oath. "Blimey," he bellowed in surprise, his mace rising and falling, swooping in front of him in a low arc, trying to bat away the knights who were advancing on him. Two of them were caught and went careening down the low steps. Another knight was quicker and dashed in with his spear before the giant's swing could return. The blade pierced the enormous man under his left armpit, causing him to shriek and stagger. Then, roaring in rage, he raised his mace, but before he could shift his momentum forward into what would have certainly been a horrifically fatal blow, the knight twisted the spear, buying him another moment as the giant reeled in renewed pain.

This moment was all that was needed for the other knights. Two more came to their companion's aid and threw their weight on the spear, forcing it upward, and the giant back.

Another spear thrust upward, pinning the giant on the right breast. Crying out in obvious pain, he fell backward on the iron doors, his legs buckling. Seizing the opportunity, more knights moved in and hacked and stabbed the giant around the waist. Red gashes opened beneath his loosely woven clothes. Axes swung and the giant slumped forward on his knees, entrails snaking slowly out of his belly and onto the stone floor. Eventually his chest collapsed as the air went from his lungs, his body falling to one side. The knights let go of their weapons before the strain broke them. Only when he was completely dead did they go forward to retrieve their spears.

The courtyard was now completely still, and they all stood

in silence, listening for sounds of the attackers outside the walls. They couldn't hear anything. Benjamin was panting and his arm was becoming numb where Alex was gripping it.

"Are you okay?" Alex asked him in a low voice.

Benjamin only nodded and wiped some of the sweat off his face.

Alex raised his voice and began shouting orders. "Roll the body away from the door! Some of you men get up on that wall!"

Something overhead caught Benjamin's eye. He looked up and could just make out large shadows circling the darkness of the roof above them. He tugged on Alex's arm and pointed. Alex nodded and told the knights to hurry up clearing the giant away from the door. He and Benjamin stepped to the side as its body was rolled forward, over the dead yfelgópes. Alex went to the door and banged on it with the hilt of his sword.

"Open up! It's us!" he shouted at the closed doors, one of which had warped slightly under the giant's blows.

After a few moments there was a scraping sound and then the doors opened inward. A pool of very frightened children peered up at the battle-worn knights, Gemma at the head of them.

"Is everyone okay?" Alex asked.

"Yes," said a small boy who moved to the front. "We closed the door when we saw them coming. We almost didn't, but—it was pretty close." Alex finally let go of Benjamin's arm as they walked into the Langtorr. Then he turned and shouted outside, "Get the wounded in here! Be quick, these doors will be shut again in three minutes!"

CHAPTER SEVEN

The First Sacrifice

I

Freya kept her jaw clenched tight, trying not to breathe. Modwyn's skin and flesh were already cold, and the dead weight of her body was hard to control with anything even approaching grace as Freya removed it from the rubble pile of the hero's throne. She tried not to look at how the body bent, or what caught and what gaped open on the rocks. After a series of terrible efforts, the body was down at the foot of the heap. Once during the ordeal, Freya happened to look up at Ealdstan; he peered down at her with a kind of detached amusement—like someone would at a child seriously engaged in a playful task. She hated him all the more for that. Through it he kept talking, his voice a constant, monotonous drone that made Freya's head feel as though it were stuffed with cotton.

"... the deeds of His we do not understand we explain as 'mysterious,' which implies a purpose we do not comprehend. But how do we truly know they are not nonsensical? Or even just random happenstance, devoid of any intent at all? Are we merely excusing a meaninglessly causal universe of blind action and reaction as somehow adhering to a divine will or an overarching plan? And if an action made by mere chance of hazard manages to benefit us personally—as how could it not, at some arbitrary point—then we declare this the culmination of the plan, the end of the design. But this is only a dressing we put on an otherwise arbitrary event, or series of circumstances. I have lived for over a thousand years and seen the worst of humanity and have yet to see any heavenly parent's corrective hand."

The elves had parted to let Freya at the body. But now they closed ranks as she dragged the body into the ellipse formation the Norns were now standing in.

"The only thing I can see that keeps any sort of check on evil and destruction—if we are to even believe in those terms as objective notions—is that what we choose to define as wrong or bad systems are subject to the same effects of entropy and decay as those we label as good. Rage and oppression are as unsustainable as kindness and beneficence in a closed system, and if there is no God or greater force to pour energy into our system, then the universe truly is closed—however many dimensions we acknowledge as existing either physical, spiritual, or mental. The fundamental design of the created does point strongly to the Creator but how much of our human condition are we to project upon Him, and what of what we wish in a deity are we to ascribe to . . ."

Freya laid Modwyn's arms across her chest, which still showed a small slit where the stone knife had kept her body separate from her spirit so that she could protect the Langtorr. What did death actually mean in this place? "I'm sorry," Freya said quietly, smoothing the cloth on Modwyn's arm. The long, bloody gashes in her chest that soaked Modwyn's green fabric to almost black didn't make it seem like she would ever move again. Freya wanted to put her hands over her eyes and close her lids, but couldn't quite bring herself to do it. "I'm sorry," she said to Ealdstan, standing up. "But you keep talking and talking—are you under the impression that someone is listening?"

Ealdstan chuckled. "You speak facetiously, but that comment underscores one of my fundamental complaints: so much talking, and where does it fetch us up? Can we, by talking, change our circumstances? No, action is the only personal meaning we can enforce on the world we inhabit. Do I speak because I cannot act? Yes. But it is only because I have taken every action I can think to. I have set our corner of creation on a path to destruction, and it is only by direct, outside action that it can be saved. Ignore me or no, you have been a tool I have concentrated much attention on. In fact, you are my hope of salvation."

"What does *that* mean?"

"Not that I literally believe you will save me," Ealdstan said. "But that you are now the sole possibility of redeeming the work and effort I have exerted over the centuries. You are the chance I have given the Creator to salvage the situation. Do you know how diamonds are formed?"

"Yes."

"Just ordinary seams of dust—ash, really—that are compressed by purely immense pressures. This changes the rough material into something hard enough to resist such pressure—into a dense, almost flawless lattice structure." Ealdstan clenched his fist tightly and then let it go. He smiled, his face beaming magnanimously.

"That's what Gád and I have done to you and the boy—taken dust and squeezed and squeezed and squeezed." Again he clenched his fist. "The hidden entrances of this nation I have designed to be a trap for children, the purest souls. Not just you, but countless others have fallen into it. And the quest I subsequently sent you on—and the others like you—was not a real thing at all. Gád and I devised in concert the challenges faced in order to exert the most pressure on those who ran the gauntlet. All failed—all failed . . . except for you and the boy Daniel. And so when it was time to use you, I sent Robin Ploughright—who came to sharpen you both and draw you back into the fight. I had to be certain that you were the strongest I could possibly make you in order to stand against what I have put in place."

"That doesn't make sense. Why would you make it easier for someone to stop you?"

"Not easy—possible. You won't. But you see, I don't want to shut and bar the door against God. I want to fling it wide open, to lay out the carpet for Him, so when He still fails to show the shame of those who believed He will be all the greater."

"And meanwhile?" Freya asked. "What about the rest of us?"

"What about you? If life has no meaning, then it doesn't matter one jot what happens."

"But if life *does* have meaning, just not the meaning you want?"

"Then . . . I don't care. I don't want to be a part of this universe if it makes all of my life—my work, my every effort—up to this moment irrelevant."

"Daniel's and my life obviously don't mean as much as yours— or anyone else around you," Freya said, gesturing to Modwyn. "Or you wouldn't have played around with us like you have. What makes you so important?"

"Power. I was given much, and much was demanded of me. I have lived up to those demands—who could have done more than I? And what was the object? I have given back to God. And will He not now return the investment—to honour the demands made to me? Or will He let those greater talents languish?"

Freya stood quietly and then sighed. So much was tangled up in her head, it was hard to tease it out into any sort of sense. "I don't know, Ealdstan. You certainly have a point of view. It seems crazy to me, but maybe I'm not smart enough to follow it. I rather think that if you really were right and justified in your actions, then so many people wouldn't get hurt while you just sit up on your big chair, wait for things to happen, and watch everyone else suffer."

||

Vivienne finished doing the head count. Twelve villagers were now with her, as well as the two knights. That was all that she could persuade to come with her, and unfortunately Dr. Sarraf was not one of them. Against her persuading, he had decided to stay and administer to the wounded.

Twelve of them was so few. Vivienne had done all she could to convince everyone, but it started to sound absurd even to her. Arguments spiralled out of control as the line was drawn between the villagers who were going to stay and those who were going to leave. Both she and Dr. Sarraf tried hard to maintain tone, but they were on distantly opposing sides of the issue. He was arguing that someone was bound to come and help them. She countered that it had been almost two hours now and no one had. There were insults, bitter recriminations, and there may even have been blows, actual blood spilt, but Vivienne drew it all to a close by demanding that those who were going to leave needed to leave now—there was no more time for discussion, and it was too unsafe to stay any longer. Really, she was mostly worried for the children, all alone except for their small escort.

When they had finally come away, when Vivienne and those following her had made it back down the massive piles of rubble that was once the open fields around the village and rejoined the children, these twelve had joined her—about a third of those she estimated were still around the village site. She prayed they would be okay from here on out, that help really would come to them from somewhere.

"Oh no," one of the villagers said as they started to descend the rubble. "Are these the missing children?"

"Just some of them," Vivienne said, looking across at the couple hundred clearly restless children who were beginning to make a lot of noise—bickering and joking and playing around as they were. "They'll have to be a mite quieter than that though."

"Sasha?" one of the mothers shouted, causing over a hundred heads to turn up toward them. "Sasha, where are you? Sasha, it's mummy!"

"Shush!" Vivienne shouted. "Don't make such a din! We don't want to attract—"

Her words had absolutely no effect on the woman, who continued to shout her daughter's name and climb down the unstable pile of rocks as fast as she could—which was faster than she should have. What started as a controlled slide got quickly out of hand and she fell in a stream of loose earth and large rocks. She screeched as she fell, but her voice was quickly muffled as she was buried by the scree and dirt.

Vivienne gasped and continued her descent as quickly and safely as she could, heading directly to where she had seen the woman go under.

"Stay away!" she called out to some of the children who had started to jog over to look or help the woman. "It's still too unstable!"

The knights on the ground had seen all this take place and were already digging the woman out. Their arms moved quickly as they flung loose rocks and pebbles away into the air behind them. It was just seconds later—very long seconds later—that Vivienne heard sputtering, a series of coughs, and the renewed calling of the mother for her Sasha.

Vivienne touched down and although her limbs and just about every joint that she had were aching, she raced over to where the woman—not even bothering to pull herself fully out of the rock she was buried in—was still crying out at the top of her lungs.

"Sasha! Sasha! Sasha!"

"*Tusht,* woman! Quiet with you now." Vivienne spoke urgently but the woman continued regardless. Vivienne crawled up toward her, legs churning in the soft earth. She could feel the panicked frenzy of the situation overtaking her as well as she scrabbled up the heap. She needed to keep control.

"Silence!" she said. She flung herself forward and grabbed the woman's shoulders, pushing her back against the rocks and stones. "Will you be quiet!" she shouted, and the woman took a deep breath, and then another, beginning to hyperventilate. "She's not here. She's *not . . . here!*"

Tears streaked the woman's face, making clean, pink tracks in the mud that was now caked there. Her husband slid down beside her and grabbed her shoulders trying, awkwardly, to hold and comfort her.

"She's not here," Vivienne repeated again, slowly and in a calmer tone of voice. "But there are many, many more children back in the city and trust you me, I want to get to them as desperately as you do. But we can't do it yelling our heads off all the way and getting ourselves into these sorts of scrapes. Is that understood?"

The woman nodded, sobbing now, and made a noise from her throat that might have been "sorry."

"Grand. Now, we're going to dig you out, as swiftly as possible, but try to find if you've damaged yourself in any way in your fall. If so, I'll get one of the knights to carry you, and it won't be a big fuss. Is that acceptable?"

The woman nodded and Vivienne, with the help of one of the knights, extricated the woman; her leg had been twisted, possibly sprained. She was able to walk with the assistance of her sheepish and apologetic-looking husband.

The rest of the adults in the meantime had mixed with the children and, to everyone's surprise, one couple had actually located their son. The father was now carrying him, clutching him tightly as the boy's mother hung on to his arm, and they were walking off, looking to Vivienne as if they were looking for a way back into the rubble.

"Where are you going?" she shouted at them, jogging back to the group.

"We've found him, we're taking him back home."

"You can't—"

"We certainly can!" the father shouted.

"But . . . your home doesn't exist any more. It's all rubble. You have to come with the rest of us."

"We're getting him to safety," the father said. "We're getting him away from this whole scene. I don't know what's going on here, but we want no part of it."

"You don't know if that way's safe."

"Can you guarantee that your way is any safer?"

"Yes. I believe so."

"You *believe*? Well, I believe you're wrong, how about that?"

"Please—you—"

"Don't tell us what's best for our son!" the mother shouted. Vivienne shut her mouth and watched them walk away.

"Okay, everyone, I'm sorry about that," Vivienne said. The altercation had obviously disturbed the children, they looked spooked and needed reassuring. "The only thing I have on my mind now is getting all of you to safety. And it's best if we get back to the tower, if we all stay together. There are exits there that I'm certain we can use, and a lot of knights to protect us while we figure out how to get to them. But we all need to stay together, so don't anyone wander off. If you feel tired, come and talk to me or one of the knights about slowing down. Am I understood?"

There were nods and murmurs of ascent.

"Good." Vivienne turned to one of the knights. "We need to get to the beacon," she said. "I've become a little disoriented. Can you tell where that is?"

"I believe I can, my lady," he answered in broken Gaelic.

"Good. Everyone! Can I have everyone's attention? Let's all go this way, please. We're following him."

III

Dr. Sarraf watched them vanish from sight, slowly picking their way through the ruins. He wanted to say one last thing, to call after them the perfect few words that would make them realise how stupid and idiotic they were being, but there was just no telling some people. No telling *most* people, actually, in his experience. Just about anyone would continue to do what was worst for them, for completely irrational reasons, either because they liked it, or they were too lazy to change, because they were afraid, or because they were in just plain denial at the consequences.

And there wasn't one of the group he counted leaving who was not afraid, and he included Vivienne and her odd friends alongside them. She was terrified and had managed to pass that terror onto some very confused people, and now they were off to get themselves in even greater danger; perhaps some of them would die.

But he couldn't stop them, any more than he could stop

anyone in his practice from making decisions he knew to be directly harmful. People made a big deal about the Hippocratic oath, about doing no harm, but harm was all just a point of view. Often—almost always, in his experience—it was only a choice of varying degrees of harm. And then there was the paradox that the least harmful action might be the most harmful in the long run, and the most harmful would cause the least harm in the short term. And of course, everyone died. On a long enough axis, everyone's mortality was one hundred percent.

He bowed his head, pressing his chin to his chest. It wasn't time to think such thoughts—they were first-year medical school quandaries anyway, and he was needed. He turned and went back to the space he had cleared for the wounded and reviewed his triage. He lost track of both himself and the time as he assessed various injuries, patched up things as best as he could, told people to lie down and keep certain things elevated, and answered excited cries of people who had uncovered more bodies. He had plenty of supplies with him, except water. What he needed most right now was just pure, clean water. He hoped whoever was coming brought plenty of it with them. He knew time was probably passing slower than he thought it was—he had diagnosed himself with mild shock—but felt for certain that rescue people should be on the scene. He kept straining his ears for the sound of rotors. If not a big rescue helicopter loaded with men, medicine, and pulleys, then at least a small one just to look at the scope of the damage. But the skies were empty. He found this very disturbing but pushed that to one side. He needed to focus on the job at hand.

He heard shouts in the distance and immediately began to reload his medical bag with his vastly depleted supplies. He recognised the voices of the men; they must have discovered another survivor or another body. He wiped stinging sweat from his eyes. He needed rest—they all did. When would help arrive? He began to make his way slowly toward the shouts that, he now realised, had not stopped and were shriller and louder than they needed to be to attract just him. Something was wrong. He looked up then and tried to focus on the landscape, which was so bizarrely distorted that it was hard to pull focus, to understand the unusual in a scene where nothing was as it usually was.

There was a smash, the sound of subsidence, and renewed screaming. He amended his path to go toward the cries—it sounded like people were being caught in a collapse of some sort. He tried to move quicker, mere seconds could be extremely valuable in a circumstance like this.

The screaming did not let up, nor did the smashing sounds. He hurried, and then a strange movement caught his eye. "What in the—" He stopped completely, not believing what he was seeing. It looked to be something that was roughly humanoid, pounding its fists into the ground. And then he saw the people around it and gasped—it must be twelve feet tall. It seemed to have mud and embedded rocks compacted around it or . . . could it have been made from rock?

It was attacking the people around it, its fists, he realised, bloody. Some men were unaccountably running toward it. Dr. Sarraf raised his hand, trying to call out to them to turn away, but no sound came out of his mouth. Then another enormous figure loomed behind them, taking huge steps forward, and then he realised the people were not running at the first monster, they were trying to run past it. They were pursued by another and, behind that, another. There were four monsters, moving through the ruins of the village, pounding everything that moved into pulp and dust, systematically finishing what the cave-in had started.

Dr. Sarraf had been proud all his life of being a rational man, of not having any superstitions or unreasonable beliefs. But from the depths of his unconscious came floating up an idea from his childhood. As a boy he had once heard a tale that had frightened him to the depths of his soul—that had, in fact, put his feet forever on the path of the rational and real. It was a tale about inanimate objects that were enchanted and made animate—yet given only a single purpose, a single task they would continue to carry out with unreasoning, inhuman constancy; an irrational creature made yet even more irrational by its thoughtless actions. It was this that he had feared as a child, and it was this that he gazed on at the end of his life.

His lips parted as he said a name of two syllables that he had never before allowed to pass—his last superstition from boyhood.

"Golem."

One of the creatures noticed him. He stared blankly up at it and as its shadow fell upon him he turned and tried to run. It was all he could do, and it was his final act in life.

IV

Alex forced himself to relax, pushing a deep breath from inside his chest and rolling his head around his shoulders. They had managed to create a little space of safety for now, but that didn't mean they could let their guard down. He climbed the steps of the completely circular wall that surrounded the Langtorr, casting a critical eye on the knights who paced there. Many of them had spears and pikestaffs, a few carried bows and arrows, which were very useful in a siege condition, but ammunition was limited.

Alex came to stand next to Ecgbryt, whose face looked no less grim than his own. Looking out over the horde, it began to sink in how vastly outnumbered they were. Even if every child with them in the Langtorr was a warrior, even if they were each an ancient, mystic knight, they still wouldn't stand a chance. Before now they had not faced anything like the full warhost. The attackers must have been already in the act of falling back when Alex and his knights had reached them at the gates of the Langtorr. Some of the withdrawing force had not resisted the opportunity to try and take potshots at the defenders, but these skirmishes were not in earnest and they quickly turned back.

The creatures that made up the army now arrayed against them were truly horrifying. Looking out into the amassing forces, he saw not just yfelgópes but also giants, trolls, and ogres. There were enormous serpents and wyrms, their bodies and tails snaking along the ground, shimmering scales glimpsed past the legs on the rest of the beseigers. There were massive armoured bears that made ferocious growls as they became more and more anxious for attack. Wyverns with riders flapped their wings, eager to take to the air. Many of these creatures he had encountered in the last eight years, tracking them down by himself or with Ecgbryt. But there were others he had not seen before, small leathery things with thick limbs, tall and thin creatures with hollow faces, and dark, flapping shapes that hovered and glided above the still growing assemblage. There were also humans in the group. They were hard to spot, but they stalked in between the other mystical creatures, their eyes trained on the defending knights. At first, Alex didn't know what they were doing, and what their purpose might be, but then Ecgbryt drew his attention to one of them who was holding his arm in front of him. It was aflame with a blue-green fire that didn't burn him, and then Alex understood they were warlocks and witches.

"There are more of them by the second," Alex said. "The attack just now on the tower—that wasn't an attack in earnest, it was an attack of opportunity. Wherever they're coming from—it was just something to keep us distracted while they got their game together."

"Aye, the battle has not yet begun." Ecgbryt clenched his axe tighter in his fists, twisting its shaft between them. "We have only tasted of the opening skirmish."

"How are the troops?"

The huge knight turned an eye down on him. "Their spirits are high—perhaps too high. This is the fulfilment of their purpose— what they have been awaiting all these centuries. They believe they cannot fail. I would judge that most of them desire nothing more than to charge out immediately and chase all comers into the sea."

"Which would be fine for them, but there's the children to think about."

"Swa swa, there is them to think on, and that is what stays them—for now. But their determination and faith notwithstanding . . . they will tire."

"What do you mean?"

"They are mortal now, Alex. They can kill and be killed. This is not the full host we were promised—so many of their number have been lost already—but few times, if any, has a host of such expert fighters been assembled. Yet they will grow weary. Their blood is up now, they are hot—why *not* attack now, if attack there is to be?"

"I would have agreed with you twenty-four hours ago. That's why we got all these guys here, after all. But the children—what part do they play in this?"

Ecgbryt folded powerful and thick arms across his chest. "I do not know. All of my faith up to this point—for nearly my entire life—has been in Ealdstan. I am loath, very loath, to forsake that now. I believe all be well in the end."

"This isn't what I signed up for, Ecgbryt."

Ecgbryt harrumphed. "The old rules do not apply anymore. The enchantments all have been broken."

"I suppose you're right. Wait, what do you mean?"

"Ealdstan has broken them—the act of killing Modwyn was not just it. Did you not mark what he said? 'I break all my enchantments'?"

Alex smacked his forehead. "Of course . . ." He gasped. "Of course!"

"What of course?" Ecgbryt asked in an annoyed tone. "What has occurred to you?"

"Just that if you're right, there may be a way for us to escape after all. Stay here. I need to check something out."

V

Vivienne had everyone sit on the ground and wait while she and a small group of knights checked out the area around the Beacon. They were getting nearer the city now, but she hoped they were still far enough away that they wouldn't be spotted. The daylight was noticeably starting to fade. The sky through the fissure was still light, but direct sunlight was not coming through anymore. By Vivienne's watch it was only a little after four in the afternoon. And the flat nature of the underground plain, interrupted only by a stream that cut a ridge through it, was very disorienting and made distances rather difficult to judge. But she hoped they would be able to spot anything dangerous as soon as anything dangerous spotted them.

"Where's the entrance?" Vivienne asked, her voice low. The building looked like a squat lighthouse. There were windows layered at different levels, but they had all apparently been barricaded from the inside with metal bars and stone slabs. There was an open upper level at the top where an enormous rock crystal lens had once diffused light from the beacon across the Niðerplain in the city's glory days, but Vivienne could not see it.

"It is this way, my lady."

Taking a moment to scan the horizon—not the horizon, she corrected herself, they were below that here . . . what was the word she was looking for? Was there even a vocabulary for it?—she searched for any sign of threat and then crossed over to where the knights were now gathered, making low muttering noises to each other. They were standing in front of an elaborately carved arched entryway, made with no less artistry than the rest of Niðergeard. And like the rest of Niðergeard, it had clearly seen better days. An enormous chunk of rock had been wedged into the arch to prevent anyone from passing. Gaps had been plugged with long metal panels that may have been benches, or possibly stairs.

"How are we going to get through that?" she asked aloud.

One of the knights said something to her in a language she didn't understand. She thought the language might be Slavic and she silently cursed herself for neglecting to study any Eastern European languages. One of the other knights stepped forward—she remembered his name being Tugdal. "Do you understand him? What did he say?" she asked him in Old English. "*Hwaet er es gesegen?*"

"He says perhaps it would be best to find a new route into the city," the knight replied.

"No, no. I've used this one before, this is the safest. If we can actually get inside." She knew there were people in there—perhaps she could get them to unbarricade the entrance? But they were so despondent, so dissociated, she didn't hold out much hope for that.

"Perhaps we can get up to the top somehow . . . ?" She took a few steps back and again tried to gauge how far it was to the top and if they could possibly scale it somehow. Or would that be barricaded as well? "Keep looking around. Even a single window would be enough to use if we could force our way through it."

They kept circling the building, looking for a way in. There were windows, yes, but they were very high up on a sheer face. Perhaps . . . perhaps they could make a sort of pyramid with the knights that the children could climb up. But they would need to find a window that they could push in, and none of them looked any more promising than the other. What was the plan if they couldn't get in?

They arrived back at the entrance. "We have seen nothing, my lady," one of them informed her. "It seems impenetrable. Again, I would suggest—there may perhaps be another way into the city—into the Langtorr itself."

"No, there *must* be something," Vivienne insisted, starting to circle the building once again. She reached out and put her hand on the wall. Up close it looked so solid and immovable, but from even just a few paces away it looked fragile, like an egg that was shattering in a dozen different places. Her fingers traced a vertical crack in the wall and flaked off a thin layer of it. It fell to the ground with a small but audible *plink* and shattered.

She took a step back and looked up at the wall, suddenly seeing it differently. There were two deep, divergent cracks running down from one of the windows, making a sort of wedge shape.

"I have an idea," she said. "I'll tell you what it is, and I want you three to get busy while I go get the others."

VI

Alex reached the top of the stairs moderately out of breath. He'd climbed the Langtorr as quickly as he could, but not as quickly as he wanted, since there was something holding him back.

"How far do you think we've gone? It feels like over a mile. I'll bet it's at least a mile."

People told Alex that he spoke too much, but he didn't know. He certainly didn't talk as much as Benjamin did.

"I don't think so. In order to go a mile—"

"But we're going up as well. How many steps do you think we'd have to go in order to go a mile?"

"I don't know. It would be easy to work out if we knew the height of the stairs, we could—"

"Is it getting brighter? It feels like it's getting brighter."

"I think you're right. It also feels—"

"And that smells like fresh air!"

He was right. They must be nearing the top now, and Alex could feel that the Langtorr had definitely changed. For a start, the air was fresh and warm. It was getting lighter—sunlight was beginning to filter down from the top of the spiral staircase, casting a warm ambient glow on the walls. They could hear the whistling of wind as he came near the top now. Alex slowed his pace, and then a turn of the stairs ahead of him revealed a white slice of sky.

"Argh! That's so bright. It stings!"

"Just keep blinking. Your eyes will adjust."

"They're watering. Look, is that really the sky?"

It was. Alex smiled to himself and put up a hand to shield his eyes, pushing slowly up into the afternoon air. Wind whipped at his face and tugged his hair. His eyes were watering as he looked around, pulling himself up from the ground, putting his hands against raw, unworked stone. The stairs just finished in the ground. A few steps forward and he was standing on soft, British grass.

Everything was flat. Or at least it seemed that way. He was on the top of a very gently sloping hill that rounded away from him with very few geographical features. There was a low stone wall running to one side of him and beyond that the roof of a farmhouse. A small copse of trees sprouted to the other side of him, he could hear the sound of birds twittering. It was the normal, idyllic British countryside.

"It is. It's true. It's true."

"What's true?"

"Ecgbryt was right—Ealdstan has broken his enchantments. All the tunnels he's created have lost their magical properties— they've reverted back to normal laws of physics."

"What does that mean?"

"It means the only barriers between the surface world and Niðergeard are natural ones. Whatever . . . mechanisms there were to disguise them are gone. We can leave directly through the Langtorr now." Alex started rummaging in his rucksack for his binoculars. "You wouldn't believe the trouble we had getting through here the last time," he added under his breath.

"So wait," said Benjamin, crouching down to feel the grass. "You're telling me that we're in England now?"

"Well, yes. Of course."

"Oh."

"What? You sound disappointed."

"No, it's just . . . I don't know. I thought we were in another world. Like Narnia or . . . that place where the hobbits live."

"No, we've all only ever been in England."

"Oh. Okay."

"You wouldn't like any of the mystical realms anyway. They're really dangerous."

"What's the most dangerous one?"

"Not sure. The one with all the flying lizards is pretty horrific. There isn't any land there, but the fish can fly, sort of. The giants' world isn't any picnic either."

"Can I go to one of them one day?" Benjamin asked, plucking at a tuft of grass.

"Uhh . . . no. Never."

"Aw."

Alex lowered his binoculars and bit back a curse. "Rats!" he said.

"What?"

"I've just worked out why we can't escape through here."

"How come?"

"Everything's collapsed in a big ring. We're essentially standing on an island. There might be somewhere that hasn't collapsed completely, or a place we could climb down and up out of again fairly easily, but I can't see it from here. We would have to walk around it to be sure, but that could take hours, like eight or ten at least. We don't have that much time."

"Can I see through the binoculars?"

"No, we should get back to the others."

"Come on, let me have a quick look. I'm already up here, it won't be more than a minute."

"Yes, but you shouldn't be up here, should you? Why can't you ever stay where I tell you to stay?"

"What are those?"

"What?"

"Those things in the sky. Are they bats?"

Alex looked up and nearly jumped out of his skin. There were wyverns circling overhead, gliding in lazy arcs like buzzards. He counted seven, and then eight of them. "No, those aren't bats. Quick, get back down into the tower. I don't think they've seen us."

"But what are they?"

"I'll tell you in a second. Get back into the tower!"

VII

"Remember, all of you stay quiet, no matter how much noise *we* make, *you* must stay silent." Vivienne was speaking only loudly enough to be clearly heard by everyone sitting in front of her. "And as soon as we break through the wall, I want all of you here to wait as I and these knights check the inside of this building to make sure it's safe. And then, starting with the front row"—Vivienne pointed—"with this young girl here, I want you all to walk in a single, orderly, and—above all—a *quiet* line through the gap. There is a tunnel in there that will take us back to the tower, where the rest of the knights are, and where we'll be safe. Does everyone understand? Nod your heads if you do."

Everyone nodded.

"Raise your hands if you have any questions."

No hands were raised.

"Good. Adults . . . I would appreciate it if you would stand by and help keep things orderly. Now—how's that wall coming?"

All five knights were working on the wedge-shaped section of the wall delineated by the two cracks that ran from the window above them, trying to pull it away from the rest of the building. Three of them had spears wedged into the gap on the right-hand side and were gently trying to lever that section of wall away from the rest of it. One of the knights had actually scaled up to the window itself and was pulling at it, his feet planted on either side of the cracks, his hands actually inside the window, trying to tilt the whole thing forward.

There was a cracking sound and for several long, slow moments, the section of the wall tilted forward and then fell, the knights springing away from the sides. The knight at the top of the ten-foot pillar of stone held on and hopped off at the last second with surprising dexterity, tumbling over sideways a few times and then picking himself up.

The sound that the wall made when it hit the ground was like a clap of thunder. Vivienne quickly scanned the walls around the fallen section to see if any other loose bits of masonry were in danger of falling. She advanced, edging as close as she dared, waiting for the dust to clear so they could see inside. With three knights in front of her, she went back into the Beacon.

The air was just as foul as she remembered, and to her mild surprise, she saw there were still yfelgópes and Niðergearders here, sitting in the deep throes of depression—the dispossessed. They were staring at the intruders in blank-faced puzzlement as if they were aliens from another planet, not quite believing what they were seeing.

Vivienne couldn't see any danger here and although the building was completely collapsed inside—the floors and stairways all lying in rubble on the floor—she believed they could navigate through it fairly swiftly. "It looks safe to me, how about you?" she asked the knights.

"It will be if the roof doesn't cave in," Tugdal said, looking up at the ceiling, which was hidden in dark shadows. There was a cluster of thin pillars in the centre of the building, each one of them about the thickness of a small tree trunk; they ran the height of the tall room and supported the weight of the top floor and the roof. He went up to them and tapped his sword on the closest, testing its sturdiness. "Should be fine."

"Right, I'll get them in, then," Vivienne said. "Go ahead and clear the way through to there," she said, motioning to the short stairway that led down into the connecting tunnel. "Lift anyone out of the way who won't move."

She stuck her head out of the gap in the wall. "Okay. Quickly now— No!"

The children jumped up, startled by her cry, as a band of yfelgópes, perhaps a dozen of them, sprang out of the shadows. The knights were already moving, weapons drawn, but there were only two of them on this side. They only just managed to get themselves between the attackers and the children who all rushed as a single body toward the gap in the Beacon.

Vivienne tried to slip out, but the press of the children pushed her back inside. Unable to see in the dark, some of them tripped, falling to the ground, feet stomping all around them.

She dashed forward, picking the fallen up before they could be trampled, but the ones she didn't reach in time became very seriously hurt, and the space was starting to get extremely crowded as the frightened children stood confused, not knowing where to go. A few of the adults had pushed their way in ahead of the children and were standing uselessly to the side, at the walls, where the dispossessed Niðergearders had been pressed. Many of the children were crying, some in pain and some in fear as outside the sound of clanging swords and shrill cries of anguish ripped the air.

"There, through there!" Vivienne shouted, pointing to the archway partly set into the ground. It was only faintly illuminated by the silver lanterns inside it. "Make your way there in an *orderly* fashion!" She wasn't sure if they could hear her above the clamour, but the crowd rolled forward and started down the tunnel.

The three knights inside with her finally struggled against the tide of children to make it through the breach and join the fight outside. Vivienne did the best she could to direct and aid everyone safely through the dark and dangerous room. The number of children flooding into the Beacon tapered off, staggering through in dribs and drabs, most of them limping now. Vivienne saw with alarm that there was blood on some of them. She stopped one boy whose left side of his face was dripping with it. "Are you okay? Are you hurt? Are you injured?"

The boy's face turned to her and he shook his head and then pulled himself out of her hands and followed the rest toward the tunnel.

Vivienne was able now to get outside and she did so, cautiously. It looked like the fight had finished. The knights were standing, panting, their blood still up, also taking stock of the scene, making sure that the fallen were actually dead.

Some of the bodies lying on the ground were children. Vivienne's heart skipped a beat and the blood in her veins turned icy cold. Some of them were still moving and she gasped as she ran to the nearest of them, a boy lying flat on his back, glassy eyes staring upward, concentrating, it seemed, just on moving his chest up and down. He had a nick on the base of his neck that was dripping blood. Vivienne touched it and he winced. It was deeper than it looked.

"I'm sorry," she said to him, her voice coming out in just a whisper. "I'm sorry, this may hurt. I'm going to roll you forward in order to see how—oh my." She had only lifted his shoulder, tilting him toward her, and found that his entire back was completely soaked in blood, his clothes felt like a warm, wet sponge. His mouth, close to her face, expelled a deep, warm sigh, and then no more sound came from him.

"No—no!" She rolled him gently back onto the ground; his eyes were now looking in different directions, one of them rolled slightly up in his head. "No!" Vivienne held her bloody hands out away from the boy. "No, I didn't . . . I only touched him. No, no . . ." Vivienne pressed two fingers to the carotid artery at the left side of the boy's throat. There was no pulse. She placed her hands one on top of the other and began pushing his sternum rhythmically. "Please, God, please. I only touched him."

A large hand fell on her shoulder; a knight was above her. "*Ætstand*," a voice said. Her mind translated this: *stop.*

"No—don't . . . ," she muttered as she kept pushing her bloody palms downward.

The hand pulled her away and she twisted out of its grasp. "*Ætstand. Frēcennes.*"

Stop. Danger.

Vivienne halted, her breath catching. Of course there was more danger. There were others counting on her. Others who were still alive. She couldn't take her eyes off of the boy who had died in her hands. But there were others in danger. Others . . . others . . .

She looked up at the other bodies. A girl, only just out of her teens, also lay dead, and two more near her. But two other children were being helped up by the knights. They were pale and injured, one boy gripping his leg, the girl cradling one arm in the other.

Strong hands gripped her arms and lifted her up to her feet. Tugdal's serious face was in front of her, speaking seriously and slowly. She couldn't quite understand what he was saying, but she heard him say, "*Frēcennes*," and point over her shoulder.

She turned and looked toward the city, where a black, shifting line was advancing like a slow tidal wave. She could see the long, pointed silhouettes of spears sticking out of the mass, great lumbering hulks ranked behind many forms of smaller shapes.

"Yes. Yes. Thank you," Vivienne said quietly, gripping the knight's arm. "Come along, the both of you." She led them into the building and toward the tunnel to the Langtorr. She turned and saw the five knights standing in the gap.

"Come along if you're coming," she said.

Tugdal walked over to her and kissed two of his fingers. He laid them against the side of her face and gave a weak smile.

He's saying good-bye, Vivienne realised. They weren't coming with her. They were going to stay and fight, but how long could they fend off an army?

An ear-splitting war cry cut through the air, a high-pitched ululating. It kicked off a string of answering cries that grew louder and louder, joined by savage shrieks and growls.

"Let's go," Vivienne said to the two injured children. "Let's get to the Langtorr."

They made their way through the rubble of the Beacon. Some of the dispossessed rose around her, frightened into movement and starting to piece together, in their addled minds, what was starting to happen. "Anyone who is still here in sixty seconds will most likely be dead," she said to them. "The rest will have followed us."

There was the sound of an impact and a sharp crack. It was so close that it made Vivienne turn instinctively. Tugdal had hurled his weight at the five thin stone columns supporting the ceiling. He drew himself back and then flung himself forward again. One of the pillars cracked across the middle and the lower half fell to one side.

Vivienne had an arm around the boy and was helping him walk. "Let's go quickly," she said. "Be careful how you go."

They made good and quick progress down the tunnel. Vivienne was holding her breath, waiting for—hoping for—another sound of collapse, and it wasn't even thirty seconds before it came. It was a small rumble and shake, a mere echo of the one they had all experienced before, but it meant that the knights had collapsed the ceiling, burying themselves and the tunnel entrance beneath a massive pile of masonry.

The children stopped in their steps, looking frightful, spooked, not knowing what this new quake meant. "Carry on! Carry on!" Vivienne said to those around her above the sound of coughing and ringing in her ears. "Keep on moving. Keep on." She wiped a tear from her eye for the knights who had sacrificed themselves, and hoped it was enough to make a difference.

CHAPTER EIGHT

Warriors and Poets

---------- **I** ----------

"Okay, all of you," Freya said to the girls, who were becoming increasingly nervous. Sounds of battle could be heard from beyond the buildings around them, and occasionally fleeting shapes could be seen dashing between them. Nobody had entered the courtyard, however. "Stay close to me, stay inside this circle. I think we're safe here. The women will keep you safe."

"So . . . what's going to happen now?" one of the girls asked.

"I don't know." Freya turned to glare up at Ealdstan who glared down at her, each of them in their protective circles.

Freya looked down at the ground and tried to think. She felt she was on the edge of seeing things for what they were, of having enough perspective on the situation to know what to do, but she couldn't quite glimpse it yet—it was like something lurking just on the edge of her vision, but she couldn't quite turn her head enough . . .

"Should we kill him?"

Freya snapped out of her reverie. "What's your name?" she asked, focussing on the girl who had spoken.

"Sophie."

"I'm not sure we can, or even if we did that it would help."

"I think we could. If the angel ladies protect us like they did you, we could get up there, no problem. They'd make short work of those elves, no fear."

"I don't think that would actually solve as much as you think," Freya said. "I've seen enough of what he's talking about to believe him. He's set everything up and now he's going to watch it destroy itself. We need to tackle the actual problem he's created, not waste time on worrying about him."

"But he's right there!"

Freya bit her lip. "If I thought it might help us defeat the army he and Gád have raised, to help close the gates between the worlds . . ."

"How do you know it won't? It might be a start, in any case. He's so powerful. If we have the chance, we should take it. He certainly deserves it."

Freya shook her head slowly. Sophie turned abruptly to one of the women who was standing behind them.

"Hey, can you answer some questions?"

The woman inclined her head.

"How do we close the gates?" She pointed up at the black gash in the air above the hero's throne.

"You cannot."

"There must be a way to close them," Freya said. "It's not natural for them all to be open."

"No, it is not," the Norn woman replied. "They would close themselves off, but they are being prevented from doing so."

"So what's preventing them?" Sophie said. "What's making the gates stay open?"

"It is the souls of those who have died but have not passed on that keep the gates from closing. They have become trapped between this world and the next, wedged each one of them in a nexus. Ealdstan is very adept at the trapping of souls—at hiding from the Silver Rider. It is his greatest magic that allowed him to keep the knights asleep for centuries."

"Okay, so how do we move the souls on? Before, when I blew the Carnyx, that seemed to do something."

"That was Ealdstan's key that removed a layer of his enchantment. The souls of the living cannot affect the souls of the dead."

Freya rubbed her eyes.

"So why could *he*?" one of the other girls asked, throwing an arm up at Ealdstan. "He obviously did *something* to them."

"He did not. He merely created circumstances for the souls to be entrapped at the moment of leaving the body."

Freya shut her eyes and pinched her brow. "So can we change those circumstances? Can we somehow help push the souls through?"

"The souls of the living may not affect the souls of the dead."

"But even if we can do it for good?" Sophie said. "Even if we could save the world?"

"Even so."

"Maybe we need to think of a different way around the puzzle," another girl said—her name was Tracey. "That's what I always do when I hit a block like this."

Freya raised an eyebrow. "How old are you, anyway?"

"Eleven. Is there any way that we can raise an army to fight all these monsters down here?"

The Norn woman looked puzzled this time. "An army already exists."

"Of knights, yes," Sophie said. "We know that, but—"

"*You* are the army. You are the next army that was summoned."

"Somehow I don't think that we'll quite be up to facing an army of giants and trolls," one of the girls behind Freya said.

"Is there any way we can raise an army like the one that Gád has?" Sophie asked the woman. "An army of *good* mystical creatures, perhaps? Is that even possible?"

The woman's eyes shifted, looking not only into the distance but also the past, into her own memory. "There have been times when such beneficent creatures roamed Albion's isles. Enormous lions lived in the deep woods, righteous and wise as they were powerful—fierce and uncompromising in their nobility. There was a race of eldritch warriors who fought back the men who gave themselves over to evil. There were the hidden folk who dwelt in the forests and waterlands, virtually unseen, but who tended to the nature realms. The greenmen and -women whose skin was bark and hair were leaves were rare but friendly to travellers. Unicorns, eagles . . . even the ancient dragons themselves were not meaningly hostile.

"But as man's powers in the world grew, he fought off such beings. Some of the battles were overt violent confrontations, but more often they were subtle and unintended—the way in which he shaped the world around him left no space for such creatures. He filled every gap. In the old tongues there were many words for nobility and honour—it was so abounding and prevalent that it was necessary to devise many different words in order to distinguish it. Now there are few words for virtue and a whole catalogue of terms for vice, sin, corruption, dishonesty, wickedness, evil . . .

"That is what pushed the defenders of good out of this world, off of this island—the lack of anything to defend. They were defeated by purposelessness, not by power. It is possible that some may be reclaimed from the lands they have left to, but to force the gates open at a time other than their natural order would dictate would be to run the risk of tearing the world apart even sooner."

"Like Ealdstan has done," Freya said.

The woman nodded. "Anyone wishing to open a gate now would have to sacrifice themselves or someone else and thus put the entire world in jeopardy."

II

"Excuse me, but you're one of the knights, right? Hello? Excuse me!"

Frithfroth snapped out of his trance. He had been sitting in a near catatonic stupor, crouching on a squat stool underneath the double staircase of the Langtorr's entry hall. His eyes had been fixed on the decaying tapestry opposite him, staring at it until they could no longer see what they gazed at. They turned now, grey and milky, to look down at the small girl tugging on his shirt. She had brown eyes and dark, curly hair that corkscrewed down to her waist.

"Who are you?" he demanded, his voice cracking.

"I'm Esme. You're one of the knights, right? Someone said you used to look after all the knights here."

"Frithfroth."

"What?"

"My name is Frithfroth. And no, I never had charge of any knights. It was I who maintained this tower."

"Why aren't you maintaining things now?"

Frithfroth looked around. *What is there to maintain?* he thought, but didn't say anything. "Do you wish to hear a riddle?" he asked.

"Not really. Is it a good one?"

"You won't know unless you hear it."

"Go on, then."

Frithfroth drew a breath and began:

> *Earth that walks on earth, must from the earth earth grow*
> *Earth that earth may eat, so earth in earth earth sows.*

But if the earth the earth won't eat, then earth in earth
  shall go:
A hole in earth shall other earth make, then earth in earth
  earth stows..

Earth takes earth from out of earth—earth that's took
  with woe.
And earth will bring that earth to earth, and to that earth
  earth shows.
And earth will lay earth in the ground then earth in earth
  will stow:
So what is earth to earth returns. All earth to earth must go.

Esme looked up at the knight, expressionless. "Is that it?"

Frithfroth nodded. He noticed that other children were starting to gather around him.

"That was terrible," Esme said. "I think that's the worst poem I've ever heard."

"It is a very old riddling poem. It was one of the first that I learnt."

"I hate it. Do you know any more?"

"Yes, many more."

"Do another one," a red-headed boy behind her said.

Frithfroth frowned. His brow twitched and it looked like he was having an internal argument with himself. He eventually reached a decision and said, "Now, this is a very old poem." He cleared his throat and began:

Now must we revere the Ruler of Heaven's Riches,
The Mighty Maker, and his marvellous creation,
The works of the world's father, the wonder of his people.
Our Eternal Lord, in this way began:
He first arranged for earth's children

Heaven as a roof. Then the Holy Wright
Made the Middle-Earth and Mankind's King,
Our Eternal Lord, appointed this to its people
As our realm, O Mighty Ruler.

He looked expectantly down at his audience's lead critic. "That hymn was very popular where I came from."

"It was better," Esme said. "But it didn't really sound like a hymn. Or a poem. So is that what you are now? You don't fight anymore, you just say poetry?"

"Would you prefer that I fight?"

Esme shrugged. "It looks as if we need more people to fight than we need people for poetry."

"You don't find poetry useful right now?"

"Not your poetry."

"In my age, warriors and poets were not separate, and the best of men were both."

"That's obviously not true for you though. So what happened?"

Frithfroth twisted his lips and then he said, "I learnt, long ago, that the largest problems of this world cannot be solved by a sword. The poetry—well, that is just how I mark the time."

"I still think you should do something useful," Esme said. She sat cross-legged in front of Frithfroth. "Do some more poems. Maybe you know one I'll like."

"Yeah, do another," a boy behind her said.

All of the children in front of him seated themselves and Frithfroth anxiously racked his mind for more poetry.

The scowl returned to Frithfroth's face and he withdrew back into himself. Esme may have kept talking to him, but he didn't know, and eventually she wandered off, the rest of the children ignored him, and he was left on his own again.

III

Alex descended the stairs two at a time. Raised voices were speaking hurriedly, although not in alarm. "We're back, we're safe, for now," said a voice that he recognised very well. "I'm sorry you all had to see that down there. You were all very brave, and I'm very proud of each—each one of you. All of you."

Alex hurried down the rest of the stairs and scanned the crowd assembled in the Langtorr greeting hall for his aunt. She was easy to spot, being over a foot taller than the children around her, and she had also picked up a few adults he didn't recognise. He was so glad to see her that he cried out and rushed to embrace her.

She caught sight of him and backed away. Her tone had been calm, but now that he came closer Alex could see something was wrong. She held up her arms and Alex saw red on her palms and fingertips.

Alex felt the ground open up before him. He wasn't plunging yet, but he was on a knife's edge. "What happened?"

"I only touched him. We didn't all—we lost, I lost some, of them. I . . ." Vivienne's throat lurched and she couldn't squeeze any more words out. Alex reached forward and hugged her as she sobbed quietly into his shirt. When he felt she had started to calm down, he held her out at arm's length and studied her face. "What happened?" he asked.

In halting, incomplete sentences, she told him about the attack. When he had enough of a picture, he cut her off. "It's not your fault, Aunt Viv. It would have happened to any of us if we were out there. I'm glad you made it back," he said.

"So am I," Vivienne replied.

"I have to ask . . . Is there a clear path through to the Beacon? Because if we could get out—?"

"No. No, it's not there anymore. It's gone—we had to collapse it—destroy it. They came after us. We need to get out. We need to get everyone out of here."

"I know, I know. I'm working on that. We're all working on that. Where's Freya?"

"I don't know. We didn't find her on the way back."

"Do you think she's okay?"

"I don't know. Maybe. I hope so."

"We should try talking to my brother—your uncle Alexander—to Gád. It occurred to me, we don't really know exactly what he wants. We may not be able to avoid war altogether, but there may be some wiggle room. Perhaps we can negotiate something, for the safety of the children—take them out of harm's way."

"Hey, no fair! I want to fight!"

Startled, Alex and Vivienne turned to where Benjamin was standing, glaring up at them. "I don't want to go back until I settle this thing," he said, his fists clenched and face flushing. "The thing that called me gave me a choice: to fight or to stay at home. I chose to come and fight—all of us did. You can't send us back—we came to fight!" He punched a fist into his hand at that last word.

Vivienne rounded on the small boy. "You're under a misapprehension, young man," she said. "If you go out to fight you will quite simply die, and that is the long and the short of that. Whatever notions your action movies and morning cartoons have planted in your head contrary to that fact are very apparently false. In any case, this is not a democracy, the issue is not open for debate, and you have no say in the matter. We are going to do all we can to keep you safe and get you home; that is all you need to know."

"But we're here for a *reason*," Benjamin shot back, a whine in his voice.

"No, you are not!" Vivienne snapped, nearly frenzied. "You are *not* here for a reason! There *is* no plan! There *is* no *great design*! Not everything is solved, and not everyone gets a happy ending with lessons learned. Very few, in fact, very few get a happy ending. You children know nothing of the world, you know nothing of war, of hunger and starvation, of children younger than you dying through privation—through exploitation! Younger than you have died in less dire circumstances than this. Not everything turns out well in the end. You'll learn that as you get older—*if* you get older— which I am going to try my very hardest to see that you do."

Vivienne felt Alex's hand on her arm and she turned away.

"We're all very stressed," he said, trying to keep his voice calm and loud at the same time. "And we're all very tired. Which makes it doubly important for everyone to listen to us very carefully and to do what we tell them. No one here knows the situation better than myself, Aunt Viv, and Ecgbryt, who is standing guard out there on the walls. Those forces out there will be beaten—"

"We don't know that. We don't know that in the slightest."

Alex shot Vivienne a glare. She wasn't very loud so he didn't think many heard her. "Those forces out there *will be beaten*, but they won't be beaten by us. This is not our battle yet—I hope. As a police officer, there's nothing I like better to hear than that hundreds and hundreds of children all want to take a stand against evil and lawlessness." Alex smiled and looked around at all of the faces looking up at him. Someone was crying and he realised it was one of the adults; one of the women who had come back with Vivienne.

"But for now, the thing I need you all to do is, in a calm and very orderly fashion, to go to your rooms or wherever you have your things, and gather them up along with any blankets and warm gear you have, and food. Get ready to leave at any moment. We may not have a plan to get out of here right now, but I am absolutely certain that many good people are working on getting us out of here. God willing, that will be soon. Does everybody hear me?"

There was mostly silence but also some nods and muffled responses.

"I'll take that as a yes. Get moving."

Everyone started to move up the stairs.

"Alex, I'm—"

"It's okay, I think they needed to hear that. No harm, no foul."

"What are we going to do? We're . . . we're trapped in this stone tube!"

"Stay calm. I'm going to go outside right now and check on how the war is getting on. Maybe I can buy us some time at the very least."

"Where is Freya? I'm so worried for her."

"Yes, and Daniel as well. Isn't he supposed to be around here somewhere?"

CHAPTER NINE

Ealdstan's Hopes

---- I ----

It was a strange sense of peace he had—very strange. Not normally an analytical person, Daniel tried to dissect the feeling on his long walk back to the surface. It was not the sense of peace he'd had before, the kind that brought self-confidence with it. There was a great deal of doubt in the peace he now experienced. That was interesting. He tried to define the terms of his doubt. He doubted things were going to turn out well—that everything would be all right in the end. He doubted anything he could do could make a difference, at least a difference for good. He doubted anything he had done up until now had been even remotely helpful— actually, no . . . he was *certain* that *nothing* he had done up until now had been helpful. And it was in that certainty that a good deal of his peace was founded. That and the fact that although he didn't know exactly where he was going, or what was going to happen to him there, he knew what his reaction must be. Since talking to the dragon he had experienced a complete reevaluation of his thoughts and beliefs. He felt as though his thoughts were so many sheets of paper that were being re-sorted and reordered in his brain. He was now questioning every action he'd taken since he was young. It was as if he had been swimming against the current of a massive river his entire life up to now—desperately clawing his way forward, trying as hard as he could to make any headway at all, fighting with everything that was in him to gain just the merest inches . . . and then he finally gave up. He stopped swimming and laid back and let the relentless pull of the water carry him.

It was an apt analogy since his body did actually feel like it was floating, and his concentration wasn't on the task before him, but on the sky above him—bright, nebulous, and changing; something only partly seen and understood. All his life he had been fighting, and now he was going to give up the struggle. There was a kind of joy in that, if there was nothing to actually be joyful about in his immediate situation. And above all the uncertainty of what exactly was in his future, he had an inkling of what was to come. It wasn't really prescience, only a sort of . . . perspective; the water was going to carry him where it would.

He was approaching the enemy camp. He could see the glow from its greasy fires up ahead, but he couldn't hear a sound from it, not even a whisper of activity. It appeared they had all moved out completely. As he approached, he saw half-struck tents hanging limply on their tilting frames, gates to the stone animal pens and enclosures gaping open, and detritus of all kinds littering the ground.

To his right he saw the large standing stones that the child prisoners had been chained to, and then his eyes saw crumpled lumps lying beneath them. Appalled, he ran over, desperately hoping that he was mistaken . . . but no. He halted a few meters from the first body, letting his watering eyes flick angrily from child to child, spotting each savage wound that had brought death. Before the army had moved on the prisoners had been slaughtered, probably a very short time after he had left them here.

He passed the useless wooden pier of the *Slæpismere* and went up the tunnel that led to the stone doors of the squat tower that had guarded the Great Carnyx, and so up into Niðergeard. His legs ached and wobbled—how many miles had he walked?—but he was driven on by his own determination this time, and desperation gave him strength.

Suddenly, he became disoriented. There was daylight and fresh air ahead of him. He actually became dizzy and began to sway as he climbed the steep tunnel. Was he on the surface already? Had he been magically transported somehow? Sunlight hit his eyes and he was blinded. Shielding his eyes with his arm, he looked around. The tower of the Carnyx had been completely levelled. He saw freshly broken stones around him and the two large doors to the *Slæpismere* lying to either side of the mouth of the tunnel. Many feet had trampled through here. The light that was shining into his face were the rays from a setting sun, orange now as they shone at him from the lip of what looked to him a distant mountain, but which he suddenly realised was the edge of a kind of crater that he was in the middle of. *So,* he thought, *that noise earlier—it* had *been a collapse.* Niðergeard, it looked, had been spared destruction, but it was now exposed to the world.

Palming away the tears from his eyes, he took a few uncertain steps forward and was aware of a hush in the voices and noises around him. He blinked and tried to make out the forms that completely encircled him. There were yfelgópes, trolls, bears, giants, and things he didn't even know the name of. A short burst of laughter escaped him as he saw a few ranks of militant gnomes marching in and among the feet of those assembled around him.

Everyone and everything was looking at him, a half-naked man suddenly appearing in their midst. Daniel gave a nervous grin and took a deep breath.

"Hi, everybody. I completely and totally surrender." He held up his hands and stood as still as he could.

"I know this one," an yfelgóp said, muscling its way through the crowd. "Take him to Kelm."

Daniel smiled and nodded, allowing himself to be manhandled away, not resisting in the slightest. He was pushed in a direction south of the city, and as he was, he watched his silhouette on the walls of the city, set against a red sun that set completely in the few moments while he marvelled at its light, placing Niðergeard in twilight. The colour of the sky brought back the words of the knight Swiðgar, words that almost always returned to him at this time of day.

When the time, place, and person are all in efenheort—*which is a sort of unstable harmony—then fantastic things can happen.*

II

"The decision isn't up to you—we're not going to do it."

"I agree," said Beth.

"Well, what are our other options?" Sophie challenged.

Freya looked down at the four girls standing with her. They were all starting to become more vocal. "It's hard to explain. The last time I was here—the first time . . . I got the feeling there was another course to take than the ones being laid out for us. And it turns out I was right. We thought there were only a limited number of options, but in reality . . . well, there may have been more. If we hadn't gone on that quest, we wouldn't have advanced

Ealdstan's plan. If we'd just waited, investigated where we were a little more, asked some more questions, thought a bit harder . . ."

"Then what?"

"I don't know. But we might not be in this situation now."

"Where would we be?" said Rebecca. "Seems to me there's a problem here that's needed solving for the last hundred years or so. If you weren't there, it might have been put off, maybe until it was too late."

"Yes, maybe. But anything we did only made things worse."

"Never mind about that," Sophie said. "Right now we have to make a decision—are we going to do what the women said and open some more doorways so we can get an army together and fight these evil things off for good?"

"The ladies didn't say that!" Freya's hands went to her hips and she took a step forward, towering over the young girl. "This is what I was saying about options—we have more than we think we do. It was the ladies who told me that when I first met them. I think that's what they were trying to tell me, at least."

"Well, they're right here, you can ask them again," said Rebecca, picking at her large woolly jumper.

"But you'd better decide what to do pretty quickly," said Beth. "I don't think we have much time here."

"No, see—that's what I'm saying." Freya bit her lip. "That's *exactly* what we thought last time."

"I mean, if we don't do something, someone else might. If we want to stop them from doing something they shouldn't."

"What are you saying?"

"I think we should get back to the boys," Beth said. "Before they figure out how to summon more warriors."

Freya nodded and swallowed. She turned to one of the women. "Are you going to come with us?"

The woman lowered her face. "We will not. We shall stay

here—if you are to stay with us within our circle then you will be protected by us, but if you leave—even just a footstep outside of the ring—then you will be open to any peril."

"I see." Freya turned to Sophie and the other girls. "I think you four should stay here."

"I think we should go with you," Rebecca said, her eyes shifting to where Ealdstan sat seated with his otherworldly guards.

"It's too dangerous. You could get killed."

"There are worse things than dying," Beth said.

"True, but none of them will happen if you stay here."

"Fine. Get a move on, then. Go if you're going."

Freya nodded and turned. She also looked up to Ealdstan who was sitting attentively, listening to everything that was passing between them with quiet interest. For a moment she felt the Fear wash over her, but she immediately reminded herself that she had passed beyond fear. Beth was absolutely right—there were worse things than death, and at the moment she wasn't even facing that. Or she didn't think she was.

"How about you?" Freya asked Ealdstan. "Are you going to let me pass? Are you going to allow me to go talk to my friends, or are you going to keep me here? Kill me?"

Ealdstan continued to look intently at her, but did not move a muscle.

"No, of course. Why would I have thought that you would be even the slightest bit helpful?" she muttered to herself as she looked down at her feet. Exhaling deeply, she took a step forward that carried her out of the circle of women. Then she looked back up at Ealdstan. He was unmoved.

She took a few more cautious steps forward, heading around the stone pile of the hero's throne, toward the Langtorr. She wondered how close she would have to walk by the elves. She decided to give them a fairly wide berth, but just another couple steps would make it so that she couldn't reach the women again if they came after her. At the moment they were just watching her, just as Ealdstan was.

She took those extra couple steps and then Ealdstan spoke: "Take her," he said quietly, with a flick of his finger.

The elves were on her before she could even lift her feet to run.

III

He slowly moved a hand down his tie, as if smoothing it, and then shifted his fingers to his jacket where it crossed itself and gave it a tug. The action was a seemingly self-conscious one, but it was very practised. His manner was relaxed and in control as he looked levelly into the mid-distance past the camera lenses angled at him, as though addressing a great multitude. Of course, he was looking at nothing, but the impression his posture would give to the millions watching him would be that of a world leader addressing his nation or of a general addressing his military. They would need to get used to seeing him as such.

"As far as we know, the danger has passed. For now, we are advising people to stay in their homes or places of work. This has been a one-of-a-kind, freak geological occurrence. Yes, go ahead."

On over a billion screens all over the world people watched as Gád cocked his head to listen to an inaudible question. "No," was his response. "It was decided that it was not necessary to involve the military. With the cooperation of the British people, with their common sense to guide them"—he allowed a small grin to pull at his lips—"in staying away from this site, I see no need to bring in the military. Some of you will have seen me conversing with representatives of the armed forces earlier—that is the decision we all arrived at. Yes, another."

Again he tilted his head, keeping his face fully visible to each camera around him. He nodded as a journalist reeled off another obvious question.

"Rescue attempts are under way for those who have been directly affected by this event." He looked down to his podium and shifted a piece of paper and then looked up and swept his eyes over everyone before him in a commanding movement. "And I've been told to ask everyone to please respect the urgency of these operations and maintain as much distance as possible, for safety's sake. One more only, please. Yes."

He pointed again, this time to someone closer whose voice came as a low scratching on the microphones nearest Gád.

"No, at the moment we can see no connection between this event and that of the missing children, which of course is taking joint priority in our actions and resources at this time. Allow me to be absolutely clear on this issue: this tragedy, as disastrous as it is, will not deter in the slightest our actions in getting our children back. Our energy and attention to that problem is as resolved as ever, and we go forward confident that the resolution of the government and its people is behind us one hundred percent. Thank you all."

Gád swept his hand across the podium to collect his papers, which naturally had nothing to do with what he was saying, and strode with easy, measured steps to a cordoned-off area, out of view of the cameras, lost in a crowd of junior assistants and hastily erected tents.

The sun was setting; in under two hours it would be night. He looked at his watch and turned to a policeman standing outside a very small tent. "Has he shown up yet?"

"Yes, sir—he's inside."

Grunting, Gád pushed his way through, letting the flap close behind him. Inside, sitting patiently on a cheap plastic chair and holding a paper cup of cold tea, was a person who looked exactly like him. This was Gád's fetch, a mystical aspect of his personality, made physical by his power. It smiled as it looked up, apparently happy to see him.

"What report do you have?" Gád asked it.

"When I left Kelm, he was busy arranging the troops for the invasion of Niðergeard. Shock forces had been sent to destroy any survivors of the collapse and hidden warriors are right now circulating the site, killing all who may be spying or observing what is occurring both in those sites and in the realm beneath us.

"And the holdouts are still confined to the tower. Kelm is staying his hand, for now. The prisoners have been put to the sword. All await your arrival."

Gád nodded. As usual the fetch had anticipated him completely.

"You will stay here," Gád ordered. "You will only do that which is necessary in order to delay action and assuage suspicion. I will send for you at some point when this is over—when Niðergeard is a pile of rubble and her defenders lie dead. When the knights and the children live no longer and all my legions are ready to invade this island."

"Understood," the fetch replied placidly. "May I ask when that might be?"

Gád did not need to tell it anything in order to ensure its cooperation, but he relished the thought of how close his plans were to completion.

"When the sun next rises again, everything it shines upon shall be mine." He pushed his way back out of the tent.

"Come with me," he said to the police officer on guard, walking along the plastic tape barrier that had been rolled out along the whole circumference of the collapsed area, still about a mile from the immediate site itself.

There was a small brook that had cut a gentle slope into the landscape. Ducking under the tape, they proceeded inward. Walking along the brook, Gád and the policeman were able to approach the collapse out of the line of sight of the journalists and cameramen.

"Sir, are we going much farther? Do you want me to radio in for—?"

Gád spun instantly. His arm shot out faster than a rattlesnake, catching the policeman's neck in curled fingers. The policeman's eyes bulged and he threw a blow at Gád's head, catching him hard with an elbow. The hit would have been effective against most men, but it had no effect on Gád. Starting to panic, the policeman's hands went to his weapon, a semiautomatic that hung on a strap across his chest. His fingers, starting to become clumsy, fumbled at the trigger and safety mechanism. Gád maintained his hold, steadily crushing the life's breath from the stocky man. Finally getting his hands around his weapon, the policeman managed to swing it forward and shoot three rounds into Gád's chest. Gád could feel the impact and then also the hot bullets falling down his shirt, as effective as peas from a peashooter. Baring his teeth and sucking in a hissing breath, Gád looked around to see if there was anyone who might have heard the noise, but no one was in sight.

Life is a fascinating property, Gád reflected. Up to a point it seemed practically invincible, unable to be denied or contained. But then, at a single point, a small and thin moment, it appeared so fragile—weaker than a guttering candle flame. And it passed from one state to the next with the least perceptible movement, transisting almost undetectably.

The policeman's face, a deep and unnatural purple at this moment, started to relax as his thick tongue protruded from between his lips and his eyes rolled back in his head. Gád unclenched his hand and let the policeman's body fall to the ground. He turned away and continued striding down the ravine.

Less than fifteen minutes later the brook began splashing down the newly uncovered earth that led down into the darkness of the underground world of Niðergeard, making the ground marshy and dank.

Emerging from under the overhang that cast a very dark shadow were a line of yfelgópes and otherworldly invaders.

"Bring me to Kelm!" Gád shouted. "I wish to see the army he has arranged. I wish to give final instructions."

The yfelgópes straightened, having enough wits to recognise who was ordering them.

"Which one are you . . . ?" one of them asked. "Our master . . . or his shadow?"

Gád leapt, hands going again to a throat, but this time death was fast and frenzied.

His hands wet and dripping with warm blood, Gád turned to the others. "Well? What are we waiting for?"

One of the yfelgópes swallowed self-consciously, its head twitching. "Do . . . do you want to see the prisoner first, or after?"

"Prisoner?"

IV

"Hello. This is a nice how d'you do."

Gád tilted his head and observed the prisoner a little more closely. The prisoner was stripped to the waist, an odd collection of materials covering his legs, much like the yfelgópes guarding him. Bruises and large welts ran up and down one side of his body—some of them were fading to yellow and brown.

The prisoner smiled at the same time that Gád did. "You're Daniel, aren't you? You're one of Ealdstan's hopes. His two last, dim hopes."

The prisoner nodded. "And you've got to be Gád. It's nice to finally meet the man I killed when I was thirteen." He nodded to the back of the room where Kelm sat, his massive body folded over itself onto a squat metal chair.

When Kelm spoke, his voice was like shifting gravel. "Do not trust much to truth with this one, your highness. He lies incessantly—he has never spoken correctly to me."

"That, of course, is true," Daniel said, his eyes twinkling.

"When first we talked, he tried to convince me that he wished to join our army. I locked him away immediately. He escaped, ostensibly with the help of some traitor yfelgópes who he—"

"Oh, so they *were* actual traitors? That settles that point."

"They were some twenty-odd traitors he proceeded to kill. He returned to me with their heads as a sort of votive offering or . . . admission fee."

"Is this true?" Gád asked Daniel.

"Yes, it is," he said sadly. "I really wish I hadn't done that now. I was—pretty confused at the time. I'll probably never stop regretting what I did. To you included."

Gád came closer to Daniel. "To me? You gave me more power than I thought I would ever have in my life. That was Ealdstan's plan for me—to raise up a man to be as powerful as he was. I am the new Ealdstan, and you are the instrument by which he created me. The power I now control was delivered to me by you."

"Yes. Like I said: I'm sorry about that."

Gád drew himself up. "So, hope. If I were to let you go, to return you to your people, what would you do to try to stop me—to justify Ealdstan's trust and faith in you?"

"I would ask you to stop what you're doing—what you're planning to do. Nicely."

"And if I didn't? What would the consequence be?"

"No consequences. At least, not from me. All I'm doing is asking—nicely."

"Are you certain that I do not detect a threat behind those words? You have shown yourself to be supremely violent. From what I understand, every obstacle you have been presented with you have met with a show of force. This has suited me fairly well in the past—or at least, it has done me no harm. I am interested in the course you are set on, and I am curious as to whether or not it would be best to just let you carry on with it, unimpeded."

Daniel nearly replied, his mouth was open to do so, but he shut it. He would not now try to escape what would happen to him, but he thought it might be better to be let go. He would definitely prefer it, in any case.

"Take him away," Gád said.

The yfelgópes on either side of Daniel pulled him to his feet. Then they looked to Kelm.

"There is a well in the western end of the city with a wrought-iron frame. Chain him to that for the time being and set a watch."

Without protest or struggle, Daniel was taken away. Gád and Kelm waited until he was out of sight before conferring again.

"Do you really think he may serve any purpose?" Kelm asked. "Even at this late stage?"

"I do. I do," Gád said, turning to face the fat and odious general. Gád went to the doorway of the half-ruined building. "But you are correct. For now he is far too late to stop our winning play. So at any point that is convenient, you may allow him to escape. Now come along—rouse yourself. We must go now and meet Ealdstan."

V

Freya felt as though she were being bent like a paper clip, forced down on one knee, face close to the ground, her arm pulled up behind her, held up to the ceiling by one of Ealdstan's bodyguards.

She could see the girls, shocked and worried, but not daring to venture beyond the circle of impassive Norns.

"Allow her to stand," Ealdstan said from above.

The grip on her arm and the hand on her back eased off and Freya crumpled slightly to the ground. It was a few moments before she was able to haul herself up, and this time she found herself surrounded by a circle of hostile warriors.

"Are you going to kill me?" Freya asked.

Ealdstan took an excruciatingly long time to respond, stroking his long beard before eventually saying, "I honestly don't know."

One of the elves turned his head and said something that Freya couldn't understand.

"What did he say?" she asked.

"Someone approaches."

Freya turned to look to where the elves had turned their attention. She saw yfelgópes approaching in a clump—they always gave her a shiver of revulsion, their low, gangling walk and their pedantic way of speaking.

But there was another figure that looked strange among the strangeness of the scene. He was a slender figure with very good posture and an exquisitely tailored suit.

It had been over eight years ago, but Freya knew who he was even before his face became visible. Dread balled up inside of her as Gád's leering face emerged from the darkness. She hadn't wanted to see that face again, and all the emotions of her first meeting with him, the horror of seeing him kill Swiðgar, the helplessness of him controlling her movements, the fear of seeing him gain his power—it took her breath away. She tried to shut the door on those emotions, started counting to ten, and reminded herself to breathe.

"*Wes ðu hale*, Ealdstan!" he called out happily, throwing his arms wide.

"Hale and well met," Ealdstan called, rising. He held his staff before him, leaning his weight on it.

Freya cowered down within the circle of elves as Gád came to stand before the throne. She couldn't turn herself invisible though, and Gád spotted her. "I say, is that young Freya Reynolds?"

Freya forced her quivering legs to stand.

"You've grown into quite an attractive woman, do you know that?"

Freya couldn't speak, she only scowled as best as she could.

Gád looked back up at Ealdstan. "May I have her? I took the boy also, they should be together now, at the end."

"Daniel?" Freya blurted under her breath. She didn't expect anyone to have heard her, but Gád answered her.

"Yes, Daniel. He wandered straight into my army, apparently. Like he wanted to get caught."

Freya swallowed. So it seems he made it back from wherever he needed to be.

"Where is he?" Ealdstan asked.

"I've chained him up near here and left him to be rescued or to escape." Gád laughed and looked to Ealdstan for a reaction. Not getting one, he played to Freya instead. "Yes, in all honesty I wish him to be free. Why wouldn't I? There are those who work against us—and I would very much prefer that they be led by a brash boy who has always proven himself to rush into events without thinking his actions through. Daniel will collect and galvanise all those who oppose me and lead them in futile and ineffective attacks against us. He has already been a conduit for my own power, and even helped Kelm weed out a pocket of traitors within his own forces. If I could have released him outright without making him suspicious, I would have!"

"Enough posturing," Ealdstan said in a low, powerful voice that filled the courtyard.

"Quite," Gád said, becoming serious, turning to look back up to the hero's throne. "Give me the girl."

"What would you do with her?"

Gád shrugged. "Kill her."

Ealdstan nodded. "I certainly would not stop you. But would you consider not doing so?"

"For what reason?"

"The same reason that you released the boy."

"Oh no." Gád chuckled. "No, the girl is too close to things."

"The girl is useless and ineffective. The *boy* is dangerous."

"Oh me. Have we finally arrived at a difference of opinion after all this time?"

"The boy is a wild, rabid animal, blindly attacking everything in his path, leaving destruction behind him. The girl, what has she done? Blown an enchanted horn that any ordinary person could put their lip to."

"Nonetheless, the boy is blind. The girl is too near events." Gád turned to look at the Norns briefly, who had not moved an inch.

VI

Daniel breathed out, a deep, long breath that came from his gut. The yfelgópes had chained him to the western well, and he had to smile at that. He didn't know why, but he felt that the action was appropriate somehow—fitting. This was the place that he first entered Niðergeard through. He remembered, all those years ago, how young he was, how scared, how wide-eyed and eager. He thought that he felt that way again, for the first time in a long time—the feeling that everything around him was new, that he was travelling in a glow.

They had left him now, the yfelgópes. Tied him up and then marched away. He had expected guards or something. He felt . . .

lonely. He'd had enough time on his own on the way back from talking to the dragon; he wanted to do something. He felt that he fit into some purpose somehow, but he didn't know what. He hoped that it wasn't too late to make a difference. To do . . . something, whatever it was. If only he knew what . . .

He had been testing and straining at his bonds as he stood there thinking, but he had made no progress except that his hands were sore now. If he were held in chains then he might be able to squeeze his way through them, but this was rope of some sort, and very well tied. The more he contorted his arms, hands, and wrists, the tighter the bonds seemed to get. Instead he forced himself to close his eyes and breathe out again.

As he opened his eyes again, he saw a familiar shape illumined in the half-light of the city. He blinked a couple times and tried to remember where he'd seen it before. It looked to be the outline of a figure that he knew very well, but he couldn't seem to identify it exactly. It was turned toward him, but its face was obscured. Its bulky outline was like one of the knights, although the bright reflective shine that parts of it gave off reminded him of the Silver Rider—but Daniel knew that wasn't who it was. He drew in a breath to try to call to it and then didn't know what to say. The figure raised a hand to him.

"Hisst!"

Daniel turned instinctively, but then whipped his head back to look at the beckoning figure, just in time to see it and the one behind it turn and walk behind a building.

"Hisst!" the call came again, and Daniel looked over his shoulder. Crouching in one of the archways that lined the courtyard was a group of children.

"Uh, hi," Daniel said.

"Stay there," said one of them, the boy who was crouching nearest him. "We'll get you out of there."

"Thanks," Daniel said and watched him scamper warily forward, his head turning quickly from side to side. He came next to Daniel and then stood up, holding a sword in front of him. "Whoa!"

"Sorry. Wait." He angled the sword down and started sawing at the thick ropes that held him.

"Careful," Daniel said as the blade bit through the thick rope.

"We don't have much time," the little boy said, still sawing furiously downward.

"I know, but care—*careful*!"

Daniel pulled his wrists apart and the last few threads were torn; he was free again.

"Quick, this way," the small boy said and scurried back to the shadows. Daniel followed after him, less frantically, rubbing his wrists and arms.

There were eight children trying to make the most of the sparse cover that the columns gave. They were all carrying something sharp—some had spears, two of the boys carried axes, and all of them had swords. A few were even trying to juggle shields and others had helmets. "Are you kids from the tower?" he asked. "What are you doing here?"

"We can't get back in," the tallest girl said. "We went out to get some weapons, to arm ourselves, and now the whole place is surrounded by orcs and trolls and giants and whatever else. We're not sure what to do now. We can't find a way in, we can't find a way out—"

"We're trapped," the boy who rescued Daniel said. "We were looking around for something we could do and came across you. We were going to attack them and free you, but we started arguing. Who are you?"

"My name's Daniel. I came here with Freya when I was about your age." That brought Daniel up short. Was he really as young as these kids looked? He couldn't have been. "I tried to kill Gád, but it all turned out to be a trick. I—" He couldn't think of what to say or how to explain anything else.

"This is Jason, that's Sarah, Edward," the young boy said, introducing them all. "James, Gretchen, David, Ben, and I'm Fergus. I'm looking for my brother, have you seen him? Are there more prisoners like you?"

Daniel couldn't remember having seen any and said so.

"Well, we'll find him. But I think first we need to try and break everyone out of the Langtorr. They're trapped there, we need to break the siege somehow. I don't think we can fight our way through by ourselves, but maybe we could create a distraction. Or maybe if we could get some rope, we could tie it—"

"No, we're not going to win by doing any of that," Daniel said.

"So you have a plan? Or something that will help us out? Are there more secret tunnels?"

"Perhaps, I don't know, but we're not going to solve any more of these problems by violence. In fact—I want you all to leave your weapons here."

"What?" Fergus exclaimed, louder than he intended.

"Just put them on the ground. Lay them down."

A couple of the girls started to lower them. One of the boys holding a very heavy shield gratefully, and rather noisily, let it drop to the ground.

"Why? What do you have instead?" Fergus asked.

"Nothing."

"Do *you* want a sword? We have lots of extras. There was this pile—"

"No, I don't want anything else. None of us can have any weapons. No good will come of them. Trust me on this."

"Do you think we can't use them?" Gretchen asked. "We've already killed an yfelgóp, all by ourselves. I think you can trust us with them."

"It's not about that. Just—all of you put your weapons down now!" Daniel's voice raised. Even though he was only frustrated, he realised he sounded angry. The children started to lay their weapons on the ground, some more slowly than others. All except for Fergus.

"Fergus, I'm begging you—please put it down."

"Tell me first what your plan is."

"I don't have any plan, put the sword on the ground. You can't do any good with it. Trust me, I know, I've tried."

"But what's going to keep us safe if we run into trouble?"

Daniel opened his mouth but didn't know what to say. "Maybe nothing. But you'll be safer without it than with it. If you have it then the bad guys will come after you. And instead of capturing you, they'll kill you. That's how it works."

With a scowling face and slow movements, Fergus laid his sword against the column nearest him. "All right, now what do we do?"

"I think the idea you had was pretty good—let's go try to join everyone in the Langtorr."

Half of the kids reached for the weapons again.

"If you want them, I won't stop you—but I won't be with you. You'll be on your own." They stopped, turning apprehensive faces to him. "I know I'm asking a lot. It takes a lot more courage to face danger without anything to help you—a *lot* more courage. But we can do it. I'm not promising everything will be fine, but I am promising that everything will be *better* this way."

They straightened up.

"Thank you. Now, let's try to find out what's happening. Can we get up onto the roof of this place?" He looked up at the building that stood on the courtyard.

"Yes, we were up there when we saw you," Gretchen said. "You can see to the Langtorr from there. It's kind of scary."

"All right. Let's see what we can see, then."

They went into the building, the children leading and Daniel following.

One of the girls, Sarah, hung back and walked along with Daniel as they walked up the stairs. "You should have said that you have a plan," she said. "Even if you didn't really have a plan, you should have said you did. It makes it easier for people to trust you."

"Thanks, I'll keep that in mind."

They got to the top, hunching instinctively, and made their way to the parapet on the roof's edge. Daniel drew a sharp breath. The streets below them were awash with yfelgópes and enormous lumbering beasts.

"Oh, wow," Fergus said softly. "There're even more of them. There're *thousands* now!"

Daniel's heart sank. There were so many of them, all ready for a fight. He swallowed and tried to collect his resolve.

A twinkling gleam below him caught his eye. He saw the two silver figures again, moving away from him, into the crowd. He blinked and started nodding his head. If he ever wanted a sign, this was certainly one he was being given.

"Who *is* that?" he said, his voice barely more than a breathless squeak. "I have to go down there. I think you should all stay here, out of sight, until everything is over. I'll come and find you, if I still can."

"I think we should stay with you," Gretchen said.

"No. I'm going to go down there, by myself, unarmed." He looked at Sarah. "Without a plan."

"I'm coming too," Fergus declared. "You might need help."

"If anyone comes with me, it's very likely you'll be killed."

"I'm not scared," Fergus said defiantly.

"If you aren't then I don't know why, because I sure am,"

Daniel said, hearing his voice break. "I mean it. I fully expect to die down there. I can't protect you at all. The best you can do is all to stay together and stay hidden."

"I'm coming," Fergus insisted. "You can't stop me."

"No, I can't, but I'm begging you to stay." And, not wanting to prolong the argument, he turned and started for the stairs again.

Fergus followed him, but the others remained where they were. He followed close behind Daniel as he descended the stairs, like a puppy after its new owner. Only when they got to the bottom did Daniel turn to look at him. Fergus's face was steely with resolve. *I must have looked like that when I was his age,* Daniel thought. *Perhaps it isn't too late for him.*

"Well?" said Fergus. "Let's get going."

CHAPTER TEN

The Axe Falls

I

Alex went to the wall, racing to keep up with Ecgbryt.

"What plan have you, partner?" the knight asked.

"Och, am I needing a plan, now?"

"Somebody is in need of one."

Alex paused, stopping at the steps that scaled the wall. He felt Ecgbryt's hand on his arm. "We are ready to fight," he said earnestly. "Each one of us is willing to die for our land—it is the reason we have endured the centuries in laborious sleep. This is the reason we waked. Alex, it is our purpose."

"The time for fighting may come very shortly," Alex said.

"It cannot come soon enough," Ecgbryt said. "Heed me, if there is any opportunity to let loose our swords upon the enemy, do not hesitate to give the order—we are all of us ready."

"All right, now you listen to me," Alex said, turning and placing a hand on Ecgbryt's chest to stop him. "Don't lose focus. Our duty now is to protect the children. If we do anything to endanger them now, then you might as well hop the wall and fight alongside the enemy, because you'll be doing their work for them."

Ecgbryt pouted and Alex realised how harsh his words must have sounded. He added, "But it would be a good idea to stand at the ready anyway. If we need to attack, be ready at the gate. Take men from the wall, but do it quietly."

Ecgbryt nodded and headed back toward the steps at the back of the Langtorr as Alex started up the ones in front of him. He just needed more time. He felt if he had more time he could figure something out, but he didn't know where he was going to get it.

Cresting the steps he went to a parapet. His breath suddenly left him when he saw the army arrayed before him.

There were enemies as far as the eye could see. The yfelgóp spears were like a forest of naked trees, all perfectly ordered into neat rows between the ruined buildings of Niðergeard. There were flanks of trolls as well, and a company of strange beasts that were being wrangled by the yfelgópes. He saw armoured bears and giant serpents whose movements were controlled by thick staffs attached to their necks.

The troops had been pulled back from an area in front of the wall.

"What are they waiting for?" Alex asked Ecgbryt.

The knight raised an arm and pointed to a thin figure moving through the warhost. All that Alex could see was a white tuft of hair. All near it passed to let the figure through and it came to stop in front of the gate, and now everyone could see that it was Gád. To his left was Freya, unbound but flanked by two guards. To his right was a man with rhinoceros-thick limbs and chest, Kelm.

"Hello, Uncle," he called down, placing his forearms on the tower's defending wall.

"I say. Is that my nephew Alex?"

"When did we last see each other?"

"Let us see, you would have had to have been . . ." Gád stuck his hand out at his side. "Oh . . . about to here?"

Alex nodded. "Been awhile, then."

"I dare say. You're the spitting image of your father."

"Your sister's back here," Alex said, straightening and waving a hand behind him. "Did you want to speak to her? She's a tad busy trying to find ways to prevent you from killing us all. But if you want, I can . . . ?"

His uncle, Gád, beamed a bright smile on him. "Not necessary. I don't suppose my sister and I have much left to discuss after our last meeting."

"And me? Anything you have left to discuss with me? You've missed a few birthdays, you know." Alex's eyes flicked to Freya, standing miserable and afraid, but fighting against herself not to show it.

Gád sensed the movement. His smile slid to one side of his face. "Well, enough with the catching up. Let's get to business."

"Yes, what can I help you with, Uncle Alexander?"

"I think you know," Gád returned coyly.

Alex frowned, making a show of it. At the very least he could play for time and give Vivienne more of a chance to get everyone up the tower.

"I'm afraid I don't. Have we really got anything that you need? There aren't any magical weapons here. We've used the horn— you see where that got us. We shan't be using that again. The knights that Ecgbryt and I managed to round up, well . . . you can see for yourself. I suppose I needn't have bothered, really. They're fine warriors, every single one of them—well worth a hundred of your yfelgópes, but even at that we're outnumbered. We're outmatched, outmaneuvered, and on the back foot on top of all that. I could offer you our surrender?" Alex twisted the last statement into a question. "If you could guarantee that the children would be safe?"

"Yes, the children. Let us discuss them—I find their appearance most interesting. One of the aspects of my plan that I was, shall we say, concerned about was the Great Carnyx and the powers that it summoned."

"The powers? Do you mean me and the knights?"

"I mean the children—the next army. That surprised us all; even Ealdstan. He was unclear even at the start as to what would be the effect of his spell—the enchantment he worked on it was untested and tapped into a more fundamental, deeper magic. The best way I can explain it is to imagine if you set up a row of dominoes on a table—that is Ealdstan playing tin soldiers with this nation's history. Now imagine that the horn blowing is not a toppling of the lead domino, but a violent kick at one of the legs of the table. That is what happened when this girl blew that horn—the spiritual foundations of this island were rocked and a host of defenders poured forth to protect it in complete disorder and all at once. From where I stand, she's practically a war criminal, putting all those children in harm's way like that."

"Into *your* way, you mean," Alex said. He was feeling a good deal more assured right now. Gád was obviously willing to talk and talk. That was absolutely fine with him. But he was starting to be disturbed by a noise he could hear in the distance: a sharp, cold sound like a pickaxe working on stone. It seemed there were two different pitches to the sound, as though something were operating in syncopation. "There's no one threatening them but you and your army."

"But I am a *liberator*, my dear nephew. A freedom fighter. And this idea of a new spiritual army fills me with grave worry. If these children one day grow into the army that will defeat my planned liberation—if I have to destroy them to save future generations, future children, hundreds of thousands, millions of unborn children, then I shall destroy them. It shall be unpleasant, but I will."

Alex looked out over the enemy army. "And what then, Gád? What happens after that? What are you really liberating us from? Or to? I feel that we live in a pretty free society."

"You do not. You absolutely do not. I am freeing you from the past—from history. From the established order that judges and subjugates the advancement of the people of these isles. The weight that has crushed them, that has taken them from the height they once attained—the pinnacle of civilisation and advancement. They could have flown to the stars by now if it wasn't for the backward glances, the ties to an ancient world that should have been severed immediately the instant they took root."

Alex sensed movement beneath him. Ecgbryt had assembled a band of knights and was positioning them at the gateway, ready for a command of attack.

"You are born into this world without choices," Gád was saying, "already bound, already blinkered. As you grow you are raised in the darkness and educated into blindness. You are shown the walls of your prison and taught that the movement between them is freedom. I want to tear those walls down."

"So does Ealdstan," Alex said. He looked up to where a thin line of dark blue night sky was showing. "Literally. He seems as eager for you to destroy everything that he's made as you are."

"Naturally," Gád said, spinning around. "We are of an accord, he and I. And why shouldn't we be? We are wise men who have seen the truth behind the world."

"I guess I'm not so clever," Alex said. "Where you're losing me is when your plan for liberation necessitates killing children."

"I've worked long and hard—the next army is an unknown factor, one that may easily multiply in the future. I have the ability

to rub it out now before it grows and endangers my plans totally—
and therefore the world."

Looking for ways to stall, Alex decided to play a little more
line on the spool of sophistry. "Ah, the end justifies the means
argument. As a police officer, I hear that one all the time. I'm
more process oriented. The means *are* the ends. Or rather, there
are no ends, only a pause between means."

"Is there no opportunity for improvement, or even change?
That sounds a cynical view to me."

"Just as yours, to me, sounds deluded."

"Mine seems to be winning right now."

"Might is right? Odd to think that those people usually lose—
in the end."

Gád smiled and relaxed into his former posture of hands
clasped behind his back, his head bent slightly forward. "I can
see that I missed more than just birthdays. I've missed a lot of
interesting conversations with you. I could stand here and discuss
these topics all night—I truly could. And so, I suspect, could you.
But are you not concerned that you are running out of time?"

"It is pressing, I admit. But . . ." Alex caught a gleam in Gád's
eye that seemed to convey that he knew something Alex didn't
yet—something he hadn't figured out. "What do you mean, time?"

"You hear that noise?" Gád said, tilting his head and imitating
it. "Tac—tac—tac—tac—tac . . ."

"What is it?"

"It is my giants. Have you not noticed they are not with us?
They are industriously at work, they have taken a leaf from your
own warriors' book. They are just now attacking the far southern
pillar that supports this ceiling of rock above us."

"You're going to collapse the ceiling unless we do as you
say? Unless we surrender?" As he said this, an yfelgóp sidled up
to Kelm and gave a message in his ear. The large general gave a

snorting grunt that shook his body and then hobbled off to the perimeter of his line.

"*Would* you surrender? Would you entertain such a thought?"

"It depends on the terms."

"The terms are these—join us in the destruction of all that has been established. Turn over command of the next army to me to be destroyed."

"You wouldn't. Why would you?"

Gád shrugged. "Why would I possibly want to preserve this place? It is a relic. You have to see it from my point of view. You must see these actions dispassionately, as movements in a game. Why mourn for a few pawns if their sacrifice will win the game? That is what we are negotiating right now—the exchange of pieces. But you are limited—walled in—by irrelevant sentimentality, a short-sighted morality that prevents harming a plague-carrying mosquito because it is a living thing, uncaring of the fact that it endangers many more significant lives. Ealdstan understands that, and Ealdstan agrees with me!" Gád became fervent while making these points, but caught himself and straightened, bringing his emotions under control with a stage actor's sincerity. "But it makes no difference. I shall kill you in either case. No doubt you are working on a plan to have them saved, but you should know—no one is going to help you. The hands of this nation's government have been tied. Which only further serves to prove my point, of course. You will die. And if it is not in a manner of your choosing, then it shall be mine. Ask yourself only how long you wish to prolong your own suffering."

Gád's attention went to Freya, cowering at his side. "That said," he continued, "I made a promise to an old man who gave me a lot of help. And so I am delivering this girl back to you. Incongruous, I know, but there it is. It was a condition owed and one I am more than happy to honour. My comfort is that I would far sooner have her against me than Ealdstan himself."

Alex raised a hand and rubbed his brow, turning his head to the side as he did so, glancing down at the courtyard. Ecgbryt was there, poised at the head of a column of knights—maybe thirty of them, standing at the ready for a signal from him. The gates were very quietly being unbarred.

Alex turned his attention quickly back to those below him. Gád nodded at Kelm, who swung around and made a hand signal into the sea of yfelgópes, then addressed Alex again. "Events transpire," he said with a smile. "It's a funny old world, isn't it? It turns out we've caught the other one—Daniel Tully. Seems we can't *stop* capturing him. This makes the fourth time, I believe, that he's just walked straight into our arms. Practically given himself up. His persistence to be caught is matched only by our apparent willingness to allow him to escape . . ."

Alex was taken aback—he had assumed Daniel was still in the tower somewhere. He frowned as he saw him being pushed forward by a gang of yfelgópes, his body scratched, bloody, and sooty. He was hunched over, attentive to something at his side that Alex couldn't quite see. Then he straightened and Alex saw that it was one of the children, Fergus, the boy who had lost his brother. They were both manhandled to stand next to Kelm, on the opposite end of the line from Freya. Daniel kept a protective hand on Fergus at all times, who was so terrified he was visibly shaking.

"Well," Gád said with sparkling amusement, his head turning from Daniel to Freya and back again. His manner was like that of a game-show host's—it was all a grand performance, and one that he was enjoying immensely. "Here we all are. Do you know, I remember reading in a book once that there are two states in which one meets so many old friends. One is in a dream, the other is the end of the world. Do you think that's true?"

Alex himself looked from Daniel to Freya and back to Gád again. "I'll be sure to think the point over," he said, suddenly feeling nervous and impatient. "In any case, we're not going to surrender. Why don't you and your forces retreat, leave Freya and Daniel at the gate, and we'll continue our futile escape attempts while you bring the roof down on top of our heads."

"I'm afraid that the obligation I suffer under Ealdstan only nominated Freya as the conditional party. But not the boys. As I see it, I am free to do with them as I wish." Gád stroked his chin. "I think I shall kill them both."

Alex raised an arm and then brought it down again quickly. That was the signal and Ecgbryt and his knights instantly leapt into action, charging forward even as the guards were still swinging the gates open. Guards from the walls hurled their spears down at Kelm and Gád.

Everyone below reacted at once. Daniel ducked, hunching over Fergus as a spear entered Kelm's leg. He howled in pain as Gád was knocked back by two spears that had hit him in the chest, stumbling backward and eventually falling over. Freya flinched and started running toward the tower; she was slightly ahead of Daniel, who only started moving when he saw the gates swing open. He pulled Fergus—who was staring wide-eyed at Kelm and the yfelgópes who were helping support his weight—with him. Kelm was barking incoherently at them, spittle flying in the air, trying to order them to leave him alone and secure the prisoners instead.

The confusion worked in Daniel, Freya, and Fergus's favour for the first vital moments, but that was as long as it took for all of the forces arrayed behind them to realise what was happening and charge forward.

The knights poured forth from the opened gates.

The sound that came when the yfelgópes and the knights met

was a rapid series of ear-splitting noises of metal against metal. Yfelgópes fell beneath the large knights, their small and frail forms a very poor match against the bulky power of their attackers. Alex could only watch the movements beneath him, his senses heightened, heart beating quickly and the salty, battery taste of adrenaline in his mouth.

Daniel and Freya passed the doors of the gate itself and Alex released a breath in a sigh—it looked as if they had managed the nearly impossible and rescued Daniel and Freya from Gád's grasp.

"They're in!" Alex shouted from the parapet. "Get back in! Shut the gates! Get back in!" His orders were drowned in a sharp screech cut above the din and reverberated between the stone structures. The wyverns were coming in for an attack. Alex only had enough time to duck down and press himself against the wall next to him as a shadow, deadly and fast, whistled past him, its outstretched talons tearing through the empty space that he had occupied less than a second before. Alex drew his sword. Across the courtyard he could see a group of defenders were not so lucky in fending off the creatures, as one of them was snatched and carried off, the small dragon's wings flapping fast, carrying the knight swiftly upward before flipping him up in the air and then smacking him with his tail at the top of his arc. The knight disappeared into the darkness.

Daniel, Freya, and Fergus were now up the steps and Alex saw them slide through the crack in the Langtorr door. Drawing a deep breath, he hazarded a quick look over the wall, to see how the knights were doing at the gate.

They were coping well, but certainly would not be able to hold out much longer. The sheer press of bodies was working against them. Had they been fighting a small band of attackers, their wide and powerful strokes would have easily kept them at bay, but the crush was starting to overwhelm them as enemy forces, uncaring of the safety of those before them, crowded each other forward in a relentless crush. Those at the front were very quickly dispatched, but opportune strikes by frenzied yfelgópes were becoming more frequent, and already some of them had proved fatal. Knights had fallen, their bodies trampled and buried by dead yfelgópes. But what was more threatening was the sight of angered trolls thundering across the stone ground, ploughing through the sea of bodies.

"Why aren't they retreating? Sound retreat!" Alex yelled at the knights around him. "Get everyone down! Down from the walls! Back into the tower!"

A knight near him raised a horn to his lips and gave three blows on it. The knights began falling back, gradually giving ground to the enemy. Alex and the knights on the wall started circling around to the stairs, and the wyverns with their yfelgóp riders noticed this and began a barrage of attacks on them. Alex hacked at the swooping legs and claws and instead of going for the head of the stairway, he jumped down onto one of the landings. A wyvern had just made an unsuccessful attack, but saw Alex and twisted around to try and reach him. Sharp claws raked across Alex's back and he was flung off the landing, hitting the ground hard on one leg and then falling against the corner where the wall met the ground.

A piercing pain leapt up through his leg and his breath left him completely. He lay for a full five seconds, trying to suck air back into his lungs and then hands were on him, hauling him upward. He kicked his feet against the ground and then hands were on him and he was pushed into the Langtorr. Alex staggered to the door and turned to see the knight who had pushed him lifted into the air in a flap of leathery wings. Knights were flooding into the tower and Alex was forced to step back to allow them through. Between the passing bodies Alex could see three of his men still in the courtyard; two of them were working as hard as they could to close the metal gate on the third one, who was standing in the arch, fighting an entire army away from the doors. Alex knew instantly that it was Ecgbryt. He danced expertly, his strong axe whirling around him, slicing off anything that came into its path. Yfelgópes fell before him like stalks of grass, and the sluggish trolls couldn't lay a finger on him.

But from the midst of the sea of attackers rose Kelm's ugly form, limping, his weight supported by the spear he had torn from his own leg. Out of the range of Ecgbryt's axe he hefted it to his shoulder and then threw it with tremendous velocity. Alex only had time to draw in a breath to shout and it pierced Ecgbryt right through the centre of his chest.

Tilting backward, Ecgbryt's final act was to alter slightly the swoop of his axe and fling it at the yfelgóp warlord who was having difficulty righting himself from his throw. The axe spun through the air and lodged directly in his neck, from shoulder blade to chin.

That was all that Alex saw. Ecgbryt's body hadn't even fallen to the ground before the gates closed and were quickly barred with the four large metal bracers. The last two retreating knights sprinted across the courtyard and into the Langtorr.

Alex closed the door, his eyes beginning to water. He stepped away as others made it secure. He felt long, delicate hands encircle him and he turned, collapsing into Freya's arms.

"*Shh*," she said. "*Shh*. You have to be strong now—you must mourn later. We're all counting on you to be strong. Breathe out, all the way out—" Alex forced air up from the bottom of his lungs. "Now breathe in, a deep breath. Wipe your eyes and stand up."

Alex palmed away tears and blinked to clear his vision. Freya was before him, her face sympathetic, but stern and resolved. Daniel was on the floor, his legs crumpled beneath him as if he were kneeling for prayer, his face pale, shocked eyes staring, unseeing, at the door. The whole hall and every step of the double staircase was filled with children, looking expectantly at him and the other adults. An icy chill flooded Alex's heart as the reality of the situation was driven into him once again. The hopelessness of it all came crashing down on him and he suddenly didn't see a point of making a pretence of it all. He let himself fall back down to the ground. He was done.

— **II** —

Freya looked down at Alex, who was concentrating on the small space of cold stone in front of him. She reached down to shake him out of his stupor. He grabbed hold of her arms and leapt up, furious. "Get your hands off of me," he growled. "Don't touch me. They're coming, don't you see? They'll be inside here any minute now. Ecgbryt killed Kelm. He . . . he . . ."

"Kelm is dead? But surely that would buy us some time?"

"Don't bet on it! Kelm kept all those things in line. Now that he's dead his forces are angry, confused, and after revenge. Listen! Listen! Do you hear that? They're breaking the wall down. Not just the doors, the entire wall!"

Freya drew back. Alex was beneath her, and huddled against a near wall was Vivienne, in a similar state to her nephew. She was now the only adult still on her feet, and all eyes were on her.

She cleared her throat. "I think the first thing to tell all of you is—we're sorry. I think we adults thought that we could figure out a way to get out of here—out of this situation—but it looks like we were wrong. I don't see this ending well. There is an army out there that is determined to kill us, and it will only be a matter of time before they get in here. We're completely trapped.

"I know how you must feel—helplessly caught up in something much, much bigger than you are—manipulated by people you don't know and used in their games for power. The same thing happened to me when I was your age, and in the end it's brought me here with you, in exactly the same position that you are.

"So while I can't promise you that we'll keep you safe and get you home to your families, I can promise that we'll be with you right up to the end. You won't be alone."

Freya looked around at all the faces looking down at her.

"So I think you should all think about that. If you have good-byes or prayers that you want to say, go ahead and say them. If you all want to stay here, together, then that's great. If some of you want to go off and find a space on your own, then that's okay too."

Freya turned to look at Alex and Vivienne again. They were calmer now, still, at rest. "Have you got anything to add?" Freya asked in a quiet voice.

"Why don't we fight?"

The question came from a girl on the stairs.

"We were summoned here," Gemma Woodcote said, "to fight—to be the next army. So why don't we go out and fight? There's a chance we might win."

Freya tried to smile a sympathetic smile. "I understand why you feel that way, but that's not how it's going to happen. Things don't always turn out like we want them to."

"I don't mind dying if it's for a good cause," Gemma declared defiantly. "But I don't want to just sit here and wait for it. Even if it is hopeless—I'm not going down without a fight!"

"Neither am I!" shouted someone else.

"Fight!" shouted another.

"Fight! Fight! Fight! Fight! Fight!"

The children were chanting, stomping their feet, banging their fists against their palms. The cacophony shook her physically and all she could do was let them keep at it, tire themselves out. It was useless to try and speak above them, and she wasn't in a rush anymore.

"*No!*"

Daniel sprang to his feet and screamed again above the din. "NO!"

His defiant voice pierced the noise and the clamour trailed off and died out completely. He came to stand by Freya, his face red, the veins on his neck pulsing. "That's what we've been doing wrong all this time!" he shouted. "We've been fighting, trying to kill! It's not the way to solve this situation—any situation! Trust me, I know!" He had everyone's complete attention now and he lowered his voice.

"I know—I'm the worst one here! I've had blood on my hands since I was thirteen years old. I've killed yfelgópes wherever I could find them, I've even assassinated a powerful prince—and none of it has ever done any good . . . *ever*! All it did was lead to more violence—more pain and misery."

Daniel's words rattled against the stone walls of the Langtorr. This was such a turnabout for him, Freya was breathless.

"I've seen things I don't . . . I don't think I could describe them. Or if I could, you wouldn't believe them. I've . . . I've seen things from the outside. History before it began. Violence has been with us since the beginning, and it's never been the answer. It's never helped. I've never helped . . ."

Daniel became quiet, and there was complete silence throughout the tower.

"But I'm not going to be a part of the problem anymore. And neither are you, if I can help it. Here's what I'm going to do—" He was interrupted by a clap of thunder and a shockwave that shook the tower and knocked some of the children to the ground. One of the tapestries fell from the wall and a stream of dust rained down through the centre of the tower.

"They did it . . . they actually managed it," Alex said, rising to his feet. "That was one of the pillars! I didn't think they could do it, but they did. They collapsed it. He's really serious. He's really going to wipe us all out."

"What do we do?" cried one of the children.

"Yes, tell us! What do we do?"

More and more started crying and screaming. Daniel put his hands out and waited for them all to be quiet. "Here's what I'm going to do. I'm going to go out and march against that army, unarmed. And if they kill me . . .

"Freya says we are all going to die, and I believe that's true. Anyone who wants to come with me is welcome at my side—as long as you do it without any weapons and without any more violence. And if these are the last words you hear me say, I want you to know, all of you, that I'm sorry. I'm sorry that I helped make such a violent world for you." Daniel turned to Freya. "I'm sorry."

She smiled at him.

"I'm coming with you." Fergus walked forward and stood right in front of Daniel.

"I'm going as well."

More children came forward. Less than one in ten did so, but that added up to nearly a hundred, all crowding around Daniel.

"No, you can't," said Vivienne. "Freya, Alex, we can't allow them to do this. My brother will kill them—he will certainly kill them. If you expect him to show mercy at the last moment . . . he won't. He simply won't. This isn't some sort of sanitised Disney movie. It won't end well."

"No. But it will end," Freya said. "I think Daniel's right. I think he should go out, and I think anyone who wants to go with him should go as well."

"It doesn't sound like it makes sense," Daniel said, "but I've seen behind the curtain, seen the way things really are. Not every-one is going—just the ones who feel they should."

From his dark space under the stairs, Godmund emerged. Scowling as deeply as ever, he slowly pushed through the crowd of children, going straight for Daniel.

When he was still half a dozen feet from him, Godmund drew his sword. Everyone cleared a space from around him. Stopping, he raised its wide and flat blade above his head and then dropped to one knee and brought it down, blade first on the stone floor of the hall. It shattered to pieces that went skittering along the ground, ringing like bells. Godmund stood again and dropped the empty hilt without even a glance. It landed with a hollow *thunk* on the bare floor and, stepping over the scar he had just made at his feet, he leant forward and embraced Daniel tightly.

"Thank you, boy—thank you," the old knight said. "I shall walk with you until the end."

"It's senseless," Vivienne said, becoming exasperated. "Simply senseless."

"When are you going?" Freya asked Daniel.

"No time like the present."

CHAPTER ELEVEN

The Battle of the Martyrs

---- I ----

The doors opened to an empty courtyard, which was still except for the explosive pounding on the metal doors of the circular wall. Each hit caused the tense atmosphere to quiver, as though it were made of glass and could shatter at any instant.

They quietly stepped out into the courtyard, Daniel in front and the children behind him. Godmund was the last out of the tower along with a few of the Niðergearders. He clapped Frithfroth on the arm and nodded to Vivienne, Alex, and Freya, who were the only ones left standing in the doorway.

Daniel looked out over the assembled children behind him, his heart thumping like a jackhammer. He was finding it hard to breathe; his throat felt tense and tight, like a clenched fist.

They all looked so frail and frightened, licking their lips and blinking their eyes.

"Stay together," Daniel said, his voice sounding thin and

scratchy. He was having to pause and speak between the thunderous blasts of the enemy hammering at the gates. "Remember to stay together. And don't fight or push back at anyone. If something happens . . . let it happen. It will all be over soon enough, one way or another. And if there's any sort of world after this . . . I'll see you there."

He looked up and saw the windows of the Langtorr were filled with faces, those of the ones who were staying behind.

He turned and breathed out, his breath misting in front of him, hoping no one could see him trembling. He had to stand tall and walk straight. He stared at the flat, blank metal of the gate, which was shivering in front of him, about to fall off of its hinges. He felt a small hand grip his. He looked down and saw Fergus looking up at him, hanging on his arm. The boy gave him an encouraging smile and Daniel smiled back.

"We're coming out!" Daniel shouted up at the doors.

The pounding stopped. Daniel strained to hear any noise beyond the ringing in his ears, but there was none.

"Open them," he said, and Godmund and the Niðergearders who had circled around the group removed the bars and pushed the doors open.

The attackers had withdrawn—there was nobody waiting for them immediately outside the doors—even the dead had been carried away. But looking more carefully, he saw sharp, black silhouettes beyond the first line of buildings. For the briefest of moments he had thought that maybe the army had vanished somehow and they would all be allowed to leave, but that hope became stillborn in the space of a breath as he noticed the lines of spears on the rooftops.

Daniel took a single step forward. It was hesitant and jerky, and as difficult as pulling his foot out of a pit of mud. The second and third steps were just as hard as the first, but after that it became easier. He still held Fergus's hand as the others fell in step behind him.

They walked slowly and steadily. Rolling his tongue around his dry mouth, Daniel realised he didn't have any sort of route planned. He kept going straight ahead, his eyes fixed unblinkingly on the roofless building about a hundred yards in front of him, and the night sky that could now be seen with stars shining through that seemed unnaturally bright.

Daniel felt that his legs would buckle after every step. He marvelled at the human condition—walking had never been this hard and it was unreasonable that it should be so now. His mind was calm, his heart was clear, but his body was terrified. He heard sounds of crying from behind him and also at his side.

"Look at the stars, Fergus," Daniel said as black shapes started to detach themselves from the darkness between the buildings and come closer to them. "See how bright they are? Do you know that I've travelled between them? They're so far away, and so far apart from each other that you can't imagine. And their beauty . . . the light when you get close to them . . ."

One of the children from behind took his other hand, and then he felt more hands on him, holding on to his arms, grabbing his belt. His footsteps slowed but remained steady, and he somehow found it easier to walk.

"Stay together," he called out as the dark shapes became more distinct. "Don't let anyone fall behind." He took a last look behind him. The outer wall of the Langtorr was lined with light. The children were standing on the ramparts, holding the silver lanterns in order to see them. Freya would be up there watching, along with Alex and Vivienne. He didn't know if what happened to them would be any more pleasant than what was about to happen to him, but he prayed anyway. There weren't many words to his prayer, because he didn't know what to say, and the concept was unfamiliar to him, but he needed to reach out to something at that moment for strength.

"Keep up the pace," Daniel said. "Don't fall behind." Godmund was herding them all from the rear, his arms outstretched as if to support the entire group as it walked. He caught the burly captain's eyes and gave him a nod; Godmund gave him a smile in return.

Yfelgópes appeared between the buildings, moving in a mob, walking alongside Daniel and the children, weapons drawn, predatory grins baring sharp teeth. They were close enough that he was able to smell them, but they made no aggressive movements.

Daniel kept walking until the yfelgópes refused to move out of the way of the small group. The crying had stopped now; they were all breathless. Daniel stared into the eyes of an yfelgóp standing directly in front of him, who glared back with hateful eyes, a flared nose, and vicious sneer. There was no sympathy there, no humanity, unless irrational hate was an inherently human quality.

Some of the yfelgópes' attention was not on the group, but on a building up ahead and to their right. Daniel looked and saw a clutch of yfelgópes, bristling with weapons, standing on its roof. Several of them were holding burning torches, and in the orange smouldering light they gave off, he could see Gád, perfectly illuminated. He was looking down at them imperiously, his face stony and hateful. At any moment he would open his mouth, give an order, and Daniel knew it would be the end. He pulled the children near him closer. A movement on the building opposite caught Daniel's attention and he saw Ealdstan's outline, approaching the edge of the roof with his elf bodyguards.

They kept walking, but at a slower pace than before, on track to pass between the two men. Moving along with the mob around them Daniel saw a sparkle of light, just a small triangle of bright white, which . . . which looked like a shoulder. He craned his neck and saw the figure that had appeared to him when he had been chained at the western well. But this time he recognised him.

"Swiðgar . . . ," Daniel said, doing little more than only mouthing the name. There was no doubt about it, it was Swiðgar, the wise knight and sword-brother of Ecgbryt. Daniel hadn't seen him since they parted in the sewers when he was a boy, but here he was again, as large as life and shining like silver. He laughed at Daniel's astonished face. Daniel realised he hadn't actually seen Swiðgar laugh much at all in life, but he was doing so now, and Daniel was encouraged.

"*Hweat*, young Daniel," he said as he moved through the ranks of angry warriors, his voice booming. No one else near the supernatural knight gave any sign of seeing or hearing him, but to Daniel he seemed more real than anything else in sight. "How is my little *aetheling* this fine evening?"

Another figure of light stepped out from behind Swiðgar; a smaller, more slender figure—Modwyn. And behind her, Ecgbryt.

"Kieran!" Fergus whispered breathlessly beside him, yanking his arm. "Daniel, it's my brother, Kieran!" Daniel followed his line of sight but couldn't see anything. "He's here. He's shining . . . he's . . . he's gone."

Daniel turned back to the three silver figures he could see. Swiðgar held up a hand to him. "Be at peace," the knight said, and then vanished, along with Modwyn and Ecgbryt.

"Draw arms." Gád's voice sounded clearly in the still darkness. Those who weren't holding weapons at the ready did so, swords scraping against scabbards, shields and spears rattling.

"Don't do this!" Daniel shouted up at Gád. "You don't have to do this! Let us go!"

"Stand ready!" Gád raised an arm, his fingers stretching straight up toward the sky.

"Please!" Daniel shouted desperately. "Please!"

"Kill them," Gád said and let his hand fall.

The yfelgópes leapt forward, their swords slashing through the air. Daniel closed his eyes and shouted as they fell into the children at his side. He felt the hands on him gradually fall away and then there was a sharp, biting sensation at his arm. Children were crying out and something pierced his side, penetrating his bare flesh. Cold metal slid into his gut and scraped against his ribs. His jaw clenched, teeth grinding against each other, as blood and salty bile rose in his throat. He opened his eyes and saw that his hands were tightly gripping a spear that was protruding from his belly. He tried to lift his head to look at who had stabbed him, but instead he reeled forward, everything spinning around him, and the ground coming up to meet him at an angle. He put out an arm to hold it back and rested there, trying to draw a breath but finding that to be almost impossible. He was suffocating, he realised. Then there was a blow at the back of his head and he swooned.

The wails of horror and pain became less frequent and the deep red that now filled his vision grew darker and darker still until all was black.

CHAPTER TWELVE

Triumph

I

The shouts, cries, and sounds of weapons clinking in the night gradually stopped and silence spread through Niðergeard once more. Whatever was happening had happened. Freya stood on the Langtorr outer wall and wondered what was coming next.

From where they were, and with the lanterns positioned as they were, they could now see that the yfelgópes were marching back to them. Gád was at their head, striding confidently, as the others crept in around him. Freya looked for the children and Daniel—any small sign of them, in fact, maybe some of them had been taken prisoner, she thought—but there were spatters of blood on the weapons and bodies of those she saw before her.

Gád strode into the light, his face beaming with a grimacing leer. Behind him three yfelgópes carried a messy, ragged bundle, which Gád directed to be placed at his feet. The bundle fell and unfolded, arms splaying outward, legs twisted beneath it. Freya gasped as Daniel's pale, white face lolled lifelessly at Gád's feet.

"What did you hope to achieve?" Gád shouted up at them. "Did you think I was only posturing? That I would have a change of heart at the last moment? A crisis of conscience? Your generation does not know war. You send unarmed children onto a battlefield—what do you expect?"

He waved at the yfelgópes behind him and pointed at Daniel. A few of them slunk forward and grabbed his shoulders and chest, hoisting him upright.

"I want to share this moment with you," he said. "This is the very beginning of my time of triumph. He still lives," he said in a marvelling voice, pointing at Daniel. "But not for long." He drew the sword of an yfelgóp near him. "This is for all of you to see!" he bellowed, the sword dangling in his hand. "All negotiations, all preparations are over! Ealdstan has failed. An age of darkness and stupidity ends now, with a piercing strike!" He angled the sword down toward Daniel's neck.

Freya described what happened next constantly for the rest of her life. It was a highly scrutinised incident, referred to in countless books and articles, and although not everyone completely agreed to seeing exactly the same thing, her account was given the most weight.

As Gád let go of the sword's handle, Daniel's body began to shimmer with light. Patches of silver danced across his body, breaking through the skin and then submerging behind it. Gád backed away and the yfelgópes holding up Daniel dropped him and retreated, and Daniel's body then did two things: it fell to the ground, and it remained where it was.

The dark, broken mass of bloody skin and revealed flesh crumpled into an indistinct pile, but the silver form of Daniel remained where it was. It wasn't a mere ghostly outline, but a body made out of light, every inch and contour of his skin radiant and illumined. It hurt her eyes to look at it but also, strangely, she longed to keep looking at it forever. The silver image of Daniel unfolded himself as the human shell crumpled beneath him. His head came up and he blinked bright, shining eyes, as though he were waking up from a deep sleep. The scars and hurt were gone from his face—the permanently hostile set of his expression had vanished, even though his features were completely unchanged. He was as old as he had been, but to Freya he looked much more like the boy that she had first known, that she had grown up with, shared birthdays with, and come to Niðergeard with.

He looked languidly from side to side and then down at his chest. The hilt of a silver sword still protruded from it. He frowned and raised a hand to touch it, his arm moving in a slow, graceful arc. His fingertips brushed the shining hilt and then gripped it fully. He pulled on it, slowly drawing the blade out of his chest.

The sword's blade was long and thin, delicate like a needle. Daniel swung it upward in a high arc and it seemed to grow, extending in a flaming halo of light. All eyes were on it and Daniel's expression of awe was no less than anyone else's. Behind him, Gád's mouth was moving violently; it looked like he was shouting, but Freya could not hear what he was saying. He made frantic movements with his hands, clenching them and thrusting them forward. They twisted into patterns and made symbols in the air in front of him. When Daniel had finished studying the sword he turned to Gád, and with a fast, natural movement, lowered the sword and flicked it out at him. It sliced clean through Gád's own chest, but did not cut him.

Daniel took a step back, as Gád staggered back, a look of horror on his face. He clutched at his chest and moved his hand, searching for a wound, but he found not so much as a scratch on himself. And although Freya didn't know exactly what had happened to him just then, she found out that at that moment his soul, his spirit, had been killed, and his supernatural abilities and powers were completely destroyed. Daniel turned away from him. Gád's face was contorted into a hideous expression of terror and anger. He rushed at Daniel in desperation, his fists clenched. Freya expected him to pass right through Daniel, but Daniel was as real and solid as a brick wall and Gád bounced off of him, reeling and then falling, and eventually sprawling on the ground.

Daniel did not even look up, his head instead was still bowed, concentrating on something. Then around him began to appear little points of light that darted up from between the yfelgópes. The lights brightened and grew and solidified into other figures. Freya blinked her eyes and squinted. Next to Daniel was Fergus, and beside him was a taller boy, who may have been his brother who was captured. The two turned their heads to each other—one looking up and one looking down—and smiled.

On Daniel's other side Swiðgar appeared. He looked up and waved at Freya. Her heart leapt into her throat and she raised her own hand to wave. Ecgbryt was next to him, wearing his old armour, teeth gleaming with a joyful grin, clutching a silver axe in his hands.

The figures of light were appearing faster now. Freya saw Godmund, looking young and unscarred, and the children who had gone with him and Daniel were clustered around him.

But there were more. Hundreds of knights appeared, and then more hundreds and more, completely filling the underground plain. Who were they all? Not all of them were clothed in armour, and many were women, wearing old-fashioned dresses. Near the wall she spotted some men who were clothed in clerical garb; others were in cassocks. There were women in nuns' habits.

They filled every inch of the Niðerplane, standing between the rows of attackers and spreading out behind them in a sea of light.

There were thousands of them by now—the martyrs of Britain's history had assembled. The light they generated was so bright and so intense that Freya had to hold her arms up to shield her eyes.

All at once they took to the air, swooping and diving into the enemy army, picking out and lifting up the mystical creatures, their outlines appearing black within the sea of light. The snakes, trolls, beasts, and even the giants became airborne, many bright hands grasping them and hoisting them into the cyclonic tempest that was now whipping around the Langtorr. They went spinning off in different directions—the trolls went one way, the snakes in another, the armoured bears in a third, the wyverns in still another, and so on. They were all being separated and borne away for some reason, all of them except the yfelgópes, who were pushed to the ground and remained huddling there. Freya wasn't sure exactly why they were being sorted like this until she saw the white bodies wrestling with the flapping shadow creatures, and taking them back through the torn-open gate above the hero's throne that Ealdstan had opened when he killed Modwyn. And when they had all been forced back to where they came from, the bright, flying shapes clustered around the hole and closed it up behind them. In time, and no one could ever agree on how long that was, the Niðerplane became quiet and dark once again. The yfelgópes still remained, lying or kneeling on the ground. Freya saw Gád below her was lying flat on his back next to Daniel's body. He was rocking his head slightly from side to side, mechanically and with no apparent purpose.

The yfelgópes that could get up did so. They took off into the darkness as quickly as they could move, stepping on and over the bodies of those still on the ground. Soon the entire city was deserted.

The children on the wall started to cheer. Freya was being shaken and she turned to Alex, who began shouting in her face, "We made it, Freya! We've won! Daniel won! We're safe—we're safe!"

Vivienne stared out, her hands covering her mouth as she cried tears of relief. The children started flooding down from the wall and the knights who had remained in the tower unbarred the doors. Freya joined them as everyone walked out into the city. It was completely quiet, peaceful, and the rising sunlight brightened even the darkest shadow. The sky from beneath the overhang was starting to turn to a pastel grey, and as they walked deeper into the city it brightened into hues of orange.

By the time Freya had fetched a blanket from the tower and wrapped up Daniel's body, warm rays from the morning sun shone down onto her face.

A new day had dawned.

CHAPTER THIRTEEN

The Rise of Niðergeard

—————————— I ——————————

Stories give us the illusion of endings, but nothing truly does. A crisis had arisen in Niðergeard and catastrophe for the world had been avoided, but the story didn't end—that was just one incident in the long and continuing history of Britain. Stories start and finish at moments of great change, but life continues on.

—————————— II ——————————

And life continued on in Niðergeard, which could no longer be counted among the secret cities of the world. Once Gád's power had been stripped from him and his spells had been broken, the enchantments he had sown within the government dissipated and the goblins, kobolds, and elves had been carried away by the storm of martyrs. The rulers of the country came to their senses again, the collapsed area was properly and cautiously investigated, and emergency forces started moving into the area.

What they first encountered were fleeing yfelgópes, every single one of which insisted on surrendering. Temporary jails were set up in nearby school halls. It was hard for the legal community to untangle exactly what crimes they could be charged for, but the yfelgópes were pretty helpful in volunteering testimony against themselves and keeping their compatriots accountable. Those who could be charged, were charged; the rest were kept for study and rehabilitation. Although they had been living a feral, animalistic existence, their names and previous identities started coming back to them, after a time.

Next the rescuers came across a young man who claimed to be a Scottish police officer, who was leading thousands of the missing children out of the dark sinkhole. He was asked many questions, and he answered almost none of them to the satisfaction of the responding teams, but all of his answers were upheld by the children he was leading and the adults who were with him.

The children were driven to a nearby town where they were fed, their names taken, and parents contacted. Only a small group of emergency workers—two paramedics, two police officers, a British army captain, and three infantrymen—continued farther on into the wide, dark cavern, coming eventually to the city of Niðergeard itself. They shone powerful lights up into the ruined buildings, which still retained some of the marks of splendour they had once displayed proudly and in full.

When they came to the centre of the city, they found a young woman standing outside the gates of an enormous walled tower, wearing a silver crown traced in gold that was wrought into the shape of a dragon. She was flanked by eight large men in armour holding spears and shields, and looking up at the wall behind her they could see many more lining it. Wrapped at her feet was the body of a young man with brown hair who had been horribly mutilated. He was now laid out, his arms on his chest. Crouched against one of the doors was an elderly gentleman in a dark suit being tended by a woman in her fifties who was wearing hiking gear. The man was found to be Alexander Simpson, civil servant, and he was in a complete catatonic stupor, his eyes open and staring, but unresponsive to anything around him. The woman, Vivienne Simpson, claimed to be his sister.

The army captain interviewed the young woman and she told them she was Freya Reynolds, the ruler of Niðergeard. She asked if the children had been rescued yet, and she was assured that they had.

Freya turned to the police officers and told them that a number of children had also been killed and their bodies would need to be recovered. She did not know exactly where they were, but she gave them directions to where they might be. And she told them not to disturb the bodies of anyone who was dressed like the knights behind her, that those bodies would be brought to her here at the tower.

The medics took Simpson away in the company of Vivienne, and the police and military men needed to return to the surface to report on what they had found—no satellite communication could get through the massive stone ceiling above them and it would still be awhile before temporary line-of-sight radio equipment could be set up. They left the imperious girl at the tower in the company of her knights.

III

The children returned to their families and started undergoing trauma counseling. It was soon discovered that none of them needed it and every single one of the "Niðergeard survivors" went on to lead remarkable lives. They were welcome to return to Niðergeard whenever they pleased.

The bodies of those who were killed with Daniel were identified and buried privately by their families, although a public memorial service was held several weeks later. A statue was commissioned and placed near the Marble Arch entrance of Hyde Park. It is a bronze casting made from wax showing 217 children, their hands raised, supporting a map of the British Isles. On the site where they were killed in Niðergeard lie the same number of flat stones arranged to form a cairn. A wreath is placed in honour of the Niðergeard martyrs at Westminster on Memorial Day, the eleventh of November.

IV

The knowledge of Niðergeard's existence, as well as what, exactly, happened there, was kept secret for as long as possible, which was almost three days. Newspapers started reporting what they could piece together from the different accounts of the adults they were allowed to interview and then a few photographers managed to sneak past the cordons one night. Picture spreads ran in newspapers and magazines and video footage was seen on the news and other online media sites the very next day.

Officials needed time to inspect Niðergeard, but after four days it was decided safe. They allowed Freya's family to come and see her, followed shortly after by the prime minister. His arrival kicked off several days of arduously long and unfocussed meetings with Freya. Eventually she persuaded him and the other cabinet members and officials to allow the last three members of the "Niðergeard Cannies"—Vivienne, Alex, and James Simpson—into the talks and things seemed to go smoother. There was a wealth of ancient documentation going back nearly a thousand years, variously signed by Alfred the Great, William I, Henry II, Richard II, Henry VI, John I, Elizabeth I, James I, Oliver Cromwell, and Queen Victoria, among others. This completely flummoxed the bevy of lawyers who had descended into the city. Copies of these documents were made and taken away to be studied by the appropriate experts and historians. James Simpson accompanied them all. He was excited to finally be able to talk about something that had been a secret his entire life and he was chattering nineteen to the dozen all the way back up to the surface.

The presentation of these documents brought about a welcome hiatus to the meetings. It was another week before discussions started up again, and then over a year before everything was officially sorted out.

What they decided was that Niðergeard was not a separate, sovereign nation apart from Great Britain, but had been a part of it since Ealdstan first built it. Freya could no longer call herself the queen of Niðergeard, but she would be given a title and a seat in the House of Lords, as would her successors. The city itself would be preserved as an English Heritage site and restored and made open to the public.

Today you can visit Niðergeard and walk along wooden boards through roped-off paths and see the existing wonders of what still stands before seeing models and interactive computer displays of what it looked like before it was ruined. There is a room with display cases showing weaponry, armour, and other artefacts that have been uncovered, and there is a separate building that has been designed and constructed as a memorial for everyone who had given their lives on that last day. You can buy keychains and paperweights and peruse a growing number of picture books and academic works on the city. Many of the reformed yfelgópes work as tour guides. Opening hours are 10:00 a.m. to 6:00 p.m. weekdays, 8:00 a.m. to 10:00 p.m. on Saturday. The standard entry fee is £45 with various concessionary rates (large groups must book in advance).

Alternatively, you may apply to an office at an address in Oxford to live as a volunteer or as a part of the "Sojourner" program in Niðergeard, joining the community that works and studies there, maintaining and restoring the buildings or serving those who do so. While there you will eat, sleep, and work alongside those who have lived in Niðergeard for hundreds of years. There are a limited number of very highly sought-after positions for history students to interview these witnesses of past ages, and to study, catalogue, and photograph the texts that line the shelves in Ealdstan's study.

V

Ealdstan was not found for many, many years. Not until the tunnels in and around Niðergeard started to be excavated and mapped was the body of an old man found. When examined, it showed every sign of extreme old age and was presumed to have died very shortly after the battle, of cold and starvation, in a very lonely corner of the dark caverns.

VI

Frithfroth continued to live in the Langtorr. Handicapped and nearly blind, he continued to occupy the office of steward of the Langtorr, which was strictly ceremonial since there were more than enough people to look after the running of the city and the people who lived there. He was willing to talk and tell stories as long as anyone was willing to listen; he didn't care how many times he repeated himself.

When the topic came up, he expressed much grief at not

having gone with Daniel and the children when they marched against Gád. He wished he had been a part of that, and hoped it was still not too late for him to get his body of light. Yet if he had to be a martyr to the continued service and upkeep of Niðergeard and die in that task, then that would not be too much to ask.

He eventually did die, only seven years after Niðergeard was uncovered. And although he would often, understandably, slide into bouts of depression and hostility, Freya also saw glimpses of the man she had first met in Niðergeard, who was so merry sitting at a bench, drinking ale and guessing at riddles with his friends. Always a gruff character, the Sojourners who took the time to get to know him were rewarded with many fascinating forgotten tales and epic poems. But riddles were his favourite, and in time they were recorded, written down, and published in several books under his name.

VII

Freya was uncertain about living in Niðergeard at first. She felt her position there was more one of duty and necessity, rather than her own desire—the city still needed to be protected, she believed. But as she stayed and she saw things being rebuilt, and young people coming and studying and living in this incredible place and then going back out into the world with a new perspective and different ideas about life and the universe, she came to truly love every day that she spent there. The grip that pain and trauma had over her heart lessened as time went by, and she became thankful for the circumstances that had brought her to where she was, horrible as those were at the time. She never married and never had children, but she meant as much as any mother ever did to many of the young people who came to live at Niðergeard. When she died, the number of people who counted themselves her children—and the children they had—ran into the hundreds. If anyone wants a happy ending, you could say this about Freya: she was never lonely or unloved for any of the rest of her days. And although what happens to us when we are youngest stays with us the longest, the eight years of terror and misery she had experienced in Niðergeard became less important than the sixty-seven years of happiness that she spent there. Like a strong thread in a tapestry, she held long and well.

But she didn't forget the boy who had given up his life for the city and for the world. She still thought of him as a boy, an eager twelve-year-old boy who loved quests and adventures.

VIII

She did meet with Daniel again, although she did not remember doing so. She talked with him in a dream, which she entirely forgot, even before she woke up.

They were sitting on a bench, looking out at Niðergeard as it had been before it was nearly destroyed, the tree-carved stone wall of trees still visible and even more striking in the daylight, because they were also in the open air, with grass fields around them.

"I wish I knew why I was hurt so much," Freya said to Daniel.

"For the part that I played in your pain," Daniel said, "I am truly sorry. Pain is never easy, but neither is it all bad. Your pain was not like my pain. The pain I suffered pushed me to the light, and I am grateful for it. Change is always painful, and I needed to change a lot."

"What does it all mean?" she asked. "Changing or not? Feeling pain or not? Living or not?"

"It means there is something greater. In this life, we are like seeds in the ground, trying to find nourishment enough to allow us to break out of the darkness, isolation, and confusion. A seed is not a tree, only the promise of one, and once we've fought through the dark we will grow into the promises of ourselves in the garden where every living thing stretches upward toward the sun transformed, beautiful, and fulfilling every promise placed into our souls."

A tree as tall as the Langtorr itself appeared before them, and then another just as big behind it, and then they were in a whole forest of trees as large as skyscrapers.

"Good-bye, Freya."

"Good-bye, Daniel."

The gates of heaven are fearful gates
Worse than the gates of hell;
Not I would break the splendours barred
Or seek to know the thing they guard,
Which is too good to tell.

—G. K. Chesterton,
The Ballad of the White Horse

About the Author

Author photo by Colin Munro

Ross Lawhead was born in America but grew up in England. He studied screenplay writing at Bournemouth University before moving on to pencil the *!Hero* graphic novel and coauthor the *!Hero* novel trilogy with his father. He has also coauthored humorous books of poetry and created a theological superhero. Find him at rosslawhead.com/blog.

AN EXCERPT FROM

THE PARADISE WAR

SONG OF ALBION ~ BOOK 1

STEPHEN R. LAWHEAD

Since all the world is but a story,
it were well for thee to buy
the more enduring story rather than
the story that is less enduring.

THE JUDGMENT OF ST. COLUM CILLE
(St. Columba of Scotland)

1

An Aurochs in
the Works

It all began with the aurochs.

We were having breakfast in our rooms at college. Simon was presiding over the table with his accustomed critique on the world as evidenced by the morning's paper. "Oh, splendid," he sniffed. "It looks as if we have been invaded by a pack of free-loading foreign photographers keen on exposing their film—and who knows what else—to the exotic delights of Dear Old Blighty. Lock up your daughters, Bognor Regis! European paparazzi are loose in the land!"

He rambled on awhile and then announced, "Hold on! Have a gawk at this!" He snapped the paper sharp and sat up straight—an uncommon posture for Simon.

"Gawk at what?" I asked idly. This thing of his—reading the paper aloud to a running commentary of facile contempt, scorn, and sarcasm, well mixed and peppered with his own unique blend of cynicism—had long since ceased to amuse me. I had learned to grunt agreeably while eating my egg and toast. This saved having to pay attention to his tirades, eloquent though they often were.

"Some bewildered Scotsman has found an aurochs in his patch."

"You don't say." I dipped a corner of toast triangle into the molten center of a soft-boiled egg and read an item about a disgruntled driver on the London Underground refusing to stop to let off passengers, thereby compelling a train full of frantic commuters to ride the Circle Line for over five hours. "That's interesting."

"Apparently the beast wandered out of a nearby wood and collapsed in the middle of a hay field twenty miles or so east of Inverness." Simon lowered the paper and gazed at me over the top. "Did you hear what I just said?"

"Every word. Wandered out of the forest and fell down next to Inverness—probably from boredom," I replied. "I know just how he felt."

Simon stared at me. "Don't you realize what this means?"

"It means that the local branch of the RSPCA gets a phone call. Big deal." I took a sip of coffee and returned to the sports page before me. "I wouldn't call it news exactly."

"You don't know what an aurochs is, do you?" he accused. "You haven't a clue."

"A beast of some sort—you said so yourself just now," I protested. "Really, Simon, the papers you read—" I flicked his upraised tabloid with a disdainful finger. "Look at these so-called headlines: 'Princess Linked to Alien Sex Scheme!' and 'Shock Horror Weekend for Bishop with Massage Parlor Turk!' Honestly, you only read those rags to fuel your pessimism."

He was not moved. "You haven't the slightest notion what an aurochs is. Go on, Lewis, admit it."

I took a wild stab. "It's a breed of pig."

"Nice try!" Simon tossed his head back and laughed. He had a nasty little fox-bark that he used when he wanted to deride some-one's ignorance. Simon was extremely adept at derision—a master of disdain, mockery, and ridicule in general.

I refused to be drawn. I returned to my paper and stuffed the toast into my mouth.

"A pig? Is that what you said?" He laughed again.

"Okay, okay! What, pray tell, is an aurochs, Professor Rawnson?"

Simon folded the paper in half and then in quarters. He creased it and held it before me. "An aurochs is a sort of ox."

"Why, think of that," I gasped in feigned astonishment. "An ox, you say? It fell down? Oh my, what *won't* they think of next?" I yawned. "Give me a break."

"Put like that it doesn't sound like much," Simon allowed. Then he added, "Only it just so happens that this particular ox is an ice-age creature that has been extinct for the last two thousand years."

"Extinct." I shook my head slowly. "Where do they get this malarkey? If you ask me, the only thing that's extinct around here is your native skepticism."

"It seems the last aurochs died out in Britain sometime before the Romans landed—although a few may have survived on the continent into the sixth century or so."

"Fascinating," I replied.

Simon shoved the folded paper under my nose. I saw a grainy, badly printed photo of a huge black mound that might or might not have been mammalian in nature. Standing next to this ill-defined mass was a grim-looking middle-aged man holding a very long, curved object in his hands, roughly the size and shape of an old-fashioned scythe. The object appeared to be attached in some way to the black bulk beside him.

"How bucolic! A man standing next to a manure heap with a

farm implement in his hands. How utterly homespun," I scoffed in a fair imitation of Simon himself.

"That manure heap, as you call it, is the aurochs, and the implement in the farmer's hands is one of the animal's horns."

I looked at the photo again and could almost make out the animal's head below the great slope of its shoulders. Judging by the size of the horn, the animal would have been enormous—easily three or four times the size of a normal cow. "Trick photography," I declared.

Simon clucked his tongue. "I am disappointed in you, Lewis. So cynical for one so young."

"You don't actually believe this"—I jabbed the paper with my finger—"this trumped-up tripe, do you? They make it up by the yard—manufacture it by the carload!"

"Well," Simon admitted, picking up his teacup and gazing into it, "you're probably right."

"You bet I'm right," I crowed. Prematurely, as it turned out. I should have known better.

"Still, it wouldn't hurt to check it out." He lifted the cup, swirled the tea, and drained it. Then, as if his mind was made up, he placed both hands flat on the tabletop and stood.

I saw the sly set of his eyes. It was a look I knew well and dreaded. "You can't be serious."

"But I am perfectly serious."

"Forget it."

"Come on. It will be an adventure."

"I've got a meeting with my adviser this afternoon. That's more than enough adventure for me."

"I want you with me," Simon insisted.

"What about Susannah?" I countered. "I thought you were supposed to meet her for lunch."

"Susannah will understand." He turned abruptly. "We'll take my car."

"No. Really. Listen, Simon, we can't go chasing after this ox thing. It's ridiculous. It's nothing. It's like those fairy rings in the cornfields that had everybody all worked up last year. It's a hoax. Besides, I can't go—I've got work to do, and so have you."

"A drive in the country will do you a world of good. Fresh air. Clear the cobwebs. Nourish the inner man." He walked briskly into the next room. I could hear him dialing the phone, and a moment later he said, "Listen, Susannah, about today . . . terribly sorry, dear heart, something's come up . . . Yes, just as soon as I get back . . . Later . . . Yes, Sunday, I won't forget . . . cross my heart and hope to die. Cheers!" He replaced the receiver and dialed again. "Rawnson here. I'll be needing the car this morning . . . Fifteen minutes. Right. Thanks, awfully."

"Simon!" I shouted. "I refuse!"

☌ ☌ ☌

This is how I came to be standing in St. Aldate's on a rainy Friday morning in the third week of Michaelmas term, drizzle dripping off my nose, waiting for Simon's car to be brought around, wondering how he did it.

We were both graduate students, Simon and I. We shared rooms, in fact. But where Simon had only to whisper into the phone and his car arrived when and where he wanted it, I couldn't even get the porter to let me lean my poor, battered bicycle against the gate for half a minute while I checked my mail. Rank hath its privileges, I guess.

Nor did the gulf between us end there. While I was little above medium height, with a build that, before the mirror, could only be described as weedy, Simon was tall and regally slim, well muscled, yet trim—the build of an Olympic fencer. The face I displayed to the world boasted plain, somewhat lumpen features, crowned with a lackluster mat the color of old walnut shells. Simon's features were sharp, well cut, and clean; he had the kind of thick, dark, curly hair women admire and openly covet. My eyes were mouse gray; his were hazel. My chin drooped; his jutted.

The effect when we appeared in public together was, I imagine, much in the order of a live before-and-after advertisement for *Nature's Own Wonder Vitamins & Handsome Tonic*. He had good looks to burn and the sort of rugged and ruthless masculinity both sexes find appealing. I had the kind of looks that often improve with age, although it was doubtful that I should live so long.

A lesser man would have been jealous of Simon's bounteous good fortune. However, I accepted my lot and was content. All right, I was jealous too—but it was a very contented jealousy.

Anyway, there we were, the two of us, standing in the rain, traffic whizzing by, buses disgorging soggy passengers on the busy pavement around us, and me muttering in lame protest. "This is dumb. It's stupid. It's childish and irresponsible, that's what it is. It's nuts."

"You're right, of course," he agreed affably. Rain pearled on his driving cap and trickled down his waxed-cotton shooting jacket.

"We can't just drop everything and go racing around the country on a whim." I crossed my arms inside my plastic poncho. "I don't know how I let you talk me into these things."

"It's my utterly irresistible charm, old son." He grinned disarmingly. "We Rawnsons have bags of it."

"Yeah, sure."

"Where's your spirit of adventure?" My lack of adventurous spirit was something he always threw at me whenever he wanted me to go along with one of his lunatic exploits. I preferred to see myself as stable, steady-handed, a both-feet-on-the-ground, practical-as-pie realist through and through.

"It's not that," I quibbled. "I just don't need to lose four days of work for nothing."

"It's Friday," he reminded me. "It's the weekend. We'll be back on Monday in plenty of time for your precious work."

"We haven't even packed toothbrushes or a change of underwear," I pointed out.

"Very well," he sighed, as if I had beaten him down at last, "you've made your point. If you don't wish to go, I won't force you."

"Good."

"I'll go alone." He stepped into the street just as a gray Jaguar Sovereign purred to a halt in front of him. A man in a black bowler hat scrambled from the driver's seat and held the door for him.

"Thank you, Mr. Bates," Simon said. The man touched the brim of his hat and hurried away to the porters' lodge. Simon glanced at me across the rain-beaded roof of the sleek automobile and smiled. "Well, chum? Going to let me have all the fun alone?"

"Curse you, Simon!" I shouted, yanked the door open, and ducked in. "I don't need this!"

Laughing, Simon slid in and slammed the door. He shifted into gear, then punched the accelerator to the floor. The tires squealed on the wet pavement as the car leapt forward. Simon yanked the wheel and executed a highly illegal U-turn in the middle of the street, to the blaring of bus horns and the curses of cyclists.

Heaven help us, we were off.

The adventure continues in
The Paradise War
by Stephen R. Lawhead